D1001659

As The Wheel Turns

As The Wheel Turns

by
ANNE TUFTS

illustrated by

ROBERT L. DOREMUS

THE JUNIOR LITERARY GUILD
AND
HENRY HOLT AND COMPANY • NEW YORK

Library of Congress Catalog Card Number: 52–9045

PRINTED IN THE UNITED STATES OF AMERICA

All characters except for historical persons mentioned are fictional.

•

ACKNOWLEDGMENTS

The research necessary for the writing of this book would have been impossible without the courtesies extended by many librarians. My thanks are especially due to the following:

Mrs. Mildred Peterson McKay, State Library, Concord, New Hampshire; Miss Beatrice M. Jenkins, formerly of the Public Library, Dover, New Hampshire; Mrs. Mary W. Vaughan, the Athenaeum, and Miss Dorothy M. Vaughan, the Public Library, Portsmouth, New Hampshire; Mrs. Grace P. Bowser, of Harvard University's Baker Library, who gave me access to Boston Manufacturing Company records dating back to the year 1813; Miss Lorena Weatherby, the Public Library, Waltham, Massachusetts; and Miss May Hoag of Friends Meeting House, New York.

To my brother

CHARLES GILMAN TUFTS

CONTENTS

Part I: Fugitive

Part II: Foothold in America

Part III: A New Hampshire Mill

Part IV: All the Twenty-Four States

Fugitive
Doremus

Go to the States!

THE MORNING was bleak, that eventful day of December, 1813, and the orange-red coals in the grate barely lessened the chill of the room. A small room, its carpet was threadbare, chairs and sofa shabby, the heavy curtains drawn. A candle flickered on the table. Books stood on shelves under the pictures of mad King George and his son, the Prince Regent.

Anthony, cold to the bone, his hair feeling like a damp cloth on his head, stretched out his hands to the warmth of the fire. He heard his father moving about in the cellar underneath. John Bryce, foremost inventor of northern England! His workshop, filled with models and designs, made the humble cottage a treasure house. John Bryce had even devised an improved pattern of the new loom that was operated by water power. As yet, the shuttle stopped dead now and then; but the mill-owner promised rich reward when the water loom ran smoothly.

Someone was muttering in the square outside! Anthony sprang to pull the curtains wide and then, his hand on the cord, drew back. It was absurd to fear on his father's account. Days of mill riots were over; days when displaced hand-workers smashed the new machines, shot at mill-owners, inventors too. The cruel convictions of the year drawing to a close had ended riots. Whoever stood outside only grumbled over the early morning cold.

He returned to the fire. From the kitchen came the faint clink of china, as his mother cleared away, after their breakfast of porridge and tea. She joined him presently, a little breathless because of her tired heart, but wanting to see her husband set out for the cotton mill.

"Your father is late in leaving, this morning," she said. Her head had a proud lift as she seated herself on the small sofa, and Anthony thought she made a picture—in her plain dark gown, the brooch set with garnets and pearls at her throat. He went over and tucked a cushion behind her.

"You have said nothing about the party last evening," she remarked.

"It was very agreeable." Invited to the mill-owner's house, he had enjoyed meeting the man's daughter and the other young people assembled there.

"Next month," his mother went on slowly, "you will be eighteen years of age. Your father was seventeen, when we were married, and I was sixteen."

"I have no marriage plans," Anthony replied. He thought his mother looked worn, and it was little wonder. Born to ease, she had seen the homes his father provided grow smaller and meaner until now she lived in a four-room cottage in the shabby mill-workers' row. But with the water loom so nearly perfected, her days of hardship were almost over.

The knocker sounded, its three slow raps echoing ominously. Anthony hurried to the hall. A scrap of paper lay on the floor, and he read the smudged scrawl: IF JOHN BRYCE KNOWS WHAT'S GOOD FOR HIM HE WON'T GO NEAR MILL TODAY.

Jerking the door open, Anthony stepped outside. A dozen men idled, here and there, in front of the row of cottages that formed the western side of the cobble-stoned square, and a scrawny dog howled. The mills made the northern boundary; and there, a line of weary women and children waited their turn at the company-owned store. Directly across, gun over his shoulder, a guard paced the length of the vast warehouse. At the square's southern end, all was quiet around the mill-owner's house and park.

Anthony's gaze returned to the shabby cottage row. No

sign of trouble anywhere! Men would be fools to start trouble now; cavalry would surely be sent to mow them down. Yet a warning had been slipped under the door. Uneasy, he stuffed the smudged paper into a pocket.

"Someone knocked at the wrong house," he told his mother when he went inside.

His father came into the small parlor, tall though stooped, a blue woolen muffler in his hand. "Anthony," he began, "I've left a deal for you to do, downstairs. The spinner needs adjustment. The warp should be set up for the loom model . . ."

Anthony saw his mother rise and go to the window.

"John," she interrupted, "don't go to the mill today."

"But I must, Margaret. The idea I needed came when I waked this morning. My invention is completed." His eyes lighted as he laid his hand over a pocket.

"Look!" She drew the curtains wide apart. In the interval since Anthony had gone outside, a crowd had poured into the square; men, women and children, their faces desperate, hands clutching at ragged shawls.

"Poor souls, they're hungry," John Bryce said gently. "If they'll only be patient, I can teach hand-weavers to tend machines and—"

"You talk about next month, next year," his wife broke in. "These people are hungry now, and they blame your inventions."

Grave, he shook his head. "They can't understand that it's the war with the States that has cut our orders. No American vessels stop at our ports now. But when the war ends, we won't be able to find workers enough, if we comb the entire mill valley. My inventions will aid in getting rid of child labor, other evils."

"Father, someone knocked a few minutes ago and I found—this." Anthony had decided to hand over the scrap of paper.

John Bryce glanced at the scrawl. "I've had similar warnings for years. All inventors get them." He smiled wryly.

His wife sank into a chair, her eyes worried.

"Father, let me go to the mill with you," Anthony begged. "I can—"

"No." The voice that cut him off was unwontedly stern. "You'll help more by looking after things downstairs."

Meeting his father's eyes, Anthony read the message in them: he was expected to protect the treasure in the cellar shop, whatever happened. And something *might* happen. "Very well, sir."

He felt a tightness in his throat. Everything in the room stood out unusually clearly. His mother, very pale in the chair. His father by the door, tall in spite of stooping, the blue muffler in his slender hand. And outside, the crowd was growing larger!

"Son, go to the States when you get a chance." John Bryce tossed the muffler around his neck. "In the young republic you will do—things I may fail to do in England."

"What can Anthony do better than you, John?" Margaret asked, her voice a little sharp. "And the law forbids a mechanic to leave England."

John Bryce crossed the room and bent to kiss his wife. Back at the door, he gave Anthony a meaningful look as his deft fingers twisted the muffler ends. "Well, I'm off." With a smile he went outside.

The crowd at first were quiet and made way for him to pass. Then there were angry mutters: "There's John Bryce, him with the blue muffler. . . . We've our own spies. We know he's making a new machine. Design's likely on him . . ."

"Get the paper with the design!" someone shouted, egging the crowd on.

Voices turned threatening: "Another machine to take more work away. . . . Get the design! Tear it to pieces!"

The crowd had a single purpose now. "Tear up the design!" it clamored, surging back and forth.

Anthony dashed from the house. "John Bryce is your friend," he shouted. "John Bryce is trying to help you."

Nobody gave heed. He saw the crowd close around his father.

Someone screamed, "We'll no stand for the bread being took from our children's mouths."

Then, down at the southern end of the square, a rider galloped off. The mill-owner was sending for the cavalry.

Trying to reach his father's side, Anthony fought against fists and clawing hands. He bent to rescue a trampled child, and someone knocked him flat. When he got to his feet, the throng had passed. Unable to see John Bryce's tall stooping figure, he ran after the frantic mob.

There were two mobs now; one advanced upon the mill, the other upon the long warehouse. "Wreck the mill!" one mob barked. "Fire warehouse! Burn the bolts of cloth and they'll have to give us work!" the other mob yelped. Hands that had clutched at shawls hurled stones or burning flares.

Above the angry cries, Anthony heard pounding hooves. Cavalry thundered over the cobblestones. Sabres flashed.

Then he heard only shrieks, groans, and sorrowful wailing.

Two officers brought his father's body back to the house; they laid the still form on the sofa, crossed the wonder-working hands.

"The people had naught against Mr. Bryce," one officer said. "They wanted only to wreck what'd take their work away. There's no proof anyone killed Mr. Bryce. Frail, he was. Might have got them cuts on his head, falling from apoplexy. Might have died if he'd stayed at home. . . . No more trouble'll come, thanks to cavalry. And gover'ment'll want this bit of disturbance hushed up. Understand?" The pair looked sheepish as they left.

The mill-owner sent for Anthony. "You have a copy of the

design your father carried?" he asked.

"No, sir."

"You can reproduce it?"

"I had no part in my father's last invention. He completed it only a short time before he left the house."

"You examined the clothing?"

"There was—nothing."

The mill-owner tapped his fingers against the desk. "We'll keep you for a while," he said coldly, "but you're not much use to us without your father. By the way, all his models and papers belong to us. We'll send someone to go through his shop. Good afternoon."

Stumbling over cobblestones, Anthony realized he would be employed only as long as they could pick his brains of what he knew about his father's work. Trying to accustom himself to the fact that John Bryce would never receive credit for the power loom, or for anything he had invented, Anthony paused on his doorstep and looked down the shabby row. Because of the riot, several cottagers had lost their posts at the mill. Their children were hungry tonight. But down in the big house at the square's southern end, candles glowed. The mill-owner's daughter was doubtless enjoying a lavish tea.

He would not be invited to see the mill-owner's daughter again. He was a young man without prospects, now.

Rain fell on the day of the funeral, and his mother caught a cold. He nursed her as well as he could. A neighbor sat with her while he was at the mill.

The man who came to go through the shop laid claim to models here and there, but he passed most items by with the careless mention that a new inventor had been engaged. Anthony was astonished to see how little the fellow realized the significance of what lay around.

Later, he went over things himself. Could he carry on his father's project? Perfect the unfinished inventions? Fight for decent wages and homes for workers, oppose child labor?

Remembering how many people knew about the workshop, he felt a moment's misgiving. Surely, now that John Bryce was dead, the displaced workers' resentment would be for the new inventor. A curtain over the small cellar window would hide his own candle.

One evening, a week or so later, he was helping his mother in the kitchen, when he heard a crackling sound—as if glass were being shattered.

"Stay here, while I go to the other room," he bade his mother, "and don't fret!"

In the small parlor, a stone came through the window. A second followed . . . then another. He knew that men standing in shadow outside were breaking the panes; presently they would throw flares, made of twisted flax soaked in tallow, steady-burning, certain to set off whatever they touched.

He grabbed a pair of cushions and, when the first flare whistled in, smothered its flame. Flares came in swift succession, until he was leaping from wall to wall. The lace tablecloth caught . . . and the heavy curtain fringe. The carpet sent up tongues of fire. The picture of King George fell, its cord burned through. The Prince Regent crashed.

It was hard to breathe. Sparks fell all around. But he had only to hold out until someone gave warning and the cavalry came. Any minute, he would hear the clatter of iron shoes on cobblestone.

Outside, an angry voice chided: "You've no done what I told ye. *Cellar* winder, I said. Quick now, and our work'll be over afore soldiery come. We built a barrier to delay 'em."

The road the cavalry must take was blocked! And now stones shattered the glass below. The workshop, loose papers and lengths of lumber all about, was a perfect tinder-box.

Anthony ran to the kitchen, picked up his mother and carried her out the rear passageway, through the yard, and along the alley.

"Don't worry, dear," he said as he set her down. "I'm looking after things."

Back in the house, he opened the cellar door. Roaring fire met him. The house *and* shop were doomed. He raced upstairs. In his mother's bedroom, he opened drawers, emptied them into a hand-trunk, threw in clothing from the closet. In the adjoining chamber, he grabbed a few of his own things. Holding the trunk like a screen before him, he started down.

Tongues of flame licked at him. On he went, face and hands scorched, clothing riddled. He gained the rear passageway . . . and at last the yard. He had reached the alley when horses thundered into the square. There were screams, the hiss of water on hot wood and slate. The other cottages in the row could be saved, but his home had gone.

How could he care for his mother? he wondered as he ran. Then he saw her, lying on the ground. Shock had brought on a heart attack and killed her, he realized as he bent over her. The expression on her face was more peaceful than at any time since his father's death.

The day after the burial, Anthony visited his former home. Standing in the gap that had been a curtained window, he looked at the shell of charred timber. A pile of ashes marked the spot where the parlor door had been. His father had stood beside that door, a blue woolen muffler in his slender hands.

Go to the States, John Bryce had said. *In the young republic you will do—things I may fail to do in England.*

Escape

FELLOW-WORKERS showed little surprise over Anthony's leaving the mill. "Change of scene helps a body forget," they said, assuming he would settle in another mill valley. "Ye'll do better," an older man warned, "if ye don't say ye're John Bryce's son."

Anthony visited the churchyard and laid evergreen on his parents' graves. Then, wrapped in a salvaged shawl, the small leather trunk under his arm, he set out.

His way led west and south. He climbed a hill in the face of a January storm. Tall and thin as he was, the wind struck at him on the high moor, forcing him to crawl. He slept in a deserted hut; stopped at a shepherd's door for milk. Picking his way over treacherous stones, he tried to plan.

A mill mechanic, discovered leaving England, would be thrown in jail.

Yet mechanics *had* left England. Samuel Slater, disguised as a farm lad, had gone to New York twenty years before, carrying the secret of machine-spinning. He had mills in Rhode Island, the most important cotton mills in the entire United States. John Bryce had often talked about Samuel Slater's success.

A torrent racing through a bleak valley took all of Anthony's attention for a while. He ran into another storm and, with sleet striking at him, made little headway. Every now and then he had to set the small trunk down, stamp his feet, clap his hands, and shake ice out of the folds of his shawl. But he felt lighthearted, for he had a plan.

On reaching the States, he would go to Samuel Slater. The Englishman who had carried the secret of machine-spinning across the ocean would welcome an Englishman bringing the secret of machine-weaving. Anthony wished he knew where Rhode Island lay. Somewhere between Maine and Georgia, he figured.

The storm died down. He quickened his pace, his spirits drooping only when he remembered that he was planning what he would do in Rhode Island, and as yet he had not escaped from England.

He reached Liverpool on his eighteenth birthday. With the lone half-crown in his pocket, he treated himself to a supper of beef and kidney pie, and a modest lodging. The following week, he sold his mother's jewels—all but the brooch of garnets and pearls, his father's gift. He outfitted himself with a new greatcoat, a woolen suit, extra trousers, a few other things. After settling with the tailor, he had forty pounds left.

Donning leather waistcoat and apron, he practiced the stevedore's stooping walk, studying his reflection in a cracked mirror. When he felt sure that nobody would take him for a mechanic from a remote mill valley, he went boldly to the waterfront.

Liverpool, it seemed, held only idle keels. When he questioned a fellow-stevedore about continent-bound vessels, the man said gloomily: "A vessel lifts anchor, lad, and afore even sighting Channel, some devil of a Yankee sinks her. Most shipmasters stick to port. Ye're set on going to sea? Better 'list in His Majesty's service, if ye don't get shanghaied."

Shanghaied! Anthony had no wish to be drugged or clamped in irons, dragged away to do forced service in the Navy. He planned to work in Samuel Slater's cotton mills, and make his home in Rhode Island.

More wary, he continued his search. When a Dutch sloop came into port, he went to her captain. "I'll serve for half the usual wages, sir."

The shipmaster turned his back.

On the watch for another vessel, Anthony saw a man in naval uniform eye him. The officer gave a signal, and three rough fellows came towards him. In a trice, a fellow-stevedore had stepped up beside him. The trio passed sullenly. "Happen those devils caught either of us alone," his new friend said, "we'd be on our way, now."

Anthony found it hard to believe that men could be dragged off so openly. But passing a wharfside storehouse in the early dusk, he heard cries of distress. Two ruffians were dragging a man towards the water! He was about to run to the rescue when the victim's cries ceased, as if he'd been rapped on the head. Waiting, Anthony heard the swish of muffled oars. The poor fellow was being taken to a ship! . . . And then he saw another pair of ruffians coming for him.

Ducking into the storehouse, he slipped out through a door that opened on the street beyond, took a zigzag way to his lodging place. Between two perils now, jail on one hand, forced service in the Navy on the other, he shuddered at every sound.

Desperate, he thought of the Dutch sloop. He'd have to be a stowaway! Bad weather aided him. A flood of rain turned streets into rivers. It seemed as if the entire Irish sea poured into Liverpool. When the rain diminished, thick fog came. Small trunk in one hand, canvas bag in the other, Anthony set out for the wharves.

He knew he made only a shadow in the night. Yet, when a lantern bobbed or a voice rang out, he was wary. Groping his way, he stumbled once or twice; caught himself in time to avoid the clatter of a fall. At length he heard speech which he took for Dutch, since it plainly wasn't English.

Rain trickled down his neck, his teeth chattered from the cold while he waited. Not until the voices stilled, did he venture closer to the Dutch ship. In the storm, it had been moored snug against wharfside. He dropped his bag over the bulwark, threw his legs over, reached for his trunk. He crawled aft, found a hatchway he could open. No sound but snoring below and the wash of the tide! He went back for his things. And then, his heart lighter than since he had left the mill valley, he set his foot on the ladder rung.

The sloop sailed at dawn in a wind that kept all hands on deck. After the Channel-crossing, when some of the crew saw Anthony climb out of the hold, they glowered. But they were in their home port, wives or sweethearts waiting. So, after a minute, they winked and turned their backs.

Anthony stole ashore.

He had a long wait in Holland. Ruled by William, Prince of Orange, it was a sovereign government for the time; but with Napoleon beginning to meet defeat, no one knew what foreigners might try to over-run the Low Countries. Anthony saw Englishmen about, engaged in trade or politics or the war on the Continent, and carefully avoided them, knowing he could be seized—even in Holland.

He lodged away from the waterfront, and went to the wharves every day. In England, he had met one American, a man interested in cotton mills who had talked with his father several times; and he thought he would recognize the American accent. It was February when the brig, *Dolphin,* arrived, her crew boasting of having dodged a British frigate. As they unloaded tobacco, rice, and white pine, Anthony watched, admiring the Yankee air of independence.

"How much is passage to New York?" he inquired.

"Kingdom come, we're from Boston," the shipmaster roared. "No passengers is owner's orders."

"I'll work for my passage. Without wages."

"No strangers on the *Dolphin's* deck. Get out of my way!"

Another American vessel might not arrive for months. The more Anthony saw of the crew, the more he wanted to join them. He donned his leather apron and hung about, just out of range of the captain's eye.

Drays rumbled to the brig's side. Stevedores toted; the crew sweated as they stowed new cargo away. When one sailor's strength flagged, Anthony gave a helping hand. "I'm weak from scurvy," the grateful fellow told him. "My name's Bill." Anthony made a friend of Bill.

At last the casks of wine, the rolls of Belgian carpeting and bales of woman's frippery, were safe in the hold. Anthony was despairing of getting aboard the day Bill touched his arm.

"Three lads picked up dysentery ashore," Bill whispered. "Cap'n knows 't'aint safe, these times, to sail short-handed."

Again Anthony went to the officer. "Sir, if you need a man—"

"Land of Egypt!" Relief showed in the captain's eyes. "I'm that hard pressed, I'd take Satan himself. Mind, ye bargained to work for your passage. I doubt ye'll be worth the victuals ye eat. But I'll take ye, skinny towhead."

When darkness fell, the *Dolphin* stole out of the harbor. Anthony watched the lights of Europe fade. At last, he was on the way to Rhode Island.

Dawn brought heavy seas. Anthony found himself unable to leave his hammock. His mates, passing in or out of the forecastle, poked jibes at "Skinny Towhead." But Bill did his chores.

Next day, someone rushed in with word that enemy sail had been sighted. Anthony crawled up to the deck, where the crew were clamoring to fight.

"We've got two guns!" they cried.

"Be still, the pack of ye!" the captain shouted. "Our guns are for defense. We sail a merchant vessel and must keep on our way." His tone showed that he too would have enjoyed a fight.

By the time the eighty-ton *Dolphin* had rounded the perilous Irish coast, Anthony was accustomed to her roll. He swabbed decks, caulked seams, began to climb rigging. He liked his hearty mates; liked the smell of brine, the slap of sail. Often he looked up at the flag floating from the mast, counted its thirteen stripes and eighteen stars.

In spare hours, Bill taught him wrestling tricks. Their mates watched, when the deck was steady enough and tasks did not press; proud of a fellow-countryman's skill, yet not begrudging a cheer for Skinny Towhead's pluck. But Anthony was outgrowing his nickname. His shoulders had broadened, the muscles under the tanned skin turned hard; he had a sense of well-being. He gained sure balance from the practice with Bill and, by the time March gales tore at thread and timber, was one of the company's nimblest.

As mild April weather approached, the men grew bored. "Things'll be livelier," they promised Anthony with a wink, "when we're close to our own seaboard."

They talked sometimes of dishes that waited on shore: codfish cakes, beans slow-baked, turkey roasted to a turn. . . . Anthony's mouth watered as he eyed his chunk of half-rancid pork.

He thought often of what he would do when the *Dolphin* docked. None of the crew had heard of Mr. Samuel Slater, but Bill had told him where Rhode Island lay. "Mr. Slater'll be in a town on a river," Anthony said. Bill opined that Rhode Island had river towns, but he didn't know their names.

The *Dolphin* was reckoned four hours from Boston's Long Wharf when the lookout reported sail in her path.

"Give me the glass!" The captain peered through the long telescope. "British ship of the line, seventy-four guns!" He roared out orders for a change in course. Muttering against the luck that had put them on a merchant vessel, the crew turned the brig south.

"You'll see a bit of blockade-running yet," Bill promised Anthony.

Out of the man-of-war's range, they circled about. The

night and following day were clear, but the ocean turned choppy. On the second night, when the sky was so overcast that Anthony could not see beyond the *Dolphin's* nose, the captain ordered, "North by west, my lads!"

"Aye aye, sir." They gave a cheer.

Topsails reefed, lights covered, the brig moved with scarcely a sound. A fresher wind sprang up, and all Anthony saw was gray sky above, gray walls of water ahead. The *Dolphin's* deck would climb, hang suspended for a minute, and then plunge. Yet, north by west she worked her way.

Then he made out a shadow against the night sky, so vast it seemed unreal until it moved—in a direction that cut directly across their path. Was the *Dolphin* to be sliced in two?

With lightning speed, the crew tacked. Now the brig was battered by both the sea and the man-of-war's wash. She was caught in a gray-green valley; a mountain of water poured down on her. The second mate fell to the careening deck, slid towards the gray-green wall. Anthony sprang in the nick of time, gripped the man and, clinging to the mast, managed to hang on.

Slowly the sea of water receded. The brig righted. They passed so close to the enemy ship that the high stern seemed to hover over them. The vessel's sides were like a great fortress as they slid by.

And then, behind them, an English voice rang out. The warship came alive; guns were brought into action, cannon ploughed the water around them. The fog however was too thick for accurate aim. Presently they were out of range.

Within the harbor at last, the captain held out his hand. "I thank ye, Mr. Bryce," he boomed before the entire company, "for saving the second mate's life. Ye'll get full pay for the voyage."

Anthony was "Mr. Bryce" now. It was pleasant to see respect in his mates' eyes. "Didn't I say," Bill chuckled, "we'd have some blockade-running!"

It was nearing dawn when they tied up at Long Wharf. "Kingdom come," the captain crowed, "if I'd had a two-hundred-ton vessel under me, back there, I'd not had room to twist and turn." The owner, Mr. Lester, would come on board, he announced, to see that all hands were paid off. Short on sleep for two nights running, the crew trooped off to forecastle willingly.

Anthony lingered, remembering Bill had said that stagecoaches often started at crack of dawn. "If you please, sir, I'd like to go ashore."

"And lose the pay ye earned?" the captain's deep voice rumbled.

Anthony wanted the money; but several of the crew had warned him that British spies frequented port towns. If he hung around Boston for a day, some enemy agent might seize him, send him back to England. "I'll do without my pay, sir."

"Land of Egypt!" Holding up his lantern, the ship's master peered into Anthony's eyes. "Well, ye didn't sign for the voyage, like the others, and I can let ye go," he said at last. "But not a cent of pay!"

"Can you change a few English pounds into dollars?" Anthony asked.

"I'll gladly do that. Come into my cabin." The officer unlocked a battered safe, counted out the money. "Ye know your own business, lad," he said as he handed the notes over. "Watch out for prowlers round the waterfront. And good luck to ye." He shook hands cordially.

When Anthony went below, his mates were snoring. He wanted to say goodbye to Bill, but decided not to wake him. Quietly he collected his things.

Walking over Long Wharf, the boards seemed to rock. He made out a lighted window. An inn, he thought. He would inquire about the Rhode Island stage. And if there was time—sample a Yankee breakfast.

A Lad Wanting to Try New Ways

THE DRIVER of the Rhode Island stage knew where the cotton mills lay. "Pawtucket's a purty town." He nodded for emphasis. "If ye're Britainer and wanting work, Mr. Slater'll find ye something."

Rumbling over the road, Anthony thought again of the welcome he would receive from Samuel Slater. An enlightened man, of course. No stunted children turning spindles in his mills. And workers would be suitably housed; paid in cash, not in credit at a company-owned store certain to cheat them, as in England.

Pawtucket, on the Seekonk River, seemed a fair village, as the stage rolled in. The air was soft. Comfortable dwellings lined the high street, and in hot weather the trees would afford shade. Viewing the place he had chosen for his home, Anthony felt a deep content.

The mill, a wooden structure, was smaller than he had expected, but two stories and a half high. Eager to meet Mr. Slater, Anthony stepped inside.

Mr. Samuel Slater, tall, stout of frame, wearing clothes that were good but severely plain, had a firm hand-shake. "You mean to settle here, Mr. Bryce?" he asked.

"Yes, sir." Anthony thought of the long perilous journey he had taken to reach Pawtucket. But now his troubles seemed over.

"We'll employ you. Sit down. What type of work do you want?"

Anthony stated modestly that he was an inventor's son and had worked on the new water-power loom. He waited for the American to exclaim over his announcement.

Mr. Slater showed no change of expression. "I was a pioneer in machine-spinning," he said, "but have no interest in machine-weaving."

No interest in machine-weaving, in the mechanical loom! Samuel Slater did not understand.

". . . We find hand-weaving," the business-like voice went on, "entirely satisfactory. Our product is superior—we can't fill orders. Not with thirty-three mills in Rhode Island, others in Massachusetts." The voice warmed. "To obtain fair percentage of profit . . ."

Anthony drew his breath in sharply. The man he had crossed an ocean to meet wanted to talk about percentage of profit!

It was a relief when customers were announced.

"Look around," Mr. Slater invited as he rose, "and decide on the kind of work you want. Then come back, and we'll talk terms."

Following a guide over the solid-built floor, Anthony felt less secure than if he walked the deck of a sinking ship. The guide led him into a room filled with spinning-machines. The Arkwright model, used in England twenty years before but now outmoded! In another room, rows of children stood beside spindles.

"Children are a convenient height," the guide was saying, "for turning spindles. Here in Pawtucket they are fortunate. Besides earning money in pleasant surroundings, the Slater mills provide Sabbath Day schools where they are taught reading, writing, arithmetic, besides receiving moral instruction. . . . Now let me show you our company-owned store."

"Thank you, my time is limited."

Walking down the high street, Anthony tried to think. Middle-aged and prosperous, the pioneer of machine-spinning in the United States could not see the importance of machine-weaving. Yarn spun in the Slater mills was sent out to be woven on kitchen hand-looms. Slater, and the gentlemen associated with him, were benevolent, no doubt; but they had taken over the English labor system. Workers received favors, and had no rights. With less humane owners in control, all the old evils could creep in; all the abuses John Bryce had hoped his inventions would wipe out.

Anthony stepped into an inn and ordered a meal. He had no appetite, but he wanted to think. What to do? Where to go—in a country where he had no friends?

A cripple joined him. "Don't like to eat my snack alone," he said. "Newcomer to Pawtucket?"

"Just a visitor," Anthony returned.

"Friendly place, thanks to Mr. Slater." The cripple paused to hang his crutch on the chair back. "I was a weaver for Slater mills till rheumatiz got me. Legs give out, pushing treadles afore the loom all day. And my arms stiffened from throwing shuttle." The cripple's face showed a twitch as if from pain. "But I'd ruther git rheumatiz than lose my eyesight, like happens to some weavers. English?"

"Yes."

"Thought so. Round here, we like the English 'count of Mr. Slater. Otherwheres, with a war going on, folks ain't always cordial." Workers in Slater mills were well treated, the cripple went on; better off, most of them, than if they kept to farming. Mr. Slater was a kind man, who gave employment instead of alms.

"But suppose," Anthony pushed his plate aside, "suppose a man wanted to try new ways of doing things."

"A lad wanting to try new ways!" The lined face lighted. "I was that sort, once. Thought I'd make the world over. 'Member what it says in the Bible 'bout young men's visions and old men's dreams? If ye want to try new ways, go north-

'ard, lad. Go to Maine or New Hampshire. Quite a lot of Slater workers done that. The mills up there are poorer and smaller, but the folks are prouder when it comes to doing what they like."

"Have a cup of coffee with me," Anthony invited.

Thanks to the cripple, he knew where to go.

The stage for the North clattered out of Boston in the pale light of dawn. Briefly, as they rolled over Charlestown Bridge, Anthony surveyed his companions. The lanky fellow beside him, a wad of tobacco in his cheek, might be a farmer. The man across was a parson, to judge by his cloth. The woman sitting opposite the farmer looked matronly. Harmless, they seemed. And yet, questions might be troublesome.

As soon as the stage lumbered off the bridge, Anthony leaned back, feigning sleep. Sometimes he heard a dog bark. Children shouted greetings. Sometimes the farmer snorted, or the parson rustled newspaper pages. The woman remarked that houses were getting sparser. For a while there was only the coach body's rumble, the wheels' grinding, the horses' clop-clop-clop.

The coach lurched suddenly, throwing the parson against him.

"This road has thank-ye-ma'ams," the woman said, when things righted.

"Up Merrimack way where I live," the farmer twanged, "river makes smoothest road in Bay State."

"Transportation will be improved when Mr. Madison's misguided war ends." The parson spoke as if he stood in a pulpit.

They rumbled on.

"Wonder where sleeping lad's bound," the woman remarked. "Greatcoat's wrinkled, like he came off the sea."

"He ain't one of ourn." The farmer spoke too sharply for Anthony's liking. "He ain't off a privateer nor a fishing smack. Maybe he's Britainer, spying."

Anthony felt gooseflesh rising, until the parson pronounced: "The young man is a peaceable traveller."

The parson left them in the next town, where they stopped to change horses. When the coach door was opened, Anthony took deep breaths of the fresh salty air. His back ached from the long hours of lying in one position. His foot had gone to sleep, and his stomach gnawed him. However, he kept his eyes closed.

Presently the door slammed shut, and they jolted on. The road grew rougher; axles groaned on the up-hill hauls, brakes scraped on the slow descents.

With the parson gone, the farmer's tongue limbered. Afore the war, he used to take his grain and apples down Merrimack River, sell right from Newburyport wharf. His stuff went far as Georgia and West Indies. Nowadays, what with Britainers blockading and Yankees turning privateer, he let Boston merchants take the risk of shipping.

The woman said she'd been visiting her sister in Boston. More than thirty thousand souls lived there—she couldn't breathe in such a crowded town.

"The war," the farmer broke in, "upsets things for folks living near the sea. Makes a man madder'n a hornet."

"Housewives have their troubles," the woman retorted. "Here 'tis middle of April, and I ought to be sewing up cotton clothes for the young'uns. Ships don't bring calico and muslin these days, or that strong Chinese nankeen."

"Spin more flax and dress the young'uns in linen," the farmer teased.

"Cotton don't get so wringing wet on a body's back in hot weather," the woman told him. "We're coming into Newburyport." She began to gather up her things.

Anthony waited until his companions had left the coach. Probably he would never see them again, he thought as he sat up, blinking, and yet he would see them always: he had made up his mind to live among people like them. Resolute people, cringing to nobody. The Pawtucket cripple was right! And they needed cotton cloth.

In the inn yard, hostlers were running forward. A crowd of children stared at the stage that had journeyed all the way from Boston. The driver tossed the mailbag down. A paunchy landlord appeared.

"Purty day," the landlord said, picking up the mail.

"Mite chilly on top." The driver clambered down. "I don't aim to stop long in Newburyport." He swaggered off.

Anthony stepped outside and tramped up and down, easing his stiffness. Two men in linsey-woolsey led the lathered horses away. A leather-aproned fellow climbed up for the parcels on top. Four fresh horses were led out.

The driver swaggered back. "Portsmouth stage leaving!" he bawled.

As Anthony stepped inside, he saw an odd figure scurrying towards them; a little man in a long-skirted faded green coat that was too big for him, a red bandanna bundle in his hand. He looked wistfully at the driver.

"Climb up! Load's light today," the driver said.

Then the inn door opened, and a man of imposing appearance strode towards them. Tall, ruddy-faced, well turned out, swinging a cane.

He paused to shake the landlord's hand. "Prime beef," he said, genial.

"We aim to give the best, in Newburyport." The landlord beamed and pulled on his waistcoat points.

The coach sagged as the big fellow stepped inside.

"Smooth journey!" The landlord bowed and closed the door. The long whip cracked, lashing the air in slow wide circles, but never touching a horse's hide.

"Hooray!" The crowd of children applauded the driver's skill. "Hooray!"

"Whoo-up," the driver coaxed. "Whope! Git!"

The wheels began to roll.

The newcomer sat with his cane between his legs, hands clasped over its ivory head. The eyes under the tall beaver were a sharp blue. The man could have been no better clad, had he lived in England. The brown broadcloth of his coat was smooth, as if woven on a Dutch or English loom. The linen of the high stock was fine, the kerseymere breeches fitted without a wrinkle, boots and gloves were of well-cured calf. On what business, Anthony wondered, was this person of consequence bound?

They jogged by handsome houses which the passenger regarded with interest.

"We'll cross Merrimack over the new chain bridge," he said affably.

"Indeed, sir." As blue water flashed, Anthony looked out the window on his side. Merrimack was wider than the Pawtucket stream, but not as broad as Boston's Charles. He wished he could dip his hand into it, feel and taste it. Was it hard or soft water? And were there falls upstream?

The horses, stepping carefully off the bridge, picked up speed. Anthony leaned back.

"Rivers are roads," his companion stated.

"Rivers, sir, are power," Anthony returned.

The handsome fellow's eyes darkened, as if he were unaccustomed to contradiction. After a moment, he broke into easy conversation. More bridges would be built when Mr. Madison's war ended, the war that ought never to have started. More roads, too . . . converging on Boston, hub of the universe. . . .

Anthony welcomed this opportunity to learn about the country. And then, out of the flow of impersonal talk, a question leaped at him.

"Been in New England long?"

"No, sir."

"You travelled by stage from Boston?"

"Yes, sir."

"And how did you get to Boston?"

The questioning had a relentless drive; but this intelligent American was not likely to throw him in jail or send him back to England, Anthony judged.

"On the brig, *Dolphin,*" he said. "She docked yesterday before dawn."

The big man started, then said, "I hear you met an enemy ship of the line."

"Captain and crew were very clever."

"I agree with you. As it happens, I own the *Dolphin.*"

"Then you must be one of the Lester Brothers, sir."

"James Lester. How did you guess?"

"The captain and crew spoke often of you. Besides, wherever American vessels dock, and that is round the globe, men know the name of Lester—as I learned in Holland."

The words seemed to fall like music on the shipowner's ears. "Your name, my young friend?" he inquired.

"Anthony Bryce, sir."

"Glad to meet you, Mr. Bryce." Lester shook hands cordially. "I was informed that a lad got aboard the brig in Holland. Gave a good account of himself, the shipmaster said, and left with some pay due him."

"I hurried away from the waterfront," Anthony explained. "The crew warned me that British agents frequent the big ports."

The shipowner appeared amused. "If you care to say," he remarked, "I'd be interested in hearing what brings a young Englishman to Boston."

Anthony hesitated, but decided he could safely talk. He stated briefly how he had lost both his parents in December. "I'm a mill mechanic," he went on, "and I'd like to find an American interested in manufacturing cotton cloth."

"Upon my word!" Lester pushed his tall beaver back and stared.

"I think I could build a power loom for anyone with the

capital necessary," Anthony continued. "You've heard of the loom that is operated by means of water power?"

"Young man," Lester spoke at last, "we don't want factories over here."

"I heard a woman say the people need cotton cloth."

"Let me finish!" Lester raised a white fleshy hand. "From earliest times, Americans have exported raw materials, imported finished goods. Our slogan has been: *Keep the workshops in Europe*. The scarcity of cloth is very temporary. The few mills that have started up will be forced to close. This war will end soon. We shall import finished goods as before. And believe me, British laws, designed to keep monopoly of manufacturing in Britain, are wise laws. Advantageous to British trade and to ours . . ."

Any young man wanting to try new ways had better be prepared to meet opposition, Anthony reflected, as the authoritative voice went on.

"But I have a plan." Lester nodded affably. "Many people would hesitate to employ an Englishman during the war. I like you, Mr. Bryce. And I know the value of a young man who understands the prestige of Lester Brothers abroad. Give up this absurd idea of work in a cotton mill, and come to us!"

"I'm not interested in ships."

"We'll find you a post on shore."

"I wouldn't care for that, either."

Lester's eyes narrowed. "You mentioned capital, Mr. Bryce. New England money is handled mainly in Boston. The truth is, a man injures his credit in Boston if he even admits an interest in mills or factories." He paused as if to let the weight of his words sink in, and continued. "I'm picking up vessels at bargain prices. Got one at Newburyport for a song. Small shipowners can't take chances these times—one sinking wipes them out. But we who own fleets make enough from the profits of a single successful voyage to compensate for the losses of several sinkings. And when peace comes, we can't have too many keels.

"You'll go far with Lester Brothers. Boston is a pleasant town, and I have a daughter who would introduce you to the young people there."

The man was convincing, even magnetic. Anthony knew that the war kept ships short-handed. Without capital behind him, he could get nowhere in a mill. Had he better accept, for a time at least, Lester's offer?

The shipowner raised his hand to set his tall beaver straight. And the movement of the white fleshy hand with the big seal ring reminded Anthony of another hand, of slender fingers that twisted a blue muffler deftly. His father's voice rang in his ears. *Son, go to the States . . . In the young republic you can do. . . .*

For a minute his throat felt tight. Then he said, "Thank you, sir. Think I'll try to find someone who will employ me in a mill."

"You are a fool." The words lashed at him, and Lester sat stiffly.

They rode in silence now. A milestone told them when they passed from Massachusetts into New Hampshire. After long hours of being tossed about, they reached a sandy stretch where the stage wheels churned, half way to the hubs in ruts. They rolled through a growth of dark pine, and then through graceful white birch. The stage slowed down.

Lester glanced at his huge watch. "We're ahead of the scheduled time," he observed coldly. "You'll find Portsmouth a privateering town, Mr. Bryce," he went on. "The citizens will not suspect you of mischief unless you give them cause. But they'll be slow to put confidence in you."

A sly thrust, Anthony realized. Who would readily put trust in an enemy alien?

The stage halted, and a shabby seaman opened the door. "Mr. Lester?" There was deference for the man from Boston.

Lester nodded, stepped down. He turned, extending his hand. "Glad to have met you, Mr. Bryce." His tone was cold but civil. "When you come to Boston you'll find the pay due you waiting on Long Wharf."

"Thank you, sir."

"And remember," Lester went on, "it's ships that will bring the United States prosperity." With a curt nod, he followed the seaman down a lane.

The stage jogged on. It was lucky, Anthony thought, that the movement of Lester's fat hand had kept him from abandoning his purpose. He would yet make cotton cloth for proud independent people who spoke their minds, cringing to nobody.

Hands, he mused, had always interested him. The American who had visited English mills had such sensitive hands that his touch on a machine seemed a caress. He could not recall the American's name, nor the town he lived in; but he would always remember the hands. And the quiet voice asking earnestly about mill management, about the health of workers. *The people of the United States,* that voice had said, *will never be independent until they have their own mills.*

Anthony sat erect suddenly. Lester's picture of the prospect for American mills might be the prevailing view. But it was not the *only* view. Given a choice, he'd count on the man with the sensitive hands. If *he* had been a passenger in this stagecoach, it would have been a meeting!

Anthony felt hope return. Not much, but enough to go on. He looked with interest at the houses they passed. Stately homes with high-fenced gardens, fans over doorways, captain's walks. He liked the pedestrians' air of independence. He was amused by the barelegged lads who dashed out from alleys and ran alongside.

They rumbled through a street where buildings had been wrecked by a terrible fire. As they pulled to a halt, an eerie whistle rang out.

Foothold in America

The Gentleman Is My Guest

A QUEER one." The driver nodded in the direction of the little man who had climbed on top in Newburyport and now, fingers to his mouth, uttered hair-raising sounds that made the pack of boys shriek with delight. "Likes to show off," the driver added as he reached for luggage. "Here's yourn, sir."

Anthony felt in his pocket. "What's the best way to get to Maine?" he asked.

"Maine's just t'other side of the river. Ferry'll carry ye over. Thank ye, sir." The driver swaggered off.

Anthony surveyed the clutter of men and vehicles around. Had he better stay in New Hampshire or cross the river to Maine? He flipped a coin; and it came up for Maine. Well, before going on, he'd ease his hunger. An inn stood across the road—high, square, its door hospitably open.

He had almost reached the building when he felt a touch on his arm.

"Stoppin' here?" The queer little man who had ridden on top peered up at him, torn cap in one hand, bandanna bundle in the other.

Anthony had no desire for the company of the seedy stranger. But he lacked the heart to refuse him a meal. "Want to eat supper with me?"

"Aye." The faded eyes in the young-old face glowed like a dog's when a bone is tossed.

Entering from the street, the inn interior seemed dim. A smiling landlord stood by the door, a white-aproned cook tended the meat and fish that turned on the spit. Sputtering candles threw shadows on the dark panelled walls. Anthony chose a corner table, and the serving lass came promptly.

"Fried alewife, bit of bannock bread, swaller of cider," his guest ordered glibly.

Amused, thinking the fellow might know native viands, Anthony ordered similarly.

The room, fairly well filled, was restful after the jolting stage. The large table in front of the fireplace was surrounded by dignified men discussing, evidently, local problems. Anthony caught sentences now and then.

"Portsmouth had fifteen acres of valuable property destroyed in the December fire," an older man who wore his hair queued declared. "We need a law," a young man said, "limiting the height of wooden buildings." "Price of brick's too high now . . ."

The voices were drowned by the clatter of earthenware.

These men would not tell him, Anthony reflected, where to find a cotton mill. His eyes ranged over smaller tables with groups of two's and three's. A crowd sat in the corner opposite him, feet sprawled. Stevedores and rivermen, probably. *They* knew where the falls were; which mills shipped lumber, grain, and if any kept river craft busy carrying cotton fibre. But they would be close-mouthed with a stranger. Anthony overheard them grumble about vessels held in port by the blockade.

"Gal's comin'." His seedy companion patted his belly as the serving lass set down two steaming platters, a basket of bread, two mugs of cider. He wolfed his food; drank with sucking sounds, his thin scarred hands around his mug.

Anthony ate slowly, letting each morsel of alewife lie on his tongue for the savor. The hot bannock bread was flaky. He saw his companion, plate emptied, lean back on the bench.

"My name's Shadrach Nye," the little man said. "Folks call me 'Shad.' "

Anthony, mouth filled with alewife, nodded in reply.

"What's your name?"

Anthony told him, after he'd swallowed.

"Anthony!" his companion repeated. "What do folks call ye for short?"

Anthony said nothing, his eyes on a huge fellow in fustian shirt and sheepskin smallclothes who stood in the doorway. The crowd opposite greeted him with shouts. "Steve's come. . . . Landlord, more beef! A platter for Steve!"

As the newcomer strutted over the sanded floor, the landlord glanced at the center table. The men there gave no sign of disapproval.

"Them's candidates for 'lection," Shadrach Nye informed him. "Wants to be popular—anyways till after Town Meetin' Day. Steve's a boxer when he ain't loadin' ships. Some calls him 'local champion.' Land sakes! see them victuals landlord's sendin' over!"

The crowd quieted and began to eat.

"Think I'll call ye 'Tony,'" Shadrach Nye announced.

Anthony said nothing.

"My folks is dead. How's yourn?"

"Dead."

"Got a wife?"

"No."

"I ain't got a wife, neither. Female's a pesky bit of baggage to take around, and I got other interests . . ."

Anthony leaned back. In a little while he would start for Maine; rid himself of his chatty companion. But for a few minutes he would rest. He let his eyes close.

Rough guffaws from the crowd opposite roused him.

"Ye cat-napped," Shadrach Nye told him.

Anthony stretched, feeling surprisingly refreshed.

Shadrach nudged him. "Tony, listen to this I found in Newburyport paper." Holding a torn scrap close to his eyes, he slowly read: *"Nathan Long has escaped from Fowlerstown jail. . . . Whoever will apprehend said law-breaker—"*

"Shadrach Nye," Anthony broke in, "are you wanted?"

"Not in Fowlerstown. I'm Shadrach Nye, jist as I told ye. I only want ye to know I'm cute as the best of 'em."

"Cute!" Anthony repeated, wishing he had avoided Shadrach Nye.

"Aye. This feller, Nathan Long, bust out of one jail, and they can't ketch him. Now *I* bust out of a dozen jails. But here I be."

"What do you get in jail for?" inquired Anthony, his tone stern.

Shadrach winked. "Slight inability to tell *teum* from *meum*. Ye see, I know my little Latin! Grand'ther was a parson—over to Manchester way. My pa got killed, fightin' for General Washington. My ma was a poor orphan, died when I was born. Ye be eyein' my wrists? Slippin' out of handcuffs's bound to leave scars, Tony."

Was the fellow a thief? Anthony wondered. Or did some queer twist in his brain lead him to pretend he stole? The small hands slipped along the bench, slid back. Anthony said nothing.

"Mebbe ye're surprised," Shadrach prattled on, "that I ain't afeard to come into this inn. Tony, I like the country round Portsmouth, where District of Maine and Granite State meets. I like the country and the river and the folks. So I take care, nobody has charges agin' me round here."

The serving lass brought the score. Anthony reached for his wallet.

"Here 'tis, Tony." Beaming, Shadrach handed over the wallet. He explained, when the girl had gone: "Took it to show how easy I could of robbed ye, and got away while ye catnapped. But I like ye, Tony."

"Thank you," Anthony returned, his manner grave.

A stir passed over the room. The crowd opposite quieted and drew their feet in. The landlord stood at attention. The dignified men at the center table looked up. In the doorway, Anthony saw a sour-faced fellow.

" 'Tis Mark Badger," Shadrach whispered, shrinking, "and I'd as soon meet up with the devil."

The men at the center table had a different welcome. "Glad to see you in Portsmouth, Mr. Badger. . . . Won't you sit with us?"

"I am in haste this evening." The newcomer spoke as if he had no need of catering to Portsmouth men. He said something to the landlord about a tray to be sent upstairs. With a pompous air and wide-straddling gait, he started to cross the room.

At Anthony's corner he stopped short. "Shadrach Nye," he spoke loud enough for all to hear, "what is thee doing among honest men?"

Anthony bowed slightly. "The gentleman," he said curtly, "is my guest."

"Then thee is a fool he will rob, or else another thief."

"And I will thank you to keep your opinion of me to yourself," Anthony returned.

Badger, his long-nosed face dark with rage, stalked on.

One of the crowd in the corner piped: "Stranger spoke like Britainer. Maybe he's a spy."

Stillness fell over the room. Someone hit a wooden platter that clattered from the table, rolled over the sanded floor towards Badger. A young sailor cried: "Stranger should fight, Britainer or no. Fight or be reckoned thief!"

"Fight!" the crowd roared, jubilant. "We want to see a fight. And afore darkness falls."

Above the clamor one voice protested, "Mark can't fight, he's Quaker."

"Quaker can have substitute." The sailor pointed to the big fellow in the fustian shirt. "Steve'll fight for Mark Badger."

All over the room, cries rang out. "Steve'll lick stranger. . . . Let Steve fight."

Aghast, Anthony glanced at the center table. The town officers, who might have put an end to the disorder, had left. He needed the respect of responsible men if he was to find an employer! The last thing he wanted was notoriety gained in a tavern brawl. He deplored the impulse which had led him to defend Shadrach Nye, to linger here—even enter the inn. He should have crossed the river to Maine as soon as he flipped the coin. He *could* make his way through the noisy crowd, go to Maine now. Derisive cries would pursue him. Better this than a brawl! He bent to pick up his trunk.

"Tony, they won't let ye go," Shadrach whispered, worried. "Mark ain't true Quaker—I'll tell ye 'bout that, later. Point now is, crowd'll quiet when Mark leaves. He sailed loaded schooner down from brickyard where he's manager, and when tide's right, he'll sail schooner back. Tide turns soon. Act like ye're deaf and dumb, Tony."

Anthony glanced across at the window table. Dark-haired Badger sat with his back to the room, ignoring the uproar his arrogance had caused.

The men were crying out wagers. "Three to one on Steve. . . . *Five* to one. . . . Britainer has longer arms. . . . Steve's heavier. . . . *Six* to one on Steve our champion . . . Steve'll lick any snooping foreigner. . . ."

"Don't ye fight!" Shadrach begged. "Tony, I ain't a-worth it."

Shadrach's plea was useless. Anthony found himself seized and dragged towards the door. "We want a fight!" the dozen men who held him yelled.

The landlord rapped for attention. Nobody in Portsmouth objected to a fair fight, he called out, but there must be judges and rules.

"Let landlord name judges, and tell us the rules!" the men called back.

Borne out through the door, Anthony decided that if he'd got to fight, he'd *fight*. Once warmed up, the stiffness he felt from the journey would go. Life at sea had toughened him. Bill's boxing lessons had given him skill. What kind of fighting was he to meet? In England, Steve would be an elbow-fighter, with short fast punches. But here?

He was set down in the open area beside the inn. Shadrach Nye, mournful, stood beside him.

"How does Steve fight?" Anthony asked.

"Steve's mean," the little man whimpered. "Gits your eyes when he's playin', and your gizzard when he's mad."

Removing his coat, Anthony saw his opponent, on the other side of the open area, strip off his shirt. Big muscles bulged; the fellow must weigh thirteen stone, against his own ten. Noting that Steve kicked off his shoes and hose, Anthony removed his own.

"I'll look out for your things, Tony," Shadrach quavered, voice high-keyed.

Word of the fight had spread, and spectators tumbled over each other in their eagerness to find places. Young blades drilling in the square, ropewalk workers, apprentices in shops; all had come to see Steve fight. "Steve's our champion!" they yelled.

It was a pleasant April evening. The yellow sun, within a half hour of setting, threw shadows on crowded windows and fence tops, and on the noisy ranks that made a wide circle around the open area.

The landlord appeared, followed by a barelegged boy who carried a hunting horn. Blows must be struck fair, the landlord announced. Kicking was not permissible. Ten counts would make a fall, two falls out of three ended the fight. A townsman had consented to act as referee. His son Johnny was to sound start and finish of rounds.

"Hooray for landlord!" the crowd roared. "Hooray for Johnny!"

Steve strutted forward, and the cheering rose to the sky: "Hooray for our Steve!"

Anthony went to meet him. If he could take punishment long enough to learn Steve's tactics, he had a chance.

And then Johnny blew the horn.

Steve was no mere elbow-fighter. He sent punches straight from the shoulder. Anthony sparred, avoiding the big hands. Steve got in a jab on his chin; began to edge behind.

Never let your opponent get behind you, Bill had said. Anthony took ugly blows. Meeting the great hands was like running against iron hooks. A clout on the jaw knocked him flat.

"One-two-three . . ." The calling of the counts made no sense. Shadrach Nye put an arm under him. "Ye done fine, Tony," he whispered. "Take a deep breath."

With Shad's help, Anthony managed to sit up. Blood dripped from his head, but his back and legs felt sound. Now he made out what the crowd yelled: "Fun's over. Britainer got licked . . . Steve ain't never been beat." The spectators were drifting away.

"Young feller," someone cried, "ye didn't do bad, but ye got licked."

Anthony's head cleared. The story would spread that Steve had knocked him out in one round, on his first day in Portsmouth. Nobody employed a man who let others make a fool of him. He was done for in New Hampshire.

Then a girl's voice rang out, high and clear above the clamor. "Stranger did well. And he was brave."

Anthony looked around. No women were in sight.

The landlord came to shake his hand. Another man said, "I'm referee. You agree, local champion won in fair fight?"

The thought that defeat now would hurt his prospects, Shad's loyalty, the unknown girl's encouraging voice; all had braced Anthony. He got to his feet. "Local fighter won first round," he said. "I'm ready for the second."

The referee whistled softly, the landlord frowned.

"Tony," Shadrach whimpered, "Steve's only been playin'. Ye ain't seen him angered. Crowd'll let ye go, now ye're beaten. Don't fight more!"

"When I'm forced into a fight, I finish it, Shadrach Nye." With his bare hand, Anthony tried to wipe the blood off his forehead.

"Here's my hanky. And ye're to call me 'Shad.' "

"Thank you, Shad." Anthony took the ragged square.

Men shouted now: "Fight ain't over. Britainer wants more!" Spectators hurried back to their places.

Anthony eyed Steve, swinging towards him. The heaving chest, black hairs flattened, was wet with sweat; shoulders, arms and legs, were mighty. But no intelligence showed in the big round face. Someone could have taught Steve his powerful blows, and persuaded him he could never be downed. What would Steve do if he met surprise strategy? If his confidence were shaken?

"Six to one on Steve!" The wagers were being called. "I'll make it eight to one!"

But Bill had said: *Brain, not brawn, wins a fight.*

Blows came from every direction. Anthony tried to reach over his opponent, manoeuvre a rap from behind; but Steve had speed. Steve's iron arm forced him down. He fought back. Stealing the offensive, he pinned one of Steve's great hands between his own arm and body. Steve swung free.

"Tony, your eyes!" Shad shrieked. "Steve blinded a feller once."

Shielding his face, Anthony let himself be driven back. Steve tried to knee him, and nobody called the foul. Anthony lunged. Surprised, Steve was thrown off balance. When Anthony struck at his jaw, Steve went down.

"One-two-three—" Steve was on his feet, and ugly. He

lifted his right leg. Anthony dodged but got the edge of the blow in his belly.

"Steve kicked," the unknown girl's voice called. "Kicking's not permitted, according to the rules."

"Aye," someone in the crowd shouted. "Landlord said so."

Rather weakly, Johnny tooted on the horn.

Gasping, reeling, dripping sweat, Anthony gazed at the inn. The voice seemed to come from that direction. He scanned each small window pane, but no girl's face showed.

"Tony!" Shad touched his arm. "Steve's winded. Referee pertends to scold him to give him rest time. 'Tain't fair, but folks with bets on Steve wants him to win. That cut of yourn's worser."

Anthony put his hand to his head, and it came away bloody. His chest and arms were a crisscross pattern of welts. He looked over at Steve. The local fighter had no cut or serious bruise. And yet the men around him seemed anxious. Men with heavy wagers?

The fighter was returning, and his face showed dismay. So Steve had his bruise, an inward bruise! Taught he could never be beaten, he had been down long enough to hear the counts called. He had been caught in a foul.

"Luck to Steve!" someone yelled.

"Our champion!" the crowd roared.

Steve's face brightened.

Leaping at each other, they struck simultaneously. When Steve made for his eyes, Anthony threw him off. He felt the iron arm's grip, but managed to grip back. He tripped; found himself being driven to the ring's edge, strength almost spent.

Then he thought of an old old trick. Tried too often, perhaps, but all depended now on a surprise blow. Throat raw, body an agony of ache, he regained some of the ground he had lost. Then he yielded enough to let Steve feel on top, and stood as if ripe for a fall. Steve raised his arm for the final pummeling. And as the mighty arm fell, Anthony leaped to one side, letting Steve, propelled forward by the unspent force of his own blow, go flat.

"One-two-three-four-five—" The slow count sounded like a wailing.

The referee broke the stillness. "Score's even. One fall, each side."

Steve got up to finish the fight. When Johnny blew, he went through motions, as before. But he'd lost a round and didn't understand why. Sent without confidence, his blows went wide. A rap at his shoulder knocked him off balance. Falling, he broke a collar bone.

Stunned when Steve did not rise, the crowd recovered slowly. "Stranger licked Steve," someone yelled.

"Steve thought too much of himself," a voice called. "Steve needed to be tooken down."

Anthony was reeling towards the pump when Shad cried, "Tony, I'll git water."

"We'll any of us get water for winner," someone shouted.

They were all on Anthony's side now. The landlord, sensitive to customers' moods, bawled orders: "Show winner to best chamber! Carry up hot water! Carry up luggage he left by his table!"

Leaning on Shad, Anthony staggered forward. If the girl who had given him courage, when he was down, tarried within the inn, he meant to find her.

Don't Ye Be Castin' Sheep's Eyes

UP IN the East Chamber, a serving-man brought ointments, soft old linen. He lugged in a tin tub, wide-brimmed like a giant's hat, laid warm towels by. "Want, I do for you, sir?" he asked. It would be a proud boast, that he had bathed the winner!

"My friend will look after me, thank you."

The fellow looked disappointed, in spite of the coin he received.

"Now Tony, jist sit in this here tub." Hands gentle as a woman's, Shad lathered Anthony with a jelly-like soap, splashed hot water over him, rinsed with fresh water, dried the skin carefully. "A bit of old linen to cover bruises," he said, spreading ointment, "and mebbe ye can git clothes on."

It was lucky the Liverpool tailor had provided extra trousers, Anthony thought. Those he had worn in the fight were torn to ribbons.

"I'll pack up for ye," Shad offered when Anthony was dressed. "Want that I help ye down the stairs?"

"No, thanks." A bandage around his head, a patch on his cheek, his arm in a sling, Anthony limped outside.

Lighted by candles in wall sconces, the hall had a dozen closed doors. Anthony eyed them, resenting their power to bar his view. A stairway led to upper stories; but gentry would be accommodated on this floor, and he felt sure the girl he wanted to find was gently bred.

Down the hall a door opened, but only a chamber maid came out. He waited until presently another door opened. A waiter balancing a tray, this time. At the end of the hall a door stood open. In spite of sharp twinges, Anthony made his way towards it; it was a small unoccupied parlor. Was there no clue anywhere to the whereabouts of the girl?

He looked down the main stairway. The square hall at the foot was bounded by doors: the open one, on the left, led to the noisy general room; the one on the right stood an inch or two ajar; the stout street door between was closed. Anthony waited, uncertain which way to turn. Must the identity of the girl who had given him courage be a mystery he'd never solve?

And then, high and clear, a voice rang out. "Tide's right. He will be here any minute."

Anthony felt a pleasurable excitement. Forgetting his aching body, he started down the flight and had nearly gained the foot when he heard a vehicle halt outside. Immediately, the door to the right swung wide. A girl appeared, tall, wrapped in a drab-colored cape. She glanced up the stairs.

Under the bonnet's stiff brim, Anthony saw a bright face, friendly gray eyes, reddish-brown hair.

"Good evening," the girl greeted him.

"Good evening, ma'am." He was trying to find more words, when the street door was shoved open.

Mark Badger stood outside. Spying Anthony, he glowered until hostility seemed to flow from him. Then he turned to the girl.

"Tide'll not wait on thy dallying," he said sullenly.

"I am ready these five minutes," she replied calmly. A maid, carrying parcels, appeared and helped her gather up her skirt. She stepped into the waiting vehicle, the maid laid the parcels at her feet. Badger climbed in beside her.

As the wheels rolled, she gave Anthony a smile.

Returning the greeting, he stood in the doorway until the vehicle had rounded the corner. The sloping street, washed in sunset glow, seemed brighter because she had gone that way.

"If ye please, sir, the young lady wanted ye to win."

He wheeled and found the maid waiting. "She watched?"

"Nay, sir. She's Quaker, and Quakers may not look on fighting. She bade *me* stand by the window. When I said ye was hard pressed, she'd walk up and down. 'The brave young stranger!' she'd cry. 'Are they treating him fair?' she'd ask. When I told her Steve tried to knee ye, she ran to the window. And when I told her Steve kicked, she called out. But eyes closed, mind ye. She is one to mind Quaker rules! She clapped her hands when ye won. I think she took a fancy to ye. . . . Thank ye, sir."

Was the girl Mark Badger's wife? Where did she live? Anthony had a dozen questions. But the maid, coin in her hand, had vanished.

Cheers welcomed Anthony, when he entered the general room, and on all sides men invited him to join them. Acknowledging but declining the invitations, he limped to his former corner. Cautiously, he lowered himself.

Presently Shad joined him. "Took longer'n what I thought," he said. "Trunk's ready, when ye wants to start for Maine."

Strangely, Anthony found himself less inclined to go to Maine than before the fight. A girl's bright face, chestnut curls under an outlandish bonnet, kept obtruding on his thoughts. If only he knew whether or not she was married! Shad might know, but Anthony hesitated to reveal his interest.

A serving-maid brought plates of steaming chowder. "Compliments of landlord, sir, and more to follow."

"Kindly give him my regards." Famished, Anthony fell to, and Shad followed his example.

"Man in brown what rode inside stage," Shad said after a while, "saw ye fight. Him and 'nother man was drivin' a lively little piece. I always 'member hosses. T'other man wanted to go on, but him in brown was set on stoppin'. Stubborn feller, wants his way, I minded. They stayed till ye knocked Steve out."

Anthony chuckled. James Lester knew he had got into a fight almost as soon as he stepped out of the stage! Well, it didn't matter. His path and the wealthy shipowner's were unlikely to cross.

"Shad, do you know anything about New Hampshire cotton mills?" he asked.

"Cotton mills!" Shad scratched his scrubby chin. "They's three-four over to Hillsborough County. New Ipswich has one. Peterborough has one."

"How far inland is Hillsborough County?"

"Day's journey, more or less, 'cordin' to if ye travel foot or hossback."

Anthony shook his head. Moist air made the smoothest cloth. He wanted a site not more than fifteen miles from the sea. "Any mills near here?"

"Land sakes, seems like every town on a river has a half-baked critter tryin' to run a mill. Exeter, Dover, Newmarket, other towns, has cotton mills. Not to mention Forks Village. They's three-four over to Maine."

"What's the matter with Forks Village?"

"Eben Todd runs the mill, and folks call Eben the most crackbrained feller north of Boston. Always tryin' some new-fangled scheme, and always failin'."

Anthony gave a shrug. He had no desire for an incompetent employer. "I want work," he said, "in a cotton mill that has a dependable owner."

"Place in a store'd be better for an eddicated man," Shad told him. "Lessen ye can teach school or be parson, eh?"

Anthony laughed at the well-meant suggestions. "Making cotton cloth by machinery is the only thing I'm interested in," he said. Suddenly he found himself thinking of the girl who had smiled at him as she drove off with the surly Quaker.

"Where's Badger's brickyard?" he asked after hesitating.

"Mile or so this side of Forks Village. It's owned by Damon family. That was Damon gal called out, when Steve kicked . . ."

Anthony tried not to appear as interested as he was, while

Shad rambled. ". . . She must of come down on schooner for shoppin' in Portsmouth. Mother's dead, father too, and she runs the house for her uncle, Lish Damon. 'Bout sixteen she is, age when plenty of gals wed. Some say Mark has his eye on her."

So she was unmarried! Anthony's spirits rose.

"But don't ye go to Forks Village," Shad went on. "Eben Todd ain't crooked, but nothing he has a hand in pans out right. Then there's Mark Badger. Mark'd certain make trouble. He's one never to forgit how ye spoke up to him, and how ye won the fight."

In spite of Shad's warning, Anthony found himself thinking favorably of Forks Village; it was near the sea, and an incompetent owner might allow him a freer hand. As for Badger, he'd like to meet the fellow again.

Feeling reckless now, he asked, "What is Miss Damon's Christian name?"

"Don't ye be castin' sheep's eyes at her," Shad warned. "She's Quaker, has to wed inside Society of Friends."

Anthony persisted, "What is her Christian name?"

"Lemme think." Perverse suddenly, Shad leaned back, eyes on a ceiling beam. " 'Tain't Abigail, nor Jane, nor Ruth. 'Tain't Mary nor none of them names."

"See here!" Anthony gripped Shad's arm. "You remember that name or you'll get the worst shaking you ever had."

" 'Tis Charity," Shad responded with alacrity.

"Charity!" Anthony repeated softly, letting Shad's arm go.

"Now mind what I said," the little man begged. "If ye thinks of that high-steppin' Quaker, ye're madder'n what some folks say I be."

But Anthony had made his decision. "How do I get to Forks Village?"

Shad gave a long sigh. Evidently convinced that further protest was useless, he edged close enough to whisper: "Boat lies on beach 'bout five minutes' walk away. It's dark outside.

Tide's right, wind's right. Stroke of paddle now and then to steer, and ye can float up to Forks Village wharf."

Anthony drew off. "You mean, you'd send me up river in a stolen boat?"

Shad's eyes turned sly. "It's this way, Tony. Breakin' into a boathouse or other building after dark is felony. Some places, law'd hang a man. But slippin' a boat into river, when tide might of taken it anyways, that's jist cuteness." Shad had the look of a dog expecting praise.

Anthony gave no praise. He gripped the little man's arm. "When you're with me," he said, stern, "you're not to steal. Not so much as a pin. Understand?"

"Aye." Shad had the look of a dog who sees he has erred. "And now I think about it, that's how I'd best like things atween us, Tony."

Anthony eased his grip. "Tell me how to get to Forks Village."

"Gundelow leaves, early mornin'. We'd have to lie over."

"We!" Anthony exclaimed, aghast.

"Please, Tony," Shad begged. "I won't steal. Not so much as a pin."

His pleading look overcame Anthony's reluctance. "Well, then we'll lie over."

Next morning they stood aft on the river gundelow. Piscataqua ran wide and swift and shining, Maine on the right hand side, New Hampshire on the left. The squat craft, navigated by a skipper and two hands, was about forty feet long, a third as wide; with a slanting yard and lateen sail attached to a short mast, permitting the vessel to shoot under low bridges. "Ye can travel by gundelow," Shad explained, "where ye can't use a hoss."

A cuddy lay under the platform on which Shad and Anthony stood, with another cuddy forward. Passengers now shared the open hold with crates, hogsheads, kegs. Anthony pictured the space piled high with bales of cotton fibre or bolts of finished cloth.

"That's a snarl of water we jist edged round," Shad observed. "Piscataqua divides here and we come into Forks River."

The tributary stream was narrower but clear. Presently Shad pointed a finger. "There's the schooner took brick to Portsmouth! The *Augustus Damon!*" The vessel on which Charity had sailed rode lightly at her pier.

The big square house on the hill above, sheltered by a grove of pine, was the Damon home, Shad said. "Brickyard's yonder, close to highway," he explained. "The place is called 'Blue Clay Farm' account of soil being a bluish color. Land sakes, for a minute I thought feller by riverbank was Mark, but 'tain't. Dog follers him, see! Dog'd run from Mark."

As the gundelow ploughed north, Anthony kept his eyes on the hillside acres and gray clapboarded pile.

" 'Member I said Mark wan't true Quaker?" Shad inquired. "I'll tell ye 'bout that now. Mark's pa joined General Washington's army same time as Gus Damon, the gal's pa. Gus, being Quaker, cared for wounded. Mark's pa, a soldier, got killed. Well, Gus looked after his young'un. Sent young Mark away for schoolin'. Took him on the place soon's he was old enough. Jist afore Gus died, three-four year back, Mark turned Quaker. Matter of bus'ness, some says, Mark aimin' to be master, 'stead of manager, of Blue Clay Farm."

Eyes squinted, long coat-tails blowing in the wind, Shad looked thoughtful. "Gus died same time gal's ma did," he went on. "Got throat distemper. But if Gus was alive today, I doubt he'd put up with Mark's high-handed ways. And yet, Mark's smart and can make folks like him. Some say Charity c'd do worse. But I doubt she's thought much 'bout getting hitched yet. Mark's five-six year older. My guess is, she thinks more 'bout the wild hoss she rides. Big gray devil, bucks and rears. . . . Thrown? Not her. She calls the animal 'Gabriel,' but namin' a hoss after a saint don't make him one. No more'n

Mark's callin' hisself Quaker changes his nature . . ."

As Blue Clay Farm passed out of sight, Anthony decided he would learn to ride.

Presently Shad picked up his bandanna bundle. "We're close in to Forks Village Landin'," he said. "Todd Brothers Pharmacy is a mite up the street. Ye'll likely find Eben there."

"What about you, Shad?"

"I got a hide-away," the little man hunched his shoulders, "couple of mile out on Manchester road. I wanted to come up river with ye, but ye'll do better without me, now."

The gundelow's yard fell. A coiled rope whizzed.

"Shad!" a man on the wharf called, "sheriff of York County was asking for you."

Shad made a grimace and turned to Anthony. "Ye see how I'd only make things harder for ye, Tony. Ye'll have trouble enough, and Daniel Webster couldn't tell ye truer. If ye ever needs me, take Manchester road and look for tree struck by 'lectric fluid. My cabin's close by, and if I'm not there, leave a note. Not under door! Sheriff might find it! Apple tree near brook has a hole in its crotch. Drop note in, weight it down good! Whatever happens, ye can count on Shad. I ain't forgit how ye stood up for me in Portsmouth. Nor I never will." Twirling his bundle, he hopped ashore.

Anthony, so stiff he had to wait for the gundelow to be tied, watched the childish figure in the faded long-skirted coat sidle through the crowd, climb the steep street, vanish around a corner. A rascal he gladly would have avoided yesterday! Today, strangely, he felt sorry to see Shad go.

The throng on the wharf included the postmaster, storekeepers expecting consignments, stevedores and rivermen, farmers, old men, boys, idlers. There were fewer class distinctions in Forks Village than in Portsmouth, Anthony judged. Every man was as good as the next—and knew it.

He made arrangements for leaving his luggage for a while, and then limped up the steep street.

The Crackbrained Feller

THOMAS CARR pushed the hemlock broom back and forth over the pharmacy floor. When not attending school, which met in the spare room over the currier's shop, he worked for Todd Brothers. His father, the Reverend Timothy Carr, a graduate of Harvard College and the most learned man in the village, said a pharmacy was a good place for a boy of twelve years; and if a lad was not born to minister unto souls, as Thomas clearly was not, he had better learn to minister to bodies.

Thomas, red-haired, snub-nosed, enjoyed work in the pharmacy but for a different reason. Thomas liked people. He liked the matrons who came to buy physics, lozenges, the new-fashioned washballs. He liked the men wanting books, tobacco, snuff. He liked the children with pennies for taffy or gumdrops. Most of all he liked travellers, who wore strange clothes, spoke strange speech, brought strange news; and more travellers came to the pharmacy than to any place in the village—save the inn.

Dumping the pan of dirt he had swept up into the fireplace, Thomas wished a traveller would come. Mr. Dominicus Todd, working now at the small high desk in the back room, said travellers wasted time and brought little trade. But Thomas suspected that Dominicus feared a traveller might interest Eben, the younger brother, in some newfangled scheme certain to turn out a failure.

Thomas picked up the duster and went to the window. He dusted off the great pear-shaped bottle filled with pink liquid, and the mate in the other window filled with blue liquid. He dusted the brass mortars, the blue jar marked *Life Of Man.* Then Dominicus shuffled in from the back room.

He pointed a finger. "Dirt in that corner. Work smart, now!"

"Yes, sir." Thomas tucked the broom into the corner. Eben would never have spied the mite of dust—and if he had, would not have spoken.

"I'm going to the Landing. Goods due from Portsmouth." Dominicus pulled on his coat. "Tie the string tighter round them twigs! And on your way back after dinner, get more hemlock and make a fresh broom!"

"Yes, sir."

As the door slammed behind Dominicus, Thomas bent to tie the hemlock twigs tighter. He wished he had a straw broom, like the one Charity Damon brought home, last time she went to Boston. If a travelling man with straw brooms called, Dominicus would order him out of the shop; Eben would take a dozen. And this was the difference between the brothers.

Thomas went to the back room and began to sweep. Earlier in the day Mark Badger had stalked in here. He and Dominicus pow-wowed, sitting with their feet so close to the fire the place still smelled of scorched shoe leather. Then Mark went off, head in the air. Pretty soon Eben came, sat quiet while Dominicus talked. After a time Eben stood up, said, "I'll go over to the mill now." He went off, his forehead a mess of wrinkles. Anyone could see, Mark had put Dominicus up to making Eben do something he didn't like. . . . The doorlatch clicked and Thomas hurried into the shop.

A traveller stood there. He wore a queer kind of jacket, queer long trousers, his face and his hand were bandaged.

"What can I do for you, sir?" Thomas asked, bursting with curiosity.

"I'll look around, if you don't mind," the traveller said, moving towards the shelves of books.

"*I* don't mind," Thomas rejoined. He wished the traveller

would say right off what his business was, instead of looking the place over. He was taking a book off the shelf!

"Southey's *Life of Nelson,*" Thomas rattled off. "Just over from England in spite of the blockade. Two volumes in one for seventy-five cents."

"A little too large for my pocket, thank you."

He was putting the book back in place. He had a pleasant smile, though he walked as if his back hurt him. His eyes were sharp but kind. A man sharp as Dominicus, kind as Eben, ever so much younger than either, *would* be somebody to know. If only this stranger would say what his business was, before Dominicus came back and hustled him out.

"We have pungents, aromatics, essences," Thomas recited, hoping to hurry things along. "Also cephalic snuff for headaches, ointments—"

The stranger spoke at last. "Is Mr. Todd around?"

"Which Mr. Todd?" Thomas inquired, breathless.

"Mr. Eben Todd."

"No, but I can tell you where he's gone to. He—"

The doorlatch lifted, Dominicus came in. "What can I do for you?" He snatched the conversation away from Thomas.

"I was inquiring for Mr. Eben Todd."

"I'm his brother."

"Is he—around?"

"No."

"Perhaps this afternoon?"

"Can't say. We're closing for noon hour." Dominicus jingled his keys.

Slowly, very slowly, the stranger limped out.

"Thomas, you can go now." Dominicus was curt. "Be back prompt. Don't forget the hemlock."

"Yes, sir—I mean, no, sir."

Thomas ran down the street far enough to see that no limping stranger stood on the Landing; raced back in the other direction. The hemlock grove was that way, and he'd gather twigs *before* going home to dinner. It wasn't fair, Thomas thought as he ran, for Dominicus not to let Eben see anyone who asked for him. And it wasn't often that a man who looked as if he'd been in a fight came to the pharmacy. There he was, his taffy-colored hair showing under his funny cap! "Sir!" Thomas shouted.

The stranger waited until he caught up. "You're Mr. Todd's son?" he inquired as they walked along.

"No. I'm the pastor's son. But I work for the Todds. Sir, Eben's gone to a shanty he calls his cotton mill. Keep to this road till you reach the fork," Thomas got the words out fast before anyone could turn up to stop him. "You'll see a red barn—and there ain't many painted barns round here. Cock on the weather vane. A piece farther on, there's a lane on the right. Follow the lane till you come to a path, and the path'll take you straight to the shanty. I have to turn off here."

"I'm certainly obliged to you." The stranger held out his bandaged right hand.

Thomas took it carefully. He had never been treated like a grown-up person before, and he was tempted to say that Eben was in some sort of trouble, and his older brother was always trying to get the better of him. But maybe, he thought, this wouldn't do.

"Good day, sir." With a last admiring look, he plunged into the grove.

Anthony plodded on, puzzled by the chilly manner of Eben Todd's older brother. The boy was friendly at any rate. He had delayed telling the boy his errand because he had hoped to gain an idea of the kind of man Eben Todd was—from the look of the shop. But he had learned nothing.

He reached the lane. The path crossed a flooded field. He had to jump from hummock to hummock, in spite of the twinges this caused him; and now and then he missed his footing. At length an unpainted, barn-like building came into view. He heard the rush of water, and hurried to the muddy riverbank.

The falls were sufficiently high. The water fell in a silver sheet; it boiled and churned, yellowish from clay in the riverbed and, slipping around the bend, resumed its normal course towards the sea. Up and down the United States there were countless rivers with falls, waiting only for masters.

A river could carry and feed them, men said, when they settled on riverbanks. They let the river cut logs, grind crops, smooth hand-woven woolen; and they had harnessed the river, they thought. Actually, the river possessed more energy than armies.

Awed and humbled by the mystery of the river, Anthony stooped to pick up a stone. It was warm from the sun. He sent it skipping over the dam; and where it fell, he saw a break in the wall. Ice riding down from the north had worn it through. A sedgy line along the banks showed that the tide here had considerable rise.

He turned towards the mill. Someone stood at the door, head bowed, locking up.

"Mr. Todd!" he called. "Mr. Todd!"

The dark-haired man did not see him. Hurrying towards him, Anthony stepped on a plank laid over mud; one end flew up, kerplunked back with a loud slap. And still the man at the mill door did not turn.

"Mr. Todd!" Anthony stood beside him now.

Eben held a padlock in his hand. His eyes had a far-away look; as if they might see a hundred years into the future, but were blind to the basket likely to be knocked off the step. He clicked the padlock shut and slowly wheeled.

Anthony had not cared for the brother, but he liked dreamy-eyed Eben. "Mr. Todd, I understand you are interested in the making of cotton cloth."

"I was," the man returned, "but I'm through." He started to walk away.

Anthony noted a twist of cotton yarn hanging from his pocket. "I'd like to look at that yarn." He held out his hand.

"A waste of time." Eben halted, surrendering the yarn. "Not so smooth as some I spun a year ago. Shouldn't care to market it."

The yarn *was* uneven. Coarse too, though coarseness did not matter if the yarn was smooth and strong. "Your spinner has a flaw," Anthony said. "I used to work in an English mill. Perhaps I can find your trouble."

"An English mill mechanic!" Eben's face lighted, but only for a moment. "You come too late, young man," he added, shaking his head.

"Will you let me look at your spinner?"

With a shrug, Eben unfastened the padlock, opened the door. "I'll wait outside." Did he mean he could not bear to re-enter the mill?

The small interior was cluttered with boxes, cotton fibre, tools and what-not. Beyond a stone fireplace, Anthony saw the spinner. Against the opposite wall stood what was evidently intended to be a loom. He went to the spinner; turned the carding cylinders by hand, bent to examine them.

"Your trouble's easy to find," he called. "The teeth in the carding cylinders are set too straight to comb the fibre smooth."

Eben stepped inside. "The teeth did have more crook," he said with a nod. "Must be, the punctures widened with use and let the teeth fall away from the original angle. Young feller from Slater mills helped me build this spinner. Been glad to kept him. But he got restless, went West."

"What type's your water wheel?" Anthony inquired.

"Type that freezes." Eben gave a snort.

"Why don't you put it under cover?"

"Young man, you ain't met New Hampshire weather."

Anthony crossed to look at the loom.

"That thing never worked," Eben said dryly. "Feller from

Slater mills said it's one of the earliest attempts in the country and he doubted I could get a loom going. Said Rhode Island mill men don't favor machine-weaving."

"They don't," Anthony rejoined. "I've been there. You'll have to scrap the loom."

"Intend to. Metal'll come handy for defense of Portsmouth."

"That's not what I mean," Anthony said promptly, "I mean —a loom has to be built differently."

"I'm through with looms." Eben looked gloomy.

"It won't be much of a job to reset the spinner's carding teeth and get smooth yarn," Anthony assured him. "And if you had a water loom, you could make a pile of money."

"I told you I'm through with looms, spinners too. And I'm due at the store to help my brother." Eben went outside, his manner saying he had shown his mill and the visitor should leave.

Anthony walked slowly towards the barn-like door. Inducing Eben to keep on with his mill, he reflected, was likely to be a tougher job than licking Steve.

"Gorry, most knocked my dinner over." Eben, who had just discovered the basket on the step, glanced at Anthony and seemed to see his bandages for the first time. "Think I'll eat. Care to join me?" he invited with more warmth than he had previously shown.

"Thank you." Anthony managed to lower himself to a place beside Eben on the sun-warmed step.

"Wonder what I was doing," Eben mused as he removed the basket lid, "when Betsey—she's my daughter—rode over. Betsey wouldn't knock, fearing to disturb me. Nor my wife, Sary Ann. Here's cold pork, Mr.—what's your name?"

"Anthony Bryce, sir."

"Bread's in a napkin by itself, Mr. Bryce. Don't hang back. My wife sends enough for two meals, knowing I might forget it's time to go home."

Eben had forgotten he was due at the store pretty easily,

Anthony noted, and chatting about his wife's good food, he was no longer gloomy.

"Help yourself to milk." He plumped a jug and two mugs down between them.

Anthony took a long swallow of the creamy milk, then looked about. Beyond a white boulder top that rose an inch or two above the ground and was flat as a table, a tree stump showed dark against the new grass.

"Always hate to cut down a tree," Eben said, following Anthony's gaze, "but that elm spoiled my view across river. Besides, I needed space. Point of land by river bend is dangerous quicksand. Try my wife's gingerbread!"

"Thank you, I will."

"Mishap?" Eben queried, his eyes on Anthony's bandages.

Anthony told him about the fight in Portsmouth.

Eben frowned when Mark Badger's name came up, but showed interest in Shad. "Plenty of folks'd give Shad the little he needs," Eben said. "Some day a jailer'll get sore over his breaking loose and set a trap."

He sat with jacket unbuttoned, thumbs in waistcoat armholes, hat pushed back. His mood had mellowed until a smile showed around his generous mouth.

"Why are you closing your mill?" Anthony ventured to ask.

"I'll tell you, young man, though it's none of your business." Eben's mellow mood vanished. "First place, folks in this village don't want a mill. Next place, 'stead of making money like you suggest, I lose money. My own and other folks'. Just this morning my brother convinced me I better wind up here, give my whole time to the store. By cracky, I ought to be there now. Dominicus had to go to a funeral."

Helping him pile things back in the basket, Anthony felt that Eben Todd was too clever a man to be tending store.

"I see you used brick for your dam," he remarked.

"Ice broke through." Eben paused, his hand on the jug. "I used Maine brick, and it don't have the water resistance.

Another time, I'd try brick made of clay from bed of river it's to lie in."

"A higher dam would give more power."

"Another time, I'd build the dam higher. But there ain't going to be another time." Eben plumped the jug down inside the basket.

Anthony had no idea of giving up. "Mr. Todd," he said, "you're known as a cotton manufacturer. I heard your mill spoken of in Portsmouth."

"And didn't hear much good, I guess."

"You have a mill site," Anthony persisted, "a building, a spinner. I'll help you build a loom. Once you weave cloth by machinery, you'll find yourself an outstanding person. Other mill men will come to you for advice—"

"Quite an orator, Mr. Bryce," Eben broke in, "but might as well save your breath. Nobody's coming to me for advice, leastwise not about practical matters. And I don't hanker to be 'outstanding.'" He fastened the basket cover and got to his feet.

Anthony watched him pull the door shut. He had failed with Eben! He was not to live in pleasant Forks Village. Not to help this man whom he liked more and more. Not to know the girl with friendly eyes, with chestnut curls that showed under a stiff-brimmed bonnet. He saw Eben reach for the padlock.

Angry suddenly, he seized Eben's arm. "You click that padlock shut," he shouted, "and you close a mill, you think. Just one mill! Actually you close dozens of mills because you discourage other owners. And the people of the United States will never be independent until they have their own mills."

"By cracky." Eben stared, open-mouthed, and the lock fell from his hands. "Alexander Hamilton told us we're a subject people as long as we depend on foreign workshops. Now you remind me, man in next county said he'd keep his mill going long as I did—not a day longer. Gorry, ain't nothing I wouldn't do for my country."

He paused, continued. "Young feller, you been asking me questions. I'll ask you one. You say, between us, we can build a water-power loom, set this mill going. See anything might hinder?"

Anthony stifled a groan. He hated to cast any cloud over Eben's new attitude, hated to wreck his own chance. But Eben wanted the truth. "I *think* I can build a water loom," he said at last, "but I'm not dead certain and—"

"That's enough." His face brighter, Eben waved a hand. "If you'd said nothing under heaven could stop us, I'd think you get took with notions like I get took. But you got both feet on solid ground." He nodded by way of emphasis.

"Now I haven't a cent of cash. But there's sort of a chance to borrow. Man told me, if I got in deep water 't wouldn't do no harm to let him know."

"Go to him!" Anthony charged.

"Guess you're right," Eben said. "Meadow's so muddy, I left my horse and wagon out by the road. You ride down to store with me. Later I'm taking you home to my wife, Sary Ann. What say your first name is? . . . Well, I'll call you 'Anthony', and you call me 'Eben' like everyone does."

Love for his country had induced Eben to keep on, Anthony reflected as he followed him across the field. He must remember this. He did not yet feel certain of success—there was still the matter of raising funds.

And if he judged rightly, there was still Sary Ann.

It was late afternoon when they picked up Anthony's luggage.

"You can have my son's room," Eben said as they jogged along the high street. "Leak in one corner, but a pan catches rain. Winter hurricane tore some slate off the roof, been meaning to fix it. My son went West and then he joined Andy

Jackson's army. 'Most down to Gulf of Mexico, last we heard. We lost next two young'uns, throat distemper. Betsey's the only child at home. Coming thirteen, she is."

They drove into a cluttered yard. The shabby house was set well back from the road, a clump of lilac beside the kitchen door.

"My place." Eben eyed his home with pride. A man ran out from the barn towering behind. "Lightfoot's getting lazy, Joe," Eben said.

"She better perk up, hayin' time." Joe grinned as Eben climbed down.

Anthony, carrying his small trunk and greatcoat, followed Eben towards the kitchen door. A stringy girl came out.

"Betsey, this is Anthony Bryce," Eben said.

The girl nodded, an amused expression on her freckled face. Did Eben often bring strangers home?

"Sary Ann," Eben said as they entered the kitchen, "this is Anthony Bryce."

"Good evening, Mr. Bryce." Sary Ann was a little woman, with hair drawn straight back from her worn face. Her fingers twitched her dark apron, as she surveyed him.

His battered appearance didn't help matters, Anthony realized. A tawny dog howled until Betsey laid her hand on his head. An older girl, stirring a pot over the fire, looked at him oddly.

"Anthony's a cotton mill worker, just come over from England," Eben began.

Sary Ann said nothing. The others stared. Anthony felt as if he stood before a judge and jury.

"Got his bruises," Eben went on, "in a Portsmouth fight. Came up river this morning with Shadrach Nye."

Sary Ann's brows lifted. The two girls giggled.

"We been talking about the mill," Eben said, "and I brought him home to—"

"To spend the night with Joe in the barn," Sary Ann

finished crisply. "Mr. Bryce, you can take your things right out there. I'm sending Joe hot taters and meat. I'll send plenty for two."

"Thank you, ma'am." Anthony saw Eben's face fall, as he went outside. Sary Ann thought her husband had been taken in, some way. The mention of Shad hadn't helped.

Joe was cordial. "Course you can sleep here. Only two hosses, with space for six. I sleep on a cornhusk bed in one vacant stall, and there's another bed in the stall next to. Extry quilt hangs on beam up there."

The girl brought hot food. Joe produced tin plates, mugs, cutlery, chatting as they ate. Folks called him the Todds' hired man, he said, and he was—up to the time Eben started his cotton mill. For two years now, Eben couldn't pay him. A single feller, he hired out by the day. He paid the Todds for his keep by looking after hosses, lending a hand in haying time. Same way with Min, the girl in the house. She helped out for her keep and a bit of pin money.

Anthony slept in the stall next Joe's.

Next morning, Joe waked him and said, "I lugged an extry pail of water, case you want to wash."

Anthony's back gave him a twinge, as he sat up. His head felt less sore, and his hand was not as swollen as the day before.

"Ate my porridge," Joe went on. "Yours is waiting. Have to plough a man's fields today. Both hosses is fed." He pointed to a box. "I can lend you a shirt and britches'll do better than them fancy things you had on, wherever you got 'em." Joe winked as he went off.

Anthony washed, put on some of Joe's clothes. Pushing the great doors back, he let the fresh morning air blow in, while he ate.

Eben came, his face clouded. "No use going to mill before we settle a point or two," he said wearily as he harnessed Lightfoot. "I have to be at store all day. When I get home, we'll talk." He climbed into the seat, rattled off.

Anthony looked at the cluttered yard. Sary Ann might think him a tramp, but he'd be a good tramp and clear things up. Hunting through the barn, he found a wheelbarrow and rake. The barrow had a loose wheel, the rake lacked some of its prongs. He tinkered a bit.

Out in the yard, the tawny dog barked. Betsey appeared and called the animal inside. Later, she ran off, carrying a schoolbag.

Anthony stacked whatever wood would do for a fireplace beside the kitchen stoop. He picked up good tools and hung them on nails in the barn, placing whatever needed repair in a pile. He gathered up bits of broken crockery, crushed tin, other odds and ends; dumped them in a barrel. He raked up dead leaves, then burned the rubbish.

Sary Ann came with a steaming bowl and a plate of gingerbread. "I never had such a tidy yard," she said. "Stay another night, if you want to."

"Thank you, ma'am. I'd be glad to."

Feeling less stiff as a result of the morning's work, he remembered the leak in young Eben's room.

The ladder had half a dozen rungs gone, but this did not bother a man who had climbed ship's rigging. Up on the roof, he found several places where rain could get in. New flashing was needed around the big chimney. He hunted through the barn for tin and slate.

He had never patched a roof before. His lame hand handicapped him so that he worked slowly. He was not through when he heard a shout.

"Mister," Min called from the foot of a ladder, "can you fix churn? Cream's in the bucket, and handle won't turn."

He got the churn running, and Min looked at him with approval. He climbed the ladder again. It would have to rain before his success with the roof could be proved, he thought wryly. He had finished the work and put the ladder away by the time Eben's wagon rattled into the yard.

Sary Ann came out. "Mr. Bryce," she called, "you and Eben want to talk. You wait inside till Eben's ready."

She led him through the kitchen, into a room beyond, and left him.

A hand-loom stood beside the wall adjoining the kitchen. Anthony went over to examine it. Sary Ann had set up the warp with linen thread, but the shuttle carried her husband's machine-spun yarn. She evidently meant to fill in the cross-threads, the woof, with Eben's cotton yarn.

Eben came in, closing the door behind him. He pointed to the open-front stove, as they drew chairs around the fire. "Benjamin Franklin invented that contraption," he began. "Sends heat out into the room, 'stead of letting the most of it go up chimney."

The door opened, "Don't mind me," Sary Ann said briskly as she went to the loom. "I just want to work a piece before supper."

Eben spoke of the scarcity of nails. "Day for handmade nails is over," he declared. "And soon as war ends, we'll have a fever for building . . ."

Anthony watched Sary Ann work at the loom, as he listened. She was having difficulty with the shuttle. After a little, he rose.

"The warp threads are pulled too tight for filling in with that coarse yarn, ma'am," he said quietly. Reaching to the high rack that held the spools of linen, he slackened the threads, pulled them looser over the beam at the back. "Now try!" he bade.

She picked up the shuttle, threw it over and under the warp threads. It moved more easily as well as faster. He saw her catch her breath as she turned to meet his gaze. She said nothing; but walking back to his chair, Anthony knew he had convinced Sary Ann.

"We could sell machine-made nails locally," Eben was saying.

"You have a cotton mill," Anthony reminded him.

Eben reached for the tongs, turned a log in the open stove, sat back in his rocking chair. "I told you," he began, "I lost money at the mill. Truth is, I lost too much to start up again. And just this morning, I run into a man wants a nail factory." Eben rocked faster, and his face had a glow.

"What about your wanting the United States to be independent?" Anthony asked.

"I ain't forget what I said yesterday." Eben's eyes flashed. "A nail factory's a blow at British manufacturing monopolies, same as a cotton mill. Making nails, we'll get profits sooner. Maybe enough to pay back what I lost in the cotton mill."

Anthony felt alarmed suddenly. Had he won Sary Ann only to lose Eben! "Always trying some newfangled scheme and always failing," Shad had said. Shad was right. There was no getting anywhere with Eben.

"This feller," Eben was saying, "wants us to start work on Monday."

"Eben Todd," his wife broke in, "this man you speak of wants you to build his machines. And then he'll let you go. And you been listening to your brother Dominicus again. You've got the clever young mechanic to help you. Didn't I see him fix broken things around the place all day? Didn't he just fix my loom? Never mind about nails, Eben. You stick to the cotton mill!"

She was a faded little woman with mouse-colored hair drawn straight back from her lined forehead; but to Anthony she seemed beautiful as she stood there.

"You mentioned a possible loan," he reminded Eben.

Eben shook his head. "Come to think, I doubt Simeon Damon'd help."

"Simeon Damon!" Anthony cried.

Eben nodded wearily. "One of the three brothers. Lish

Damon, the oldest, lies bedridden. Gus, Charity's father, died a few years back. Simeon, the youngest, a smart trader in Boston, made sort of an offer. But come to think, I doubt he'd risk any of his money on the cotton mill."

With an opportunity to interest Charity's uncle in the mill, Anthony felt more eager than ever. "You should let him know the facts," he charged.

"I doubt it's any use, with Mark Badger mixed up in things."

"What has Badger to do with your cotton mill?"

Eben gave a shrug.

"Tell the young man!" Sary Ann bade.

"Round here," Eben said, "when you start an enterprise you get a State Charter. Folks who put money in become proprietors. Cotton mill has twenty shares, owned by twelve proprietors. Lish Damon owns three shares, Simeon owns five. Mark owns one. Only one share, mind you. But with Lish paralyzed and Simeon off in Boston, Mark has the say for nine of the twenty shares. My brother Dominicus owns two shares, and he and Mark are hand in glove. So Mark can speak for eleven shares, more'n half the total number. I own only three shares. Yesterday morning, Mark persuaded Dominicus we better close down. Then *you* come."

"And you decided not to close down," Anthony reminded him. "Go on!"

"Well, I told my brother about my new plans this morning, so he wouldn't count on my whole time at the store. Then Mark drops in. Seems he heard I had an English helper. Said he knew the man, and he was quarrelsome." Eben gave a wry smile. "Upshot is, he convinced Dominicus, making money or losing money, the mill'll do harm in the village."

"Mark's afraid of the mill," Sary Ann put in, her temper rising. "Afraid the brickyard'll take second place. I wouldn't trust Mark—far's I could see."

"Mark's smart," Eben pointed out. "His word counts with the selectmen."

"That's what makes him dangerous," Sary Ann retorted. "I hope the Quakers find out in time what a mean critter they took into their fold."

Anthony ignored the threat of Badger's power. "You must ask Simeon Damon for a loan," he charged Eben again. "At once!"

"Eben Todd," Sary Ann bade, "you go to that desk behind you and write Simeon now. Min's going down to Landing, and she'll post it."

Eben heaved himself out of the rocker. Presently his quill scratched across a page. He melted wax over a candle, folded and sealed his letter.

"Let me have it!" Sary Ann held out her hand.

"There's another thing," Eben said, giving her the letter, "we'll need a new dam. Ought to build with Damon brick—made of clay from river that dam's to stand in. I doubt Mark'll sell."

"I'll talk with him." Anthony seized the opportunity to call at Charity's home.

"There's still another thing," Eben said, his eyes on the rug in front of the stove. "Folks call the cotton mill mine, but—"

"I want Mr. Bryce to have young Eben's room tonight," Sary Ann broke in.

"His name's 'Anthony,'" Eben told her.

"I want to put fresh bandages on Anthony's wounds," Sary Ann said. "Anthony, you come out to the kitchen with me."

Supper, eaten with the family in front of the big kitchen fireplace, was a comforting meal. Eben talked cheerfully as he carved the joint. Sary Ann kept Anthony's plate filled. Betsey and Min smiled at him. The tawny dog, Ruddy, wagged his tail.

"Anything you'd like?" Eben inquired as Anthony started up the steep flight leading from the kitchen.

"I'd like to learn to ride," he said with a chuckle. "Didn't I hear you call the mare lazy?"

"Take Lightfoot," Eben bade heartily. "If I'm using her, take Whiteface."

Up in young Eben's room, Anthony set his candle on a stand. The room was furnished with a chest and small mirror, a pair of rush-bottomed chairs, a washstand with water and fresh towels. A bright patchwork quilt covered the bed. His trunk and coat had been carried up. And in one corner he noted the pan intended to catch rain water.

Young Eben's bed proved too short for him. He got up, set a chair at the foot, bagging the blankets to gain length, and tumbled in again. As he drew the quilt over him, he remembered Eben's unfinished sentence: *Folks call the cotton mill mine but*—Of course Eben meant he owned only three shares, and Mark controlled the votes. What if Simeon Damon refused to lend money? What if Mark Badger tried some deviltry? Well, he wouldn't worry over those obstacles until he met them.

Outside, the shutters rattled. A dog howled, a rider clattered by. But Anthony was conscious only of great content. His fugitive days were over. With a home, work in a cotton mill, and Charity living only a mile or so away, he had a foothold in America.

He stretched in the darkness, easing his sore muscles. And presently he slept.

A Steady Lass

IN THE upper story room set apart for the spinning, Charity plunged her hands into the silky flax. She divided it into twelve mounds, careful to toss whatever was specked aside; knowing from the wheels' smooth whir that the dozen maidens in the room worked with heads bent, fingers deft.

It was good to be alive, this bright April afternoon. To be making linen cloth, which was useful creativeness; to have charge of the unmarried sisters in the Society of Friends; to know she was spoken of as a steady lass who ran her household well. And then there was the memory of what had taken place four days before. Eyes on the flax, ears following the wheels' whir, she let herself remember.

She had sailed on the schooner to Portsmouth, because it was her sixteenth birthday. The shopping done, waiting at the inn for the tide to turn, she looked out the window and saw a tall stranger, surrounded by a rough crowd. The maid burst into the chamber. "Mark Badger provoked a quarrel," she cried, "compelling a young man to fight. Britainer he is, and fair-haired, like an angel. He'll be cruel injured, if Steve misses killing him!"

When the terrible blows began to fall, the maid took her place by the window. Recalling the girl's recital, Charity trembled even now: "Stranger's head is most cut open. Steve strikes again! Alas, poor Britainer's down. I doubt he'll rise . . ."

Twice she was moved by the Lord to call out in defense of the friendless young man. And after he was granted victory, she lingered in the inn parlor, hoping he would come down the stairs.

Since the trip to Portsmouth, she had been tied to her uncle's sickroom. Not that it mattered. Many men came to Portsmouth and vanished. Besides, the fair-haired stranger was of the world's people. And she belonged to the Friends forever. . . .

In the front row of spinners, a chair scraped.

Charity glanced around. All the maidens worked dutifully. A handful of flax fell from the table to her lap and, gathering it up, she saw her skirt ripple. Under the breadths of homespun, her foot swung with the wheels' rhythm!

Alas, responsible for keeping the others from flightiness, she had been nigh to dancing — which was indulgence of the flesh! Remorseful, she pressed both feet hard against the floorboards.

Whose chair had scraped a warning? Lucy Watson, the sister most dear to her, sat in the front row, but Lucy's smooth fair head was bent over her wheel. Rachel Foster, the one who would relish finding a fault in her, sat in the rear row. It must be, the chair had moved accidentally and she was spared anyone's seeing her lapse. But she had been too set up, since the day in Portsmouth.

There were specks of dirt in the sorted flax!

Dismayed, she went through the mounds again, chiding herself for letting her thoughts dwell on a man who got into brawls. What if Satan, not the Lord, had moved her to call out the window! Moved her to linger and greet the stranger! How was a poor girl to know?

Disquieted, she rose and made the rounds, saying an encouraging word to each spinner. Back at her table, she smoothed her unruly hair. The Friends condoned Charity Damon's chestnut curls, but preferred straight hair—like Lucy's. She resumed her work. The wheels' whir sounded smooth as the flight of birds; and as one bird leads in the sky, so Lucy's led in the spinning room. . . .

Now someone missed a turn! Rachel, by the window, watching the men on the wharf lade the schooner, had spied Mark Badger. Why must Rachel be so taken with brother Mark, who scarcely gave her word or look! Uneasy, Charity waited. Rachel's dark eyes reminded her of the slow fires that smoulder during the early part of the bricks' baking and then flare up in angry flame.

"Martha," she called, "it is near four o'clock and the tray will be ready. Thee, the youngest, may fetch it."

Thirteen-year-old Martha clattered down to the kitchen . . . clattered back. The others, glad to take feet off treadles, broke into talk: "I am famished. . . . Let us stir the fire and sit round it."

Rachel alone did not rush forward for milk and gingerbread. When Charity carried a plate and mug to her, she gave no thanks. In such a mood, any careless word might upset the girl, Charity thought, anxious.

The others chattered as they ate. Brother Tobias was fishing off Isles of Shoals, and a British ship chased him. . . . Sister Abigail had a letter from the daughter who went West. . . . Eben Todd said machines would take all drudgery off women's backs. . . . A laugh went around at the mention of Eben.

"Eben thinks he can blow glass by machinery," someone said. "But glassblowing is not his latest. The latest is, he wants to make nails by machinery."

"Perhaps Eben Todd is not foolish," Charity put in gently. "My Uncle Simeon in Boston says there is no telling what machines may do."

And then Rachel flared. "Because of the schooling in Boston, thee is always better than rest of us and must brag of Simeon Damon."

"Rachel, be still!" Lucy rebuked. "Charity is ever modest."

Rachel looked as if the fire within her raged hotter.

"Eben's very latest is," Martha set her mug down, "he's

keeping on with the cotton mill. A man told a man, what told my pa, Eben's hired a runaway Englishman. If British could ketch him, they'd cut him in pieces, put him in the pot and stew him."

"Oh, oh, oh!" Was the Englishman young or old? everyone wanted to know. Tall or short? Fair or dark? Single or wedded? A Friend—or world's people?

Martha shook her head. "The man didn't tell my pa." Her moment was over.

But Rachel burst out: "He's not one of us. He got into fight in Portsmouth, spite of brother Mark's trying to stop him. Had his head most knocked off."

The falsehoods! In the nick of time, Charity pressed her lips tight. But who had told Rachel lies?

"And I know something else." Rachel was bent on outdoing Martha. "Last evening, Julia Stone run away and married outside."

A sister had married someone not a Friend! The girls sat stunned.

Mark *had* noticed Rachel, Charity realized. An overseer of the Society of Friends, all violations of rules were reported to him. He had seen Rachel; told her about Julia's grievous error —and about the Englishman.

Slowly the maidens recovered power of speech. "Julia, so young and so misguided. . . . My ma says marriage outside is worse than death. . . . Julia'll be read out of Meeting . . ."

"But I liked sister Julia," Martha protested. "She was always kind."

"Hush!" Charity chided. "Julia is a wayward woman, and we may not call her 'sister.' " Too late she saw the anger in Rachel's eyes.

"Thee is a fine one to speak, proud Mistress Charity," Rachel taunted. "If ever thee fall in love, in or *out* of the Society, 't will be a fall."

"No, Rachel!" the others protested. "Charity'd die before

she'd wed outside. . . . Charity's the steadiest of us all. . . . Thee is wrong!"

Rachel said nothing. Presently shouts came from the river.

"Schooner's sailing," the sisters cried. "We want to see the schooner push off."

"Very well." Charity welcomed the diverting interest. "But do not call or wave to the men," she charged. "Do not let thy skirts blow in the wind."

"We will be seemly." They flew towards the stairs.

Lucy lingered. "Pay no heed to Rachel," she counselled. "Brother Mark casts some spell over her, and she is jealous because he thinks of thee."

"Of me! Brother Mark thinks of nobody but himself."

"Thee is grown harsh." Lucy's demure face clouded. "Charity, I stood by thee, when the others were present, but something has changed thee."

So it *was* Lucy's chair that had scraped a warning! Could Lucy have heard what happened in Portsmouth?

"The visits with thy Uncle Simeon unsettle thee . . ."

Only the journeys to Boston fretted Lucy! Breathing easier, Charity explained that some day all the care of Blue Clay Farm would fall on her, and her uncle wished her to be fitted for the task. "He believes a woman can be as capable as a man. Especially when no lads are in the family," she added with a laugh. "He instructs me about business, about the new progress—"

"Progress!" Lucy interrupted, indignant. "Thee should be thinking about a husband. Thee could have any of the unwedded brothers. Now *I* stand up with William Lane in Fifth Month. Thee, two months older, talks of 'progress.'"

Could Lucy tell her what the new flutter within her meant? Charity wondered. Whether it was good or evil? "Thee loves William?" she asked softly.

"Of course. William is a good man."

"When he sees thee home of an evening, does thee tremble?"

"Of course not. I listen while he talks wisely of the way of shearing that clips the most wool. And the best time for second plantings."

"But afterwards, when thee is alone. Does the whole world seem more beautiful, so thee could sing like a bird?"

"Song is for world's people," Lucy rebuked. "When William leaves me, I pray to be a good wife, to bear his children and raise them fittingly."

Charity sighed deeply. If the wild heart-beat the Englishman stirred in her was unknown to Lucy, it must be sinful. She would put all thought of the stranger out of her mind. And within the year, she would wed with one of the brethren. The one she could walk beside most calmly, her thoughts on turnips in the cellar, potatoes in the bin.

Heavy steps sounded. Hilda, the kitchen woman, entered the room. "Man downstairs, wants to buy brick," she announced in monotone.

"Tell him Mark Badger has sailed to Portsmouth," Charity bade.

"I told him. He asked for Mr. Damon. I told him Lish is sick. Then he asked for Miss Damon."

"I do not have the care of the brickyard. Bid him come when Mark is here."

"I told him. Says he won't go till he sees ye." Arms folded across her broad bosom, Hilda had a substantial look. "He's Eben Todd's new helper. Proper-seeming, save for a bruise or two."

Charity wanted to fly down the stairs. But she had just promised herself she would put all thought of the stranger out of her mind! "I cannot see him," she said. "The cloth is sore needed. I am very busy."

The faithful woman gave a shrug. "Looks like he'll just set. Name's Anthony Bryce."

"When has Charity been too busy," Lucy reproached, "to be civil to a stranger! Go down to this Anthony Bryce. I'll work with the flax." She dipped her hands into the silky pile.

Lucy, wanting to save her, was driving her towards temptation, Charity thought. Probably poor Julia's downward course had begun with a chance meeting. Yet, she must go down or Lucy would suspect that something was wrong.

"Very well. I'll be gone only a minute." As she rose, she pressed her unruly curls flat, pulled her white kerchief closer around her neck, reminded herself that Satan set traps.

"Good afternoon!" she said primly as she entered the best room. The Englishman looked handsomer even than before; tall and straight, his hair like gold, his injuries healed enough for him to do without bandages.

"Good afternoon," he returned. "I want to buy a load or two of brick."

What a struggle to stand there, not saying she was glad to see him; explaining she could not tell him about the brick. "Come when the manager is here," she finished and moved towards the door.

"Do people around here need cotton cloth?"

"Sorely." How could a girl ignore so important a question! she thought as she turned. "None comes from Europe or the Orient these war times."

He talked about the good that mills could bring, especially to women. With the welfare of the community at stake, she lingered.

"My uncle in Boston says the new machines are wondrous things," she told him.

"I'd like to show you Eben Todd's spinner."

"Some afternoon I'll ride over—" In the middle of her sentence, she remembered Julia's downfall—and Satan's traps. She made her voice sound coldly business-like. "Come when the manager is here."

His look, as she left him, gave her a wrench.

Back in the spinning room, Lucy smiled approval. "I am

glad thee was not *too* brief with Anthony Bryce. The schooner has sailed, the sisters are returning."

"I will set fresh flax by the wheels." Oh why, Charity wondered as she made the rounds, why didn't a girl feel happier over escaping Satan's trap!

A Meeting Is Called

THE MILL'S small interior, with only a single pair of windows, seemed a poor place to work on a morning that shouted of spring. Anthony gathered up crayon, chalk and drawing board and went out into the sunshine.

Wearing the breeches Joe had loaned him and a loose jacket Sary Ann had sewed up from a length of homespun, he eyed the path that led to the road. Eben was to have been on hand at eight o'clock, with a blacksmith to help adjust the spinner's carding teeth. The sun stood high in the sky, and no sign of Eben!

The fields had dried in the week since he first saw them, Anthony realized. The sun-warmed earth smelled sweet; the sky seemed loftier than any English sky. Whistling a tune, he settled himself on the white patch that marked the granite boulder's top, and began to work.

Eben's drawl roused him. "Courting pneumony, son? Chill comes off a river's lately had ice in it."

"Where's the blacksmith?" Anthony inquired, getting to his feet.

"Couldn't find one," Eben said. "With the State of New Hampshire paying dollar a day for defense workers, it don't leave much chance for my hiring. Anyways, when you read Simeon's letter, you'll likely figure we don't need a smith." He handed the letter over.

Trying to conceal the uneasiness he felt, Anthony walked with Eben to the mill, gave the smouldering fire a poke, turned up a couple of boxes to sit on, unfolded Simeon's letter.

"While I believe domestic manufactures to be of utmost importance," the Boston man wrote, "events lead me to doubt whether this is the time to invest in a mill at Forks Village. But rest assured, I shall look into the matter . . ."

"He don't intend to throw good money after bad," Eben observed, his forehead rutted like a muddy road after a cart has passed over it.

"You can't blame him for wanting to investigate," Anthony returned. His brief talk with Charity had persuaded him that Simeon Damon was progressive.

Eben looked gloomy. "Mark Badger came into store this morning," he began, eyes on the floorboards. "He heard you'd been down to Blue Clay Farm. Says he ain't got brick to spare, account of the terrible fire in Portsmouth last December. Says new law is going through, down there, forbidding structures more'n twelve feet high being built of wood. Every scrap of brick is promised in Portsmouth."

No smith, no money from Simeon, no brick! Anthony gave a shrug.

Eben unbuttoned his jacket, thrust his thumbs into his waistcoat armholes. "Travelling feller came into store this morning," he said, more cheerful. "Spoke of a new way of dyeing yarn. Seems a man over near Peterborough puts indigo into kittle, lays cannon ball in, pours on water. Then he hangs the kittle from a nail in ceiling beam and swings it."

Anthony tried to be patient, aware that once started, Eben had to run down, like a clock.

"Folks bring home-spun yarn from near and far—linen or woolen. They come early morning and, by gorry, before nightfall they go home with their yarn dyed. Not streaked, mind you. A clear blue! Now a dye factory in this corner of Granite State'd be a godsend. I got plenty of indigo, kittle too. There's a cannon ball left over from Revolution up in my barn loft . . ."

Anthony could no longer be patient. "I'm keeping on, here," he broke in. "And I want a cot to sleep on, as I mean to study the effect of atmospheric conditions on cotton fibre through the twenty-four hours."

Eben got up from his box. "Sary Ann'll let you have a cot, blankets too. Guess I better be humping along." With a curt nod, he sauntered off.

Watching Eben cross the field with his purposeless gait, Anthony resolved not to let himself be thwarted. If the worst came, he would carry on alone.

He turned to the sketch on his drawing board. You took a clutter of wood and metal, he mused; put the pieces together according to a pattern. You toiled a day, a month, a year. And, if you were lucky, you had a live thing.

He had eaten his cold dinner when thunder began to rumble. Eben had never bothered to set catches in the two window frames, so that the sashes had to be supported by sticks. He need not lower them as yet, Anthony thought, stepping to the doorway to watch the storm.

A flash of lightning streaked the dark sky, reminding him that the boy, Thomas, who came to see him nearly every day, had spoken of damage caused by "electric fluid," as local people called it. The fluid followed rivers, Thomas said; and the best way to avoid being struck was to make use of Benjamin Franklin's invention—metal rods which carried the fluid into the ground. He would build a fireproof cabinet for the safe-keeping of his designs, Anthony decided. Later, he would look into the matter of the rods.

He built his cabinet, during the following week; lined it with tin, fastened it to a wall. He borrowed a cot and blankets from Sary Ann, as well as stew-pans, a few other cooking utensils. Laying planks across trestles, he provided himself with a sturdy work-table. He set pegs in the walls for his clothes; purchased a supply of candles in case daylight failed him.

He was working at his table, one morning, when a shadow fell across the open doorway.

"How are ye, Tony?" a high voice chirped.

"Shad!" Anthony exclaimed, delighted to see his friend. The little man's clothes hung looser, the lines in his face seemed deeper, and when he grinned, even the gap where a tooth was missing looked wider. "I'll make coffee and pancakes." Anthony started towards the fireplace.

"I ain't a-hungered." Shad winked slyly as he looked around the neat interior. "I see you got things ship-shape. Seems a mite stuffy, after living in the open. Guess I'll sit where I can get a breath." Curled up on a box near the open door, in his faded green coat he looked like a wood gnome.

"I went over to your place and left a note," Anthony said.

" 'Tain't really my place," Shad explained. "Cabin belongs to feller gone privateering, but he don't mind I use it." He pulled out a chipped clay pipe, one grimy finger tamping tobacco into the bowl. He got out a tinder-box and sulphur matches. Puffing rings of smoke, he was a picture of content.

"Stayed in cabin only one night," he began after a little. "Sheriff from Maine was after me. I went south, met up with a feller, roamin' like I was. We jogged along. Trouble was, wan't nothing ripe to live on."

Anthony leaned back, knowing that Shad was likely to tell a long story.

"We milked cows in pasture, when we got a-thirst. Night time, we visited folks' kitchens and cellars. We got beef and lamb and pork. Trouble was, we hankered for chicken. Plenty of hen-houses about, but a barkin' dog always stood near. We found a place seemed safe. My pardner watched, while I looked at the roost. My, them birds felt plump and juicy! But one of them started squawkin'. Then a pesky dog set up a howlin'. Afore ye could count twice, I had a musket in my face. My pardner skipped. Don't know as I blame him. When sheriff came, I tagged along, knowin' I could git out of any coop he put me into."

"Shad!" Anthony broke in, concerned. "Eben says some

jailer'll get angry and set a trap for you, some day."

Head cocked to one side, Shad looked thoughtful. "Mebbe I do hurt jailers' feelings." He ducked and from under the insole of his shabby shoe drew out a thin blade. "See this! It'll bend or twist." From his bandanna bundle he produced a piece of red ribbon. "And this brings me luck, 'cause it come off a leddy's Sabbath Day bonnet. With my steel, and my ribbon for luck, I could git out of any jail on earth.

"But I wan't wastin' good tools on this no-account jail." He put his treasures away. "Someone had left a piece of crockery in the rickety place. I broke it sharper, and it cut through a log, half-rotted. I slipped into sheriff's kitchen and found a bird ready roasted." Shad smacked his lips. "Wrote a line, sayin' thanks for the hospital'ty. Weighted it with the crockery. Then I went to the cabin, found your note in the tree."

"Eben pays me four dollars a week and my keep," Anthony said slowly. "I need a helper. I could spare you a dollar a week and give you half my food. You could sleep here, live regularly."

"Live regular!" Shad chirruped. "Dishes on the table, bed made up, every day like the one afore it and the one comin' after. Tony, I couldn't stand it. Land sakes!" Tucking his pipe into his mouth, he puffed violently.

"One good thing about roamin'," he said after a minute, "is gittin' news. Hear how British went up river near New London, burnin' idle keel a-plenty?"

"No," Anthony replied. "I haven't heard a word about the war."

"Well, folks on seaboard are mighty scared. In Granite State, Gov'nor Gilman's ordered more defense. May send all Portsmouth sail up river."

"You remind me, Shad, I need a blacksmith," Anthony said. "Eben claims all the smiths are working on Portsmouth defenses."

"They be." Shad nodded. "But try Ivory Oldfield, lives near Landin'. He's got a paralyzed wife, and can't go far as Portsmouth. Anything else to worry ye?"

"Eben wants the new dam built of Damon brick, and Badger won't sell. I'd rather use fieldstone myself."

"Use fieldstone. Eben built the foundation of fieldstone and it ain't give way. Brick's jist one of his notions. Mebbe next time ye see him, he'll think he has to have marble or slate." Shad shrugged his thin shoulders.

Anthony was impressed by Shad's common sense. "Do you think," he asked, "I can get Simeon Damon to finance this mill?"

Shad let out a whistle, sat back on his heels and stared. "Tony," he said at last, "I'm for ye. I ain't forgit how ye stood up for me in Portsmouth. Mebbe ye think ye made a good start." His eyes ranged over the tidy interior. "Truth is, ye ain't got the seat of your pants warm in this village yet. Mark and Dominicus are set agin' ye. There ain't anybody for ye. Mark always has tricks up his sleeve. As for Simeon—" Shad spied a squirrel on the step and, pulling a crust out of his pocket, tossed crumbs that brought the small animal inside.

"Simeon," he went on, "the youngest of Damon brothers, was always in some scrape when he was a boy here. There's a wild strain in Damon blood. Simeon had it—some say the gal Charity's got a mite of it. Anyways, Simeon run away to Boston." Shad waited while the squirrel hopped on his hand, snatched the crust and scampered off.

"Turned into smart trader, Simeon did," Shad went on. "He could buy the whole of Forks Village and put it in his pocket, some say. And he's jist as likely to put money into this mill of Eben's as—as that squirrel I been feedin' is to bring back the crust he stole. Tony, I like ye and I always will. But ye ain't got a chance with this mill. Time I was movin'." He reached for his bandanna bundle and got to his feet.

"I need a horse," Anthony remarked. "I've been using Eben's mare, but I'd like a mount of my own."

"Lemme think." Shad pulled on one ear. "I 'member a mare in next county might do ye. Bit of doctorin' to change color of her hide, and her owner wouldn't know her."

"Shadrach, I want to *buy* a horse, not steal one," Anthony thundered.

"I 'member my promise." Shad slipped out of range of Anthony's grip. "I'll find ye a neat piece of hoss flesh, send owner around."

"That's what I had in mind." Seeing Shad look penitent, Anthony added, "I'm always glad to see you. And you can always live here."

"I'll turn up now and then to see how ye're gittin' on. Ye ain't got a chance, but things'd be worser if ye mated with Shadrach Nye." Flourishing his bundle, Shad trudged off.

Anthony returned to the work-table. So Charity was supposed to have some of the wild Damon blood! She had said she would ride to the mill some day. But would she! She might befriend a stranger in Portsmouth, not wanting to see him treated unfairly. Might accept his invitation to see Eben's spinner for civility. But was she likely to feel personal interest in a foreigner like himself! When she walked out of the room, the day he called at Blue Clay Farm, she was stiff and cold. Cold enough to satisfy any sour-faced country Quaker with an eye on her. He was a fool to imagine that Charity Damon would come to the mill!

He picked up a hammer and threw it at a cob-webbed corner. Then he reached for a wrench—threw it after the hammer.

One afternoon, late in May, the sun burst in at door and window; threw a slanting path across the mill floor, and made a lattice pattern on the table where Anthony worked.

The design for a loom was finished. Part of it he had drawn from memory, fighting at times to extract some small detail from the back of his brain; part was his own creation. He scanned each dot and curve and line, but could find no flaw. Things were coming along well, he thought. Someone who owed Eben had paid his debt, giving them a small supply of funds. The next day but one, a man with an ox-drawn dray was to gather fieldstone for the new dam; Ivory Oldfield would set up a forge and cast a small model of the loom. Anthony chuckled, thinking that now he could get on without brick, Mark Badger had no power to hurt him.

Hearing the thud of hooves, he went to the window. Buttercups had turned the fields into a carpet of gold, the river ran silver. Fruit trees coming into blossom cut off his view of the road, but the thud sounded nearer. Someone was riding down the tree-lined lane! Not Eben—he was off in the next county. Not Betsey—she had brought his dinner and gone. Not Thomas, who was at school. Anthony felt wild hope.

Then the girl came flying over the golden field. She swept up the path, the big gray's hooves scraped on gravel.

"Eben Todd!" she called. "Eben Todd!"

Charity had slipped from the saddle, by the time he got outside, and stood, flushed from the riding, her gray habit a cloud around her.

"Oh!" she seemed dismayed when she saw him.

He hastened to explain that Eben was helping a cousin in the next county who had fallen from a roof.

"Eben returns this evening?" she inquired, anxious.

"He planned to stay with his cousin until the end of the week."

She seemed uncertain what to say or do. If the spinner inside had faltered, he would have tightened a pin, searched for tension; but with the girl, he waited, a pulsing in his ears, and in his heart the fear that she would climb to the saddle and gallop away.

"My errand is important," she said at last. "Will thee get word to Eben, the meeting is likely to cause trouble?"

"Certainly, but what meeting?" Anthony inquired, puzzled.

"Thee did not see the notice in the JOURNAL? Under the advertisement about higher prices for cattle horns?"

He shook his head. He did not read the local paper.

"A meeting is called at Asa Howland's inn," she explained, "for proprietors of the cotton mill and others interested. Mark Badger's name was printed under the notice."

"When is the meeting?" he inquired, disturbed by the news.

"At five o'clock on Sixth Day—thee says 'Friday.' The regular meeting is never held so early, nor with less than a full week's warning."

"Badger can't make trouble for Eben. We've decided not to use brick."

"Mark Badger *can* make trouble." Her eyes darkened. "He has influence with the selectmen. He has never wanted a mill here, although he owns shares."

The meeting was to take place, Anthony realized, on the very day the smith was to start work. Badger controlled eleven out of twenty votes, Eben had said. Yes, Badger still had power to hurt him.

"Anthony Bryce, thee must attend the meeting with Eben Todd." Charity spoke with firmness now. "Thee will be sharper than Eben at seeing what goes on."

"Could you tell me something about the men who will be there? I'll get you something to sit on." He went inside for a box.

When he returned, she had knotted the bridle rein. "Off with thee, Gabriel!"

The gray reared, then headed for the riverbank.

"Point of land by the bend is quicksand!" Anthony warned.

"Trust Gabriel to keep out of quicksand." She laughed as the big horse turned sharply and made for the field. "And now, the meeting."

She seated herself, wide skirt falling over the box, hands primly folded. "The selectmen, and most of the others, can read and write. But they seldom leave the village and know nothing about the world outside. They see no need of mills . . . no need of change. Of those who count most . . ."

Anthony, seated near, listened attentively while Charity spoke of men likely to oppose the mill.

"Do not expect the mill proprietors to care about the good that machines can do," she warned. "They care mainly about the dollar in their pocket."

"I'll ride to next county, see Eben tomorrow," Anthony said.

"That is right, Anthony Bryce." Her eyes showed approval.

"Shad calls me 'Tony,' " he recklessly announced.

"The Friends never use nicknames or titles." She shook her head gently. "And 'Tony' is an alien-sounding name, fitting small dark men with tinkers' carts. Men who indulge in dance and song."

The words held a warning, but he did not heed.

" 'Anthony' is more suitable for thee," she went on, "besides being the name of a saint. Has thee been interested long in cotton mills, Anthony Bryce?"

"Always. My father was an inventor . . ." He slipped to the grass at her feet and told her about his life.

She was deeply interested; tears stood in her eyes when he finished. And she told him her story. She had grown up on the farm. . . . Her mother had nursed the sick in an epidemic, caught the dread throat distemper, both parents dying of it within the week. . . . She attended a Friends' school in Boston until her aunt died, and then came home to care for Uncle Elisha and run the household. . . .

The echo of the village clock sounded over the fields five times. The big gray ambled back to graze close by. The girl sat smiling. And Anthony, enjoying the warm companionship, forgetting the worries of the mill, broke into an old English song:

A dusty road is mine to tread,
'Tis honest toil for homely fare. . . .

He saw her wide habit ripple as her foot swung in rhythm, and sang on:

The folks in all the country places
Welcome gladly Pedlar Jim.
With fairy tales and legends gay
I cheer the lasses when I may. . . .

"Oh!" Her eyes widened suddenly. She was on her feet, in the saddle, before he could reach her. "I'm sorry to leave abruptly," she murmured, distressed. "I forgot an errand I must do. Good afternoon."

Anthony watched the girl on the galloping gray until trees hid her from view. Shad had told him that Quakers didn't like music. What a fool, not to have remembered! He hadn't shown her the spinner, or inquired about her Boston uncle.

Spring, or something, had got into him, wrecked everything.

What to Do!

REMORSEFUL, hot from the ride, Charity paused in the hall. When no sound came from the sickroom above, she went into the best room, burying her face in the bowl of lilies that stood on the table. Their cool fragrance did not ease her mind. If only she knew what to do!

Surely it was right to carry a warning to Eben Todd. Right, in Eben's absence, to tell Anthony Bryce the danger to the mill. But it was not right to linger and tell her life story to one of the world's people. The truth was that when Anthony spoke of his mother's death, she had wanted to slip her hand in his. When he sang, she had wanted his arm around her. Only the light-minded words, *legends gay, cheer the lasses,* had brought her to her proper senses.

She turned to the portrait over the mantel. In the face some journeyman artist had caught on canvas, she saw her own eyes and lips and, under a white cap, her own curls. The girl on the wall, her great-aunt Charity, had walked to meet the Indians, the day they came, chanting a warcry (as the story ran). The men were off in the fields, women and children unprotected, when the girl chided the foe; alone and with no weapon, she reminded them the Friends had ever treated them fairly until, ashamed, the savages lowered their tomahawks and stole away. . . . Another Charity, in a still earlier time, had been tied to a cart, lashed on her bare back, for defending the Friends' faith.

If only her great-aunt, granddaughter of the Charity who endured the lashing without a cry, would give her some message or sign! Tell whether her feeling for Anthony was good or evil! She had the same blood. Under trial, she too could be valiant.

No sign appeared. Charity went to the kitchen for a word with Hilda, then set out for Lucy's new cottage.

The path ran through woods. As she hurried along, bushes struck at her; yellow honeysuckle and purple columbine flaunted their color. She came upon a coiled garter snake and lifted her skirt, careful not to worry the creature.

At the highway, Lucy ran to meet her. "Thee is late," she cried, "and there is much to see before William comes from the brickyard to drive me home."

The new cottage smelled of balsam boughs laid on the hearth. Charity made the rounds: three rooms downstairs, two chambers above. Chairs and tables, maple chest, apple-wood bedstead; all were ready for the marriage day.

"And now," Lucy said as they sat on the high-backed settle in the kitchen, "I will tell thee the best thing of all. My William has a promotion. A hod-carrier no longer, he is to help old Moses Perkins at the ovens and receive more wages. We owe it to Mark Badger—though of course William earned it."

"Of course," Charity agreed. Not for the world would she dim Lucy's pleasure by revealing that she had asked Uncle Simeon, as her own wedding gift, to have William promoted.

"Moses knows the secret of the baking process," Lucy went on proudly. "He will teach William. Some day, William may have full charge of the ovens."

Again Charity agreed. And Lucy chattered happily on.

"William and I cannot decide whether to paint the cottage white or let the clapboards weather. It seems . . ."

Listening, Charity felt a touch of envy. Lucy would soon move from her parents' home to the cottage William had built near the brickyard; children would come; in time, William would have charge of the ovens. The years were likely to bring Lucy no more vexing problem than whether to paint—or not paint.

"Why is it," the girl was saying, "that thee never looks at any man?"

She had concealed her perturbed state well, Charity thought.

"All the village knows," Lucy went on, "Mark Badger has hoped to be thy husband, and thee puts him off."

Charity started. She *had* put Mark off, when he brought up the matter of marriage; but it distressed her to hear that the village knew of it. "Uncle Elisha needs me," she said. "It's hard to lie in bed, unable to speak."

"Brother Mark would aid in the sickroom."

Indeed, Mark stood in high favor—since the promotion!

"Mark is industrious and thrifty," the girl continued. "Sometimes he seems a mite overbearing, but this is only because he is lonely, living in the dreary riverbank cottage. With thee to smile at him, he would change."

Charity said nothing. It was useless to point out Mark's faults to Lucy, blinded by happiness as well as gratitude for the promotion.

"If thee cannot care for Mark," the girl said, "there are other young men. My William tells me, four of the brethren have vowed they will not take a wife until Charity Damon has chosen a husband. Maidens kept waiting will not love thee."

Charity sighed. She did not wish to complicate the unmarried sisters' lives.

"Dear sister," Lucy took her hand, "thee has no mother. Mine taught me that while the man rules in outward ways, the woman rules—through him. I have but to raise my finger, and William will do what I wish. Married to Mark, thee could correct his flaws of character."

Charity recalled her wish when she stood before her ancestor's portrait. Great-aunt Charity was sending her an answer in words from her closest friend!

"Married to Mark," Lucy was saying, "thee will please the sisters impatient for husbands, make Mark happier and better. . . . But I hear William's cart!" She sprang up, her thoughts only of William.

"Thee has helped me," Charity said softly as Lucy made the door fast.

The girl climbed into the cart beside William. Watching the pair drive off, as she crossed the road to the woods path, Charity again felt a touch of envy.

She would marry Mark, she resolved, and forget the turmoil the Englishman roused in her. Gentle, patient like Lucy, she would teach Mark to become the benevolent, broad-minded man she wanted her husband to be. And her life in the big house would be as smooth as Lucy's in the cottage.

If she settled matters at once, the mill proprietors' meeting need have no unfortunate outcome. Betrothed to Mark, her first request would be that he support the cause of the mill. This time of year, he inspected the well each evening to make sure no unwholesome drainage seeped into it. She would wait by the well-house.

On reaching the clearing, she found herself moved by the beauty around her. The great house, hoary with age, crowned the hill. Trees lifted their boughs to the sky, the green lawn sloped to the river's edge. There was never a Damon born who did not love Blue Clay Farm!

Coming up the hill, halfway between the schooner's pier and the house, she saw Mark. And something cold gripped her. Yet she compelled herself to look at him with a betrothed's eyes. Narrow across the shoulders, he was wiry and tall. The straddling gait that led some to think he strutted from pride only meant that his long legs covered ground rapidly; Mark walked with purpose, a dependable man.

Mark came nearer. His nose was long. Coarse black hair fell from under the broadbrimmed beaver. Well, when he became the man she wanted him to be, she would not mind his nose or his hair. She caught herself wondering how Anthony would look, swinging up the slope, a song on his lips.

She put the thought from her. Her life was as good as settled; she would forget the Englishman.

Then the terrier, Columbine, scampering across the slope, crouched suddenly, turned tail and fled in the opposite direction. Had Mark ever kicked Columbine? A shiver went through her. Of course not! The little dog had taken a notion to chase some cat or rabbit. She walked on, towards Mark.

They met at the vine-covered well-house. "Good evening, brother Mark." She sat down on the bench.

Breathing heavily, Mark settled himself beside her. He made a presentable appearance; not handsome but solid, and it was silly to object to the black line his eyebrows made, almost cutting his long face in two.

"I come from Lucy's cottage," she began. "The path is overgrown."

"The men can't clear it till they finish sowing."

His voice was gruff, but she'd get used to it. "Lucy and William," she went on, "are grateful for the promotion."

Mark snorted. Did he resent Uncle Simeon's instruction? She had not meant to irritate Mark—quite the contrary. "Lucy is so happy," she said, "I envy her."

"Thee could be equally happy."

For a moment, she felt he took a deal for granted. But he was a plain-spoken man, she reminded herself. This was his way of renewing his offer, and she would encourage him. "I regret—letting the opportunity pass," she said softly.

"It has not passed." He edged closer. When he reached for her hand, she let him have it. Drawing in his breath sharply, he bent over her.

She took his short hard kiss. Her first caress from a man outside the family, it gave her no pleasure—nor pain. Other women enjoyed a husband's kiss, and she could learn.

Mark, smiling broadly, still held her hand in his. "William and Lucy," he said meaningly, "stand up, next First Day Meeting."

She nodded to show she understood. Mindful of Lucy's counsel, she talked matters over with him. She had preparations to make; Uncle Simeon expected a visit soon, and while in Boston she would shop. In a month's time, she could be ready for marriage.

"I'll have our names read out in Meeting," he said, breathing heavily.

She was pledged to Mark! How simple it all was! Now Lucy would be relieved, the unmarried sisters need not blame Charity Damon for keeping them from husbands, and presently Mark's arrogance would vanish. Already, he seemed less self-centered. Lucy was right. His marriage day in sight, Mark was a better-tempered man.

She spoke of relatives to be invited, aware that Mark resented William's marriage coming before his own. She must never forget that Mark could not bear anyone's getting ahead of him! Things settled, she rose.

"I want to make sure that Uncle Elisha has his extra blanket," she said.

"Just a minute!" Mark seized her arm. "There is another matter. This afternoon thee gallivanted to Eben Todd's shanty and dallied with the foreigner."

She felt hot with anger. But she had been remiss, she realized after a moment. Indeed penitence had brought about this meeting. As overseer of the Society, Mark had the right to admonish her. "I am sorry," she said humbly.

"Afterwards," Mark's voice was harsher, "thee galloped through the village, causing all men to turn. The horse is too wild and makes thee conspicuous."

Again the hot blood rushed to her face. Yet she said nothing.

"This morning," Mark went on, "the animal nipped at me. No man on the place can handle him. He should be sold."

"William can handle Gabriel!" she burst out.

Mark turned white with rage. Too late she remembered he

could not bear anyone's getting ahead of him. Lucy would never have blundered so.

She laid her hand on his arm. "Dear brother Mark, soon to be my husband, Gabriel is jealous of thee. He has loved me since the day he was born."

Mark snorted but seemed mollified. "Thee may have the horse," he rasped, "but keep away from the Englishman."

It was hard to be patient, like gentle Lucy, to remember that Mark's faults could not be changed in a twinkling. "I rode to the mill this afternoon," she kept her voice low, "with a message for Eben Todd. He was away, and I talked with the Englishman. It was unseemly to linger, and I truly repent. I am not likely to see him again. But, dear Mark, one thing I beg as thy marriage gift. Do not permit the cotton mill to be closed! Our country needs mills—"

"The mill will be closed," Mark broke in. "As for the Englishman, his ideas are dangerous. He will cause discontent in the brickyard."

"Mark, tell me why."

"I am not bound to state reasons."

"Damons have always been fair with workers," she said softly. "Surely our men will not resent other workers being treated well."

"Damons have spoiled their workers, as they have spoiled thee." A glitter showed in Mark's dark eyes. "But I am master now."

Angered beyond restraint, she drew away. She could not be like Lucy, Charity realized, because she wasn't Lucy. Nor was Mark, William Lane. "I was remiss in lingering at the mill," she said, head high. "But thee errs more than I, mistaking thy will for the Lord's. I will not be thy wife until thee learns humility."

"Humility!" Mark sneered. "Thee agreed to wed me in a month. Damons keep to a bargain."

"Damons keep an honest bargain," Charity cried, eyes blazing. "When I gave my word, I supposed Mark Badger to be what he pretends. But now I see he was never a true convert. Among the Friends, a woman's soul and mind are as worthy as the man's. Man and woman work together. Neither is master."

A vein on Mark's temple throbbed. "Listen to me," he said hoarsely as he got to his feet. "Thy grandfather discovered the secret that makes Blue Clay Farm brick superior. He taught the secret to Lish and Moses Perkins. Moses taught me. Nobody else knows." He paused as if to let the meaning of his words sink in.

"Lish lies speechless," he went on. "One hour ago, banking the oven fires, Moses had a heart attack and died. I alone know the secret!"

"Moses has died! I must go to poor sister Abigail."

"Not yet." Mark gripped her wrist. "Remember, I alone know the baking secret. Without me, Damon brick will be like any other. I can carry the secret to a rival yard." He laughed, went on, "We wed next month?"

Charity faced him. "No, I will never wed thee. But I will pray that thy mind be healed of a sickness bound to end in evil."

Mark stared, as if his ears had betrayed him.

"And I warn thee," Charity said, "I shall fight for the cotton mill. Now I go to Moses' widow."

With a twist, she broke from his grip.

Trick Up His Sleeve

A MAN in a green waistcoat stood at the inn door. "Howdy, Mr. Bryce," he said. "I'm Asa Howland. Mill proprietors meet in the parlor down the hall."

Acknowledging the landlord's greeting, Anthony went on. Half a dozen men waited in the low-ceilinged room. Eben, who had consented to be present on the condition that he need not speak and that Anthony would present the case for the mill, nodded from his place in the rear.

A stocky man came forward. "I'm Henry Leavitt, publisher of the local paper. Glad to see you here, Mr. Bryce." He shook hands cordially.

Anthony chose a chair in front, near the door. Mark Badger stalked in and sat behind him. There were twelve proprietors, Eben had said, but within a few minutes more than twenty men were seated in the room. Anthony tried to recall what Charity or Eben had said about each of the notables likely to be on hand.

Lanky John Welsh, senior selectman, was chosen moderator. He had called on the Reverend Timothy Carr, Thomas's father, to offer a prayer, when the door opened. Charity and a fair-haired girl who looked frightened came in. They took seats across from Anthony on the further side of the door.

Evidently the two girls were not welcome. John Welsh, described by Eben as a stickler for the letter of the law, pulled at his beard and frowned. The parson eyed the floor, while the other men shuffled their feet. There was an awkward pause.

Then Badger said: "Ladies' sewing-bee must be upstairs.

This room's reserved for mill proprietors." A laugh went around, and the fair-haired girl looked as if she'd rather die than attend this meeting of men.

Charity rose. "The meeting was advertised," she spoke in a clear tone, "as open to all those interested in the mill. I am interested."

"Miss Damon is correct," Leavitt, the newspaper publisher, said, "I set the notice myself."

"Some of the *men* here ain't proprietors," Eben added—to Anthony's surprise. "Cloth's a matter of concern to women."

Lanky John Welsh stroked his beard, hemmed and hawed; but kept to the letter of the law and ruled that the women might remain. Once more he nodded to the tall spare clergyman. The company settled back.

We ask thy blessing for the President of these United States. . . .

Anthony stole a look at Charity. She sat, head bowed, hands folded in her lap. His spirits had risen considerably since she and her timid companion had entered the room. His untimely song might have driven her off; but she had enough faith in the mill to attend this meeting and, if she had faith in the mill, he reasoned, she had faith in him.

The parson's sonorous voice rolled on . . . *for our sons defending us by land and sea. . . .*

In the rear of the room, Eben watched a fly creep up the wall. When the fly spread wings, Eben's gaze followed it as, upside down, it walked on the ceiling.

. . . *for all in our fair village, we ask thy blessing. Amen.*

The long prayer over, chairs scraped. John Welsh rose with an air of meaning to run things off briskly. A squint-eyed man got to his feet.

"Mr. Furber has the floor," the moderator said.

"I'm a farmer and a practical man," the fellow began. "Nigh two hundred year, this village has prospered from farming. Some commerce in lumber, hides, salt-fish, so on. But mainly farming. Since brick is made from the soil, I count brick-making as farming." He bowed to Mark Badger. "I say, what's good for the first two hundred year'll bring success for the next two hundred. I say we steer clear of newfangled things like mills, and stick to farming."

Mild applause followed. Then Dominicus Todd got up.

"Some of us," he spoke with a nasal twang, "put money we could ill spare into the cotton mill. That money's gone. I'm against throwing hard-earned dollars away. I'm for closing the mill."

Dominicus wasn't even honest in his argument, Anthony realized. He implied that proprietors would have to dig into their pockets to continue with the mill. But Eben had insisted he wouldn't take a cent of villagers' money. Eben now appeared less concerned over his brother's misleading words than over the fly's seeming violation of the law of gravitation.

A shadow passed across the window behind Eben. Presently Shad peered in. He winked at Anthony, pulled on his ear, and then ducked out of sight.

The pastor rose and gave a hideous picture of the evils that mills would cause. "Let us keep the workshops in Europe!" he urged.

Charity spoke next. "Machine-made cloth," her voice was low but clear, "would be a boon to women. Spared long hours of drudgery at wheel and loom, they would be healthier, able to keep their children happier . . ."

The men, little troubled over women's drudgery, were plainly impressed by the girl's earnestness. All but Badger, who was black with anger. What could have happened that he should glare at Charity with hate!

As she sat down, Anthony got to his feet.

"A country cannot preserve her independence," he began, "when she lacks the means to provide her fighting men with clothes!"

"That's right," Leavitt put in. "We'd have won the Revolution sooner if Washington's army didn't have to go barefoot, no coats on their backs."

"How can any country defend herself," Anthony continued, with a bow to Leavitt, "if she has to rely on hand-made cannon and muskets, when her enemy manufacture better weapons a hundred times faster . . ." Summing up his points at the end of his speech, he could see that most of the men in the room agreed with him. When he sat down, murmurs of approval went around.

Then a cross-eyed fellow, recognized by the moderator as "Mr. Gragg," sprang up. "I enjoy oratory." His sarcasm got a laugh. "I'm one of the practical men," he went on, "and my position is this. I own no shares in the mill; but loaned the land on which the building stands, with the understanding that shareholders could buy the land, within two years, at a fair price. The time expires in a fortnight. Anyone want to buy?"

"If I had the means, I'd buy," Eben said.

A snicker went around. Anthony recalled Eben's speaking of Gragg. "Sharpest man in the village," Eben had said. "Deals in hides, salt-fish, anything else that comes handy. Also serves as notary."

Nobody else spoke.

"I need my land," Gragg went on after a suitable interval, "but shall keep to the agreement. If nobody buys before twelve noon on the tenth day of June, I put up a No Trespass sign."

Anthony understood now what Eben had meant when he said, "Folks call the mill mine but—" In a fortnight, Eben would have no right to step inside the mill. He was completely in the power of Mark Badger and those Badger influenced.

Badger was on his feet. "Shareholders better lay claim to the mill building and all assets, including machines and designs," he said.

"Aye," the men shouted. "Everything at the mill belongs to us."

"I move," Dominicus Todd twanged, "that the mill be closed, all assets to be held by Mr. Gragg."

"Unless a shareholder buys the land," some joker amended, "before June tenth."

Badger seconded the motion. There was no debate. The motion was carried, Eben and Henry Leavitt the only proprietors dissenting.

Anthony, waiting in the hall for Eben, told himself that Mark Badger had got even with him all right. Badger was driving him out of the village.

"You meant well, son," Eben said kindly as they walked across the yard together. "I knew, that day you found me locking up, it wan't no use keeping on with the cotton mill. Never mind. I've got hold of something better. Folks need artificial teeth. Feller brought a sample into store this morning. I'm starting to make false teeth and I'd like a partner. Have to hump along now. Later, we'll talk it over."

Anthony gave a shrug and went on towards the hitching posts.

"Anthony Bryce," a girl's voice called, "thee is right about our country's need of mills. Wherever thee has a mill, send word to Blue Clay Farm and we will buy the cloth. Come, Lucy!" Climbing into the high cart, Charity gave a friendly nod.

Watching the two girls drive off, Anthony felt new purpose. He'd known from the first, he reminded himself, he'd have to fight Badger.

Shad waited beside his new mare. "How d'ye like her, Tony?" he asked.

"Just what I needed. Her owner came around, soon after we talked, and I bought her. I've named her 'Gypsy'—for you."

Shad grinned. "Wish ye didn't have her, now ye're leavin' village?"

"I still need her." Anthony sprang into the saddle.

Shad laid his hand on the mare's brown flank. "I heard ye

speak. Ye didn't do bad, Tony, but ye hadn't a chance. 'Twas Mark put Gragg up to what he did. I knowed Mark'd have some trick up his sleeve." He shook his head dolefully, went on: "When ye're doin' well I stay away, fearin' to hinder. But ye're out of luck now. What say, we travel together?"

"I'm travelling alone this time." Seeing Shad look disappointed, Anthony added, "I'm bound for Boston to persuade Simeon Damon to buy the mill site."

"Land sakes!" Shad peered up at him. "Tony, if ye had the smallest chance, I'd wish ye luck."

"Thanks, Shad." Anthony touched the mare's side. Riding down the high street, he resolved once more not to give up the foothold he had gained in America. Now Charity was on his side, he too could have a trick up his sleeve!

A New Hampshire Mill

Sly Fox

IN LONDON, the worried English Prince Regent summoned his generals, Lords of the Admiralty, and Ministers. The continent, he pointed out, basked in a truce after the long wars. Why must England's war with the United States continue? The Yankees' toy navy had been destroyed; yet their half-armed privateers still thwarted the Royal Fleet, sinking rich cargoes until British merchants claimed they were bankrupt. Worse than this, the Americans were reported to be building mills of their own and unless these infant industries were promptly crushed, Britain was in peril of losing her closely guarded monopoly of manufacturing.

His Majesty's counsellors mapped out plans. The truce on the continent had released such vast forces that a thousand ships could be spared to tighten the American blockade, harry the seaboard from Maine to Georgia. Twenty thousand of Wellington's men could be sent; some to invade the northern States from Canada, others to seize New Orleans in the South. At the same time, Royal Commissioners would treat with John Quincy Adams and the other American delegates coming to Flanders. Soon, there would be peace!

Across the water, as the stage rumbled into Boston, Charity brushed the dust from her travelling gown and made sure that the important paper in her hand-bag was safe. Presently the coach jolted to a stop. White-maned Uncle Simeon waited, towering above the crowd.

"It is good to see thee, my dear," he greeted her, tucking her arm in his when she stepped down. Plato, his coachman, picked up her luggage.

The carriage felt restful after the long ride through the heat of the June day. They climbed Beacon Hill and nearly everyone they passed had a greeting for Simeon Damon. Near the new State House, as a weary-eyed man came towards them, Plato pulled in the pair of blacks.

"Good evening, friend Caleb," Simeon said. "This is my niece, Charity."

Governor Strong bowed civilly. Then turning to Simeon, he spoke of a report that the British were about to attack Boston.

"I doubt their ability to take the town," Simeon returned calmly. The two men discussed the situation for a few minutes.

Boston had given little support to Mr. Madison's unpopular war, Simeon explained when they drove on. The federal government in turn had stripped the forts of troops, so that defense depended on local volunteers.

"Early this very morning," Simeon said, "I met Paul Revere hurrying towards the North End, a shovel under his arm. 'Near eighty years of age, but not too old to serve my country,' Paul said."

They turned a corner. Simeon's household waited on the steps of his home. Pericles, the Negro boy, took her bag. Sappho and Theodosia, the white parlor maids, vied for her wraps. Athena, the Negro cook, beamed. Black or white, they adored Simeon—and "young missis," as they called Charity.

Up in the cool chamber that was always hers, she changed from her travelling merino to a seemly gray silk. She set a fresh starched cap on her curls, picked up her modest gray evening wrap. Then she ran down the wide curving stairs.

Theodosia was lighting candles in the high-ceilinged drawing-room. The master was engaged with a caller, she said. No wonder they worshipped Simeon, and were even proud of the Greek names he gave them, Charity thought. The parlor maids had been workhouse orphans, Plato was a slave he had freed, and he had rescued Athena from debtors' jail.

She took a chair by the window. A furbelowed lady in a carriage passed. A lad was driving his cow home from the green Common. A young man who whistled as he swung along reminded her of Anthony. Where was Anthony this evening? In some town that gave him a more cordial welcome than Forks Village had given? she wondered.

Simeon came into the room; erect, blue eyes twinkling. How his old style knee breeches became him, and the long collarless coat buttoned to his chin!

"I do not consider myself an old man," he said as he took the chair facing hers, "but I bloom in the company of the young. It is good to have thee here, my dear. Tell me, how is Elisha?"

"He lies helpless all day, and so patient it grieves one doubly."

Simeon looked grave. He inquired how many fields had been planted, how many chicks there were in poultry runs, how many cheeses were aging in damp cellars. And was that wild horse getting to be too much for her?

Gabriel too much for her! Charity laughed.

Simeon plied her with other questions. Each time she came to Boston, it seemed, he placed more responsibility on her.

"I'll move my chair to see thee better," he said. "Something has disturbed thee. Now, what is on thy mind?"

She told him how, for a short time, she had considered being Mark Badger's wife; how Moses Perkins had died and Mark threatened to take the secret of the baking to a rival brickyard. . . . Yes, she went to the widow at once. Sister Abigail said Moses had suffered a heart attack before and therefore given her the words and the figures that made the recipe for the baking. Abigail hid the paper in a crock. Charity now handed it to Simeon, tears in her eyes.

"A worthy workman has gone to his rest," he said as he took it. "And the widow is comfortable?"

"Oh yes. I would not let Mark put her out of her cottage."

"So Mark thinks he is master at Blue Clay Farm!" Simeon's voice grew stern. "My dear, Mark Badger holds no power over us."

Charity had hoped this was so, all along, but hearing the thought put into words comforted her.

"The clay at the farm," Simeon explained, "was once supposed to have special properties. The truth is, thy grandfather discovered by accident that if the fires in the kiln burn slowly during the first two days and then the heat is increased and kept very high, the brick has greater resistance. I never learned the formula. It matters little." He tucked the scrap of paper into a pocket. "Today, many brick-makers know the process which rendered our product superior. When Elisha goes to his eternal rest, perhaps sooner, it may be advisable to close our yard."

Close the brickyard! Charity could hardly imagine such a thing.

Simeon went on to say that people must adjust to changes, and perhaps a greater destiny than a brickyard awaited Forks Village. He was deeply interested in Charity's account of the proprietors' meeting and the closing of the cotton mill.

He reached for an outlandish long-handled pipe, explaining as he lighted it, that it was a gift from a shipmaster who had stopped at a Turkish port. "A neighbor came into my Cornhill shop today," he remarked. "I bade him join us for supper. He will bring his daughter, a girl about thy age."

"They are Friends?" Charity inquired.

"On the contrary, world's people. James Lester is powerful in shipping circles. His daughter Polly is one of the season's belles. It is well to have an acquaintance with those of different faith from ourselves." He blew a wide ring of smoke, continued. "I enjoy trying new things and new ways." He spoke of the changes which had taken place in Boston. Beacon Hill, between cutting down at the top and filling in at the base, had lost its three peaks and half its altitude—not to mention the monument, the original beacon.

The changes which had taken place, however, were as nothing, compared with what would come. Had she noted the paved walk on Park Street? In time, all Boston footwalks would be paved, no house steps projecting into thoroughfares, endangering pedestrians. . . . And there were very great changes in ways of thinking. The Unitarians, with their belief in a kinder God, gained converts steadily.

"At home," Charity put in, "Unitarians are called 'godless troublemakers' and are unwelcome."

"And a century and a half ago," Simeon rejoined, "the Friends were the 'cursed sect.'"

Charity smiled, remembering Lucy's warning about the visits to Boston being "unsettling."

Then a carriage drew up outside. She heard a man's deep voice, a girl's answering laugh.

Simeon laid his long pipe aside. "My dear, our guests!"

Out in the oval hall, he presented James Lester and the slender fair-haired girl. When Polly Lester let her scarlet cape slide off her shoulders, Charity barely kept from exclaiming. She had never seen a woman in formal evening attire before. The pale blue gown was narrow as a pencil, its waistline up under the bosom, neck and arms entirely bare!

"Thy daughter is a beautiful woman, James," Simeon remarked, untroubled.

James Lester bowed. "The niece is also lovely."

"Lovely!" Polly echoed, but an amused look showed in the blue eyes that ranged over Charity's high-necked, long-sleeved, gray gown.

"Let us go down to the dining room." Simeon gave Polly his arm, and Charity followed with James Lester.

After the blessing, Theodosia brought in a great platter.

"Widgeons!" James Lester exclaimed. "Simeon, you must

have gone early to market this morning."

"Before breakfast. It is my daily custom. And tomorrow, Charity will accompany me."

"About the time you selected the birds, Polly was coming home from a dance." Her father glanced at her with pride.

And she *was* pretty, Charity realized, with her golden curls dressed high and her blue gown emphasizing the deep blue of her eyes.

James complimented Simeon on his skilful carving. The talk got to public charities. "Men call you a sly fox in trading," James remarked with a bow, "but when it comes to alms for the poor, everyone says, 'Go to Simeon the Quaker.' "

"Mere selfish prudence," Simeon returned. "None of us is secure as long as another hungers."

Polly turned to Charity. "Up there in the country, what do you do?" she asked.

Did the Boston girl expect to yawn, Charity wondered, over tales of butter and candle-making? "Many pleasant things," she said. "And I have a horse that jumps the highest fences."

"Here in Boston," Polly went on, "I go to balls several times a week. There are many house-parties in Brookline and Watertown. In August, at Harvard Commencement time, my parents always give a big sailing party on one of our ships."

Theodosia brought crackers and cheese.

"Cheese needs claret, James." The wine showed sparkling red as Simeon poured.

"Let me propose the toast," James said. "To a speedy end of the war with England!"

Simeon bowed, very slightly. "For me there is need of different phrasing. Shall we say, A speedy end to all war, everywhere!"

The guest, evidently unaccustomed to correction, drank with his brow clouded, Charity noted.

When they returned to the drawing-room, candles burned in the high chandeliers. The evening had turned cool, and

Polly asked for her wrap. The girl talked entertainingly about the lads she knew. "A friend of mine," she said as she took a bonbon from the dish beside them, "has his own privateer and brings me candy from Paris."

The men, smoking long cigars, were discussing deals on Cornhill and Long Wharf when Charity heard James Lester clear his throat. "Some of us have prepared a resolution to be sent to the Congress," he said in a honeyed tone, "and we'd like Simeon Damon's name among the signers."

"An attack, I believe, on our infant industries."

How did Uncle Simeon come to be so well informed about the new mills? Charity wondered.

"Precisely," the shipowner was saying. "The war with England will end soon. We'll return to old ways: export raw material, import finished goods. Join us, Simeon, in requesting the Congress to pass no legislation favorable to domestic mills."

Charity felt hot with indignation. Just as Mark Badger and his friends had driven Anthony out of Forks Village, greedy shipowners would drive him, and others like him, out of the United States. And mills were needed so desperately!

She glanced across at Simeon. He seemed a stranger, no twinkle showing in his eyes, no teasing smile around his mouth; even his features looked sharper.

He spoke at last. "A country never returns to old ways. Thee is too late."

"Too late!" the shipowner fumed. "The war is not quite over."

"The days of New England's great carrying trade are over."

"For Salem and the small ports, perhaps, but only beginning for Boston."

"Thee forgets New York."

"Boston will remain the hub of the universe."

"With a canal bringing produce from the region of the Great Lakes to the Hudson River and New York?"

"This talk of an 'Erie Canal' is nonsense."

Back and forth, like barbed arrows, the arguments flew; the shipowner heated, Simeon cool. The air of the room grew heavy with tobacco smoke. Charity's eyes ached. Polly, beside her, looked bored.

James Lester was growing angry. "Domestic mills mean nothing but trouble," he roared, his face deep red. "Paul Revere's had a lawsuit over his copper factory."

"Thee should know where this country would be," Simeon retorted softly, "without Paul's copper on our fighting vessels' sides. As men recognize the value of mill sites, more suits will be brought. A young man came to see me a few days ago about a dispute over a mill site. An English mechanic."

Anthony could not have talked with Simeon! Charity thought. Even imagining such an idea was silly.

"*I* met an English mechanic," James Lester was saying, "in April, on the Portsmouth stage. Tall fellow, taffy-colored hair. Named 'Bryce' as I recall."

Charity saw Simeon nod. So she wasn't silly, and her uncle *had* seen Anthony!

The shipowner slapped his knee. "A stubborn fellow, I remember, liked to argue. Got into a brawl as soon as he stepped out of the stage."

"It was not a brawl," Charity declared. "He defended a man."

"Thee saw it, my dear?" Simeon inquired, amused.

"Of course not. I—I heard about it."

"I saw it, and it wasn't bad fighting," the shipowner said. "Bryce defeated the local bully. Incidentally he had crossed the ocean on one of my vessels."

"Father, you should have told me about this fascinating Englishman," Polly protested. "I'd like to meet him."

"You doubtless will. I offered him a post and expect him to turn up when he's tired of mills. But Simeon, this resolution. It seems . . ."

The shipowner got nowhere with Simeon, Charity saw. At

last he said, appeasingly: "We need not decide tonight. Think the matter over, Simeon, and let me know." He and Polly rose.

"Make no delay for me," Simeon rejoined, rising too. "I am committed to the side of the mills. This site that young Bryce came to see me about is in my native village. I agreed to buy it, in fact, finance the mill for a time. My letter, enclosing a draft on the Portsmouth bank, went on yesterday's stage."

Uncle Simeon was not letting Mark and the others drive Anthony away! The dear sly fox! Charity wanted to throw her arms around his neck, but she managed to stand quietly beside him.

"I will wager," James Lester began.

"We Quakers do not wager," Simeon broke in.

"Then I will prophesy. When it is known that Simeon Damon has purchased a mill site, men will say he has grown too old for Boston trading."

"Time will prove which of us is right."

"At any rate, we thank you for an agreeable evening." James Lester was plainly making an effort to keep from losing his temper. "If you change your mind about the resolution, let me know."

"I shall not change my mind," Simeon said firmly.

Polly covered the awkward moment which followed. "Shall you be in Boston long enough," she asked Charity, "to come to my house?"

"No," Simeon answered. "Charity goes home in two days' time as she will represent me when the deed transferring ownership of the mill site is signed."

Again, Charity wanted to throw her arms around her uncle's neck. But she waited, a gracious hostess, while the Lesters said good night.

"Uncle Simeon, I am so glad," she said as the carriage rolled away, "that thee will back the cotton mill. And I'm proud that thee trusts me with business matters."

"Trust my niece!" Simeon chuckled and laid his hand on her shoulder. "Isn't my main object educating her to carry responsibility? But thee has had a tiring journey and the hour is late." He bent and kissed her.

Alone in her room at last, Charity went to the open window. Down on Park Street, a watch was making his rounds. The croak of frogs came from the Common.

Then, off in the harbor, a gun crashed.

She waited. But no answering gun shattered the peace of the night. Had some vessel slipped through the blockade? she wondered, thinking of Anthony and the way he had come into Boston.

Watch That Wolf in Sheep's Clothing!

ANTHONY'S appointment with Matthew Gragg was for eleven o'clock on June tenth, and he took care to arrive early. A small room behind the store served as Gragg's office. The window had no shade; sun blazing in through unwashed panes revealed cobwebs in corners, rubbish in the fireplace, dust everywhere. Gragg's gloom matched the dreariness of the office.

"You're early, Mr. Bryce," he said with a sour look.

"The option expires at twelve," Anthony replied.

Gragg was silent as he cleared a space on his untidy desk. If he could find a way of not keeping the bargain, he would, Anthony saw; but he knew better than trifle with Simeon Damon.

Eben sauntered in, a changed man since he had funds to draw on. "Morning, Matt," he said cheerfully. "Here are the notes."

Gragg thumbed the money with bad grace. "Simeon's niece is coming," he growled. "Can't expect a woman to be on time."

Just as the steeple clock began to strike, Charity's cart rolled up. She joined them, cool and business-like. No longer did the office seem gloomy to Anthony. Eben looked on, thumbs in armholes, while Gragg fumed about the labor of getting clear title, about this and that. Too soon for Anthony's liking, the papers were signed and sealed.

Charity rose. "Good morning, gentlemen," she said with dignity. As if on second thought, she turned. "Anthony Bryce, will thee accompany me to see the papers properly posted to

Simeon Damon in Boston?"

"With pleasure, ma'am."

She was friendly but business-like as they walked to the post office and dispatched the papers. Afterwards, when Anthony helped her into her cart, she held out her hand. "Remember, we plan to use machine-woven cloth at Blue Clay Farm." She nodded and flicked the reins.

Her words lingered in Anthony's ears as he toiled at the mill.

Simeon had said, in Boston: "Extend the present structure, shore up the floor, tack on an upper story." Working with old Walt Hubbard, the carpenter, and his son, young Walt, Anthony thought the din of saw and hammer made a sweeter melody than the river's flow.

The spinner's carding teeth were now properly adjusted. The useless old dam was blasted away. Stone for the new dam waited. One Saturday afternoon in early July, he let his eyes range over the mill coming into new life; over the piles of planks, clapboards, nails and shingles; over old Walt, swaying on the ladder as he drove spikes home, and young Walt waiting on his father.

He walked a few yards to a spot where the field hollowed. He and young Walt had deepened the natural pit, squared it and lined it with boards. Kegs of lime stood beside it, ready for cement-mixing. Beyond, Ivory Oldfield, the smith, had set up a forge and was to cast a small model of the water-power loom.

Moreover, Anthony reminded himself, Eben, a new man now, had of his own accord journeyed to Boston to purchase supplies. With sea lanes blocked, Eben had written, and the overland route from the South terrible dear, the price of prime upland cotton had gone sky high. But he'd bought the best grade, at lowest possible figures. And he was accepting orders for cotton sheeting—to be delivered in Boston by September.

Walking back to the mill building, Anthony wished he could show Shad the progress made. He had not seen Shad since the day of the inn meeting. If the little man showed up only when things were bad, he wasn't likely to appear for some time!

Inside the mill, Anthony worked on the shuttle, a hull-shaped instrument carrying crosswise threads over and under the warp threads. As he sharpened the point, a bit of cotton fluff lighted on his hand. Unlike flax fibre, which was smooth and straight, ripe cotton fibre had a crook. The crook held the fibre closer, making cotton cloth warmer, as well as cooler, than linen; but it made cotton harder to work with. He must get his shuttle exactly right.

An hour or so later, he heard Shad's whistle. It was absurd to feel uneasy, he told himself, as he got up to greet the wanderer.

Shad had a couple of pans hanging from a shirt button. He held out his battered cap, heaped with strawberries. "Wild ones, Tony, and ain't nothin' sweeter," he said, smacking his lips.

"I'm glad to see you," Anthony said, "How are you?"

"Perky." Shad grinned as, struggling with a knotted string, he got the pans free. "I ain't bringin' what I didn't come by, honest," he declared. "A woman what was movin' and didn't have room in her wagon for rusty tinware give me these pans." He poured out the berries. "Warm as new eggs," he said, "but I'll cool 'em." He ran down to the river's edge, set the pan filled with berries on a water-lapped stone, laid the other pan over it.

Back at the mill, he perched on a nail keg and got out his chipped clay pipe. "Mill's livenin' up," he remarked. "Walt and his young'un workin' like beavers."

Anthony told him what had been done. By September he and Eben would be turning out cotton sheeting. With only one loom, they'd take small orders for a time; but as profits came in, they'd add more looms, more spinners.

"Who is it," Shad inquired, "can't go to bed without sheetin'?"

Troubled a little by his friend's jesting manner, Anthony explained that pioneer settlers in New York State and Kentucky preferred heavy cloth to the fine goods popular in the East. Eben had looked into the matter thoroughly.

Shad blew a ring of smoke, said, "Tony, I come to warn ye. Watch Mark!"

"Now Simeon Damon owns the land, I'm not worrying over Badger," Anthony replied.

"So far, ye done well." Shad nodded wisely. "Ye got Simeon to back ye, and nothin' s'prised me more. Ye got Eben interested. Ye hired the only carpenters in village—and I hope ye keeps 'em. But ye beat Mark for the second time, and he's bound to pay ye back double."

"Carpenters'll finish the outside work in another week," Anthony said.

"Mebbe."

"Then we start the new dam."

"If ye can git a mason."

"Chester Wiggin's coming from Exeter."

The peal of the village bell sounded over the fields six times. Presently old Walt appeared. "Monday, I'm working for Farmer Furber," he said.

"What!"

"Monday, I'm working for Joe Furber." Old Walt pulled out a tobacco plug, bit off a piece.

Anthony could not believe his ears. "You agreed to work for Eben," he said.

"No agreement. Said I'd help out for a while. Ask Eben."

"You're a carpenter—not a field hand."

"Round here, a man does a bit of everything. Has to. Joe Furber is haying next week, and hay can't wait." Old Walt began to chew.

"So you'll be back when Furber's hay is in," Anthony said with relief.

"Nope. Another farmer needs me then. Round here, July is haying time. Hay means fodder for cattle, and cattle is something a body can live by. Eben's mill is moonshine." He gave a shrug. "We all know Eben. Ain't no better feller, but he's full of moonshine."

' Simeon Damon is backing him."

Walt spat. "There's folks call the place here 'Simeon's Folly.' Simeon's getting old, folks say."

"We'll pay you higher wages," Anthony offered.

"Thanks, young feller," Walt nodded, "but 'tain't a mite of use. I'll drop in at store, collect what's due me. Don't want a cent more. Good day."

Before Anthony could get his breath, young Walt came. "I set ladder longside lumber pile," he said. "Monday, I'm working down to Portsmouth. Dollar a day."

"*We'll* pay you a dollar a day." Anthony felt panic.

"Nothing in a money way'd keep me, sir. English ships been trying to land on soil of the State I was born in. Ordinary times, I'd stay with Eben. But this is war time. Monday, I'll be defending New Hampshire. Good day, mister." Fifteen-year-old Walt hurried after his father.

In his bitter disappointment, Anthony walked up and down.

"Tony, don't take this to heart!" Shad begged.

"I've got to get the mill running—and before the war ends. You don't understand what I'm fighting for."

"I can guess. Partly, to earn what ye calls a livin'. Partly, pure stubbornness. And partly, 'count of Quaker gal." Shad wriggled an ear, went on. "Forks Village ain't so dull as sometimes. Think I'll stay a spell. Might even help ye. Walt will of given ye stout beams and joists. Nothing tricky 'bout Walt. I can help ye sheathe, I guess. Might do more—in a pinch."

"Six o'clock tomorrow morning!" Anthony said promptly.

"Work on Sabbath? Land sakes, that'd put a worser blight on the mill. Tony, I don't put stock in this cotton sheetin' idea, as I said afore. But I like ye. And I'm helpin' ye, Monday mornin'."

"Thanks, Shad."

"Mind, it's Mark Badger told Joe Furber to hire old Walt away from ye," Shad went on. "It's Mark been talkin' to young Walt 'bout his duty to State of New Hampshire. And it's Mark been settin' folks to call this mill 'Old Simeon's Folly.' Watch that Mark, pertendin' he's Quaker! That wolf in sheep's clothin'! But I guess them berries'll taste cool 'bout now." Shad ran down to the river's edge.

The following week brought clear hot weather. Anthony and Shad shingled the mill roof, backs aching.

" 'Tain't the work I mind," Shad jested, "but the reg'larity. And all to make sheets for softies in York State and Kentuck."

"Ouch!" Anthony had hammered his thumb instead of a nail.

"Tony!" Shad cried. "I knowed ye'd do that, 'tween bein' tuckered and in such a fever to finish."

"We've got to have a tight roof." Anthony pinched his aching finger. "Inside work can wait, but if there's no dry storage space for the cotton fibre Eben's ordered, it'll sour in the bale." He picked up the hammer.

Later in the day, as they were putting on the last row of shingles, Shad spied Eben crossing the field. "Land sakes!" he cried, "Eben's left ten year of his age in Boston."

Anthony turned. Eben did look taller and younger. He swung along, resiliency in his stride in spite of the wilting heat, and waved as he came nearer.

"Just off the stage," he called. "Carpenters quit?"

Anthony nodded, dreading the effect.

Eben seemed undisturbed. "I'll help," he said. "Shad, if you'll stick, I'll pay you fifty cents a day."

Shad peered down over the roof edge. "The money don't matter," he rejoined tartly. "I can always git what I need. But I'm stickin'."

Eben said he had ordered six months' supply of raw cotton, and the five-hundred-pound bales would come on the first vessel bound for Portsmouth. Simeon had meant to travel north with him, but had slipped on one of the rough foot-walks, broken an ankle, and would be unable to take the journey for a while. In the meantime, he wanted them to buy land, quietly and without fuss, both sides of the river. The higher dam might cause back-flowage and he meant to avoid lawsuits. "Ain't laid eyes on Sary Ann yet," Eben finished. "I'll hump along now. See you later." He strode off towards the village.

Shad laid his hand on Anthony's arm. "Tony, I hate to be harpin', but ye can't succeed without village folks behind ye. And Mark'll keep 'em agin ye. Spite of Simeon's money in the Portsmouth bank, spite of cotton bales comin'. The nigher ye seems to winnin', the nigher ye be to trouble. Tony, please watch out!"

Anthony's jaw had set. "Thanks for the warning, Shad," he said, "but Mark Badger can't stop my finishing this roof." He reached for a bundle of shingles.

On Sabbath Day, when local prejudice made work at the mill impossible, Anthony felt restless. Eager to see Charity, he convinced himself he should tell her about Eben's trip. When evening came, he hitched Gypsy to Eben's cart.

The moon was high as he drove out of the yard. How differently things looked at night! Barns loomed enormous. Sticks and stones seemed queerly distorted. Houses hugged the roadside so that sometimes he thought he would drive straight into a candle-lighted house; and then the white road twisted. Scents were stronger; the fragrance of new-mown hay, acrid barnyard odors, the sweetness of clover. . . . A great house came into view, shadowy in the moonlight.

He turned his mare into the Damon lane.

In the sickroom of the house, Charity had just drawn the the window curtains to keep the moon from shining on Uncle Elisha. She tiptoed to his four-poster bed and let the muslin that kept insects away fall around him. Then she crossed the hall to her own chamber.

The house seemed very still, as she set her lighted candle down. Her thoughts flew to Anthony. He looked so purposeful, his chin so firm, the day they sat in Matthew Gragg's office. If only she could know how he was getting on!

Wheels were rattling down the lane! Mark's gelding did not step so lightly, Mark's well-greased trap had no squeaking axle. Probably some workman wanted Mark, and presently the wagon would pass, go on to the riverbank cottage.

It had halted! Three loud raps sounded. Anthony's knock? A silly notion, she chided herself. Someone in the village was ill. Her nursing bag, filled with soft linens, herbs and ointments, was always ready. She had only to pick up bonnet and cape and fly. Now Hilda was coming for her!

"Anthony Bryce, downstairs," the woman announced.

She must seem calm, the mistress of Blue Clay Farm reminded herself, as she went down the stairs.

"Good evening, Anthony," she said as she entered the best room.

"Good evening. I'm so sorry," Anthony began, "about your uncle's accident."

"Uncle Simeon has had an accident!" She forgot she was the mistress of Blue Clay Farm and should appear calm. "Oh, please tell me!"

The mishap wasn't too serious, Anthony assured her. Simeon had the most skilful physician in Boston; but felt unable to return with Eben, as planned. . . . Eben had journeyed to Boston in the interests of the mill.

"How is the mill?" Relieved about her uncle, she seated herself at one end of the long sofa, and Anthony took the other end.

He told her about Simeon's desire to own more land, and all that Eben and he had accomplished. . . . "We hope to be filling orders for cotton sheeting by September and, as long as the war lasts, the market is unlimited," he finished.

"Thee knows I am glad that all goes well."

They talked of one thing and another. . . . The British were making landings in Maine. Three spies, prowling up river to learn the harbor's strength, had been seized. Everywhere, men were leaving home to aid with local defense. . . .

"And what about Mark Badger?" Anthony inquired.

"Uncle Elisha suffered an ill turn that kept me away from First Day Meeting," she told him. "Mark came to chide me for my absence. I told him the truth, but his eyes were filled with suspicion as he drove off."

"Old trouble-maker!" Anthony burst out.

Presently, instead of the long stretch of sofa being between them, they sat side by side. Anthony reached for Charity's hand. His arm slipped around her. . . . And then he had kissed her.

"Marry me!" he begged. "So Mark can't worry you!"

She drew away, remembering the barrier a difference in faith made.

"I love you, and you love me," Anthony declared. "We belong to each other."

She tried to shut her ears to his pleading. "I may not wed with one of the world's people," she told him. "It is mad to ask."

"I'll never try to wean you away from your faith," he promised. "I'd rather turn Quaker myself."

"If only thee *were* one of us!"

He had spoken impulsively. How could he become a Friend

as long as he thought some of their ideas a century behind the times! But there was Simeon, the most progressive man he had met in America. And he was in full accord, Anthony reminded himself, with the Friends' ideas about thrift, generosity to the poor, war, other matters. "Tell me how to be one of you," he said, after a minute.

There were difficulties, she explained. The Friends did not seek converts, and the Forks Village group was already large. Mark would be the worst obstacle.

"I'm not worrying about Mark," he said. "Just tell me what to do."

"Thee makes application," she explained eagerly, "to the senior overseer, Obadiah Andrews. He and the others will consider. The Lord may move them to overrule Mark's objections. If favorably inclined, they will map out the proper study. The Rules of Discipline are not easy for world's people."

"They'll be easy for me," he rejoined. "I want to marry you so much."

"Hark!" she warned as a clop-clop sounded. "It is Mark's cart and gelding."

They waited, silent. Mark had halted. He would see Anthony's mare, and recognize Eben's cart standing by the hitching posts! They heard an oath. Mark Badger, an overseer of the Society of Friends, was taking the Lord's name in vain. Another oath . . . and he had driven on.

"Thee must go!" Charity rose, her fingers interlaced. "Mark is a madman, deaf to reason, when he is angry. I fear he will do thee harm."

"Who can harm me, now I know that Charity loves me!" Anthony said proudly.

They did not kiss when he left. "It is better to keep to Friends' rules," Charity said softly. "Better not to meet until thee hears from Obadiah Andrews."

"I'll write to him tonight," Anthony promised.

Someone Meddlin'

NEXT MORNING, Gypsy whinnied as he pushed the barn doors wide. Knowing her bag of oats waited at the mill, she had no objection to the saddle at dawn. Anthony began a song as he cantered out of the yard, and then broke off, remembering he was almost a Quaker.

Shad, waiting on the mill step, looked doleful as Anthony rode up.

"Someone been meddlin' with pit," he said.

Anthony sprang from the saddle and hurried to the spot where Chester Wiggin had begun to work. The kegs were open, all the lime dumped into the river.

"They's been rock-blowin' too." Shad led the way to the dam.

The original foundation, as well as the new wall, were wrecked. Only explosive powder set in the riverbed could have worked such havoc. Anthony thought back to the night before. Mark, angry over finding him at Blue Clay Farm, had supplied himself with powder, come to the mill at low tide—which would have been around eleven o'clock.

"Didn't sleep here last night," Shad apologized.

"No reason why you should have." Anthony unsaddled Gypsy, in his distress not responding to her nuzzle before she buried her nose in the feed-bag.

Presently Chester Wiggin, who always left his horse near the road because of the point that was quicksand, came along the path, swinging his dinner pail.

"Boys have been up to mischief." Anthony took pains to speak casually. "It's lucky we weren't further along. There's more lime inside the mill that we can use."

Chester set his pail down, surveyed the empty kegs, and the broken dam wall. "This river don't want to be harnessed." He shook his head. "Well, man over Dover way asked me to build him a barn. Good day, young feller." He stooped for his pail.

"See here!" Anthony remonstrated. "You're not such a fool as to be frightened because a few boys got in here on a moonlight night! Besides, you agreed to build a dam."

"You got me wrong." Chester wore an injured look. "Nobody makes agreements with Eben. Changes his mind too often. And it's more'n boys been here."

Anthony watched Chester walk off. "Where can I get another mason?" he asked.

Shad pulled a piece of grass, and chewed it. "I hear Eli Durgin's got his hay in," he said at last. "Eli ain't a mason. Most any farmer can mix cement, do a mite of smithin' too."

"Where does he live?"

"Out on Manchester road, half a mile this side of my cabin. I'll stick around till ye git back," Shad added, as Anthony resaddled Gypsy.

For two weeks things went smoothly. Eli Durgin, eager to try dam-building, found a helper, and each evening they left a pile of stone, broken into gravel and ready for cement-mixing. Ivory Oldfield set up a forge. Eben and Anthony, aided by Shad and sometimes by Thomas, finished the upper-story flooring and began the outside clapboarding. Word arrived that a shipment of raw cotton had left Boston.

Anthony fretted over not hearing from the Friends, and Charity was seldom out of his thoughts. Also, Shad was looking poorly. Anthony slept at the mill now. One morning, when Shad didn't come until noon, Anthony was shocked by his wilted look.

"Shad, you've been working too hard," he said.

" 'Tain't the work but the reg'larity gits me down," his friend explained. "Ye don't need me for a while. Guess I'll roam a spell."

"Good!" Anthony rejoined. "I don't know what I'd have done without you, these last weeks. But I'm all right now. Stay away as long as you like."

Shad, already looking brighter, cocked his head to one side. "Tony, I don't put stock in your notion of turnin' out sheetin'. And I dunno what'd help ye, lessen it be the Lord or Daniel Webster. But I'm with ye." He opened his bandanna bundle, pulled out a leaf. "Ain't nothin' for luck like four-leaved clover," he said.

Anthony gripped his friend's small hand as he took the leaf. "Thanks, Shad. You've brought me luck all along."

"Soon's I perk up, I'll be back." Shad ambled off.

Except that no word came from the Friends, things continued to go well. The great bales of cotton fibre arrived and were stored in the cellar. The wall of the new dam rose. With Eben's help, Anthony built a shed where horses could have shelter. He slept on the premises every night. But no marauders came near the mill.

August brought wet weather, and Eli Durgin groaned. Unable to mix cement, he continued to break up stone. One drizzly morning, Anthony lifted his eyes from his design for a new water wheel to see a tidy rig crossing the field. The elderly man in the cart looked grave as he drew up.

"Thee is Anthony Bryce?" he inquired.

"Yes, sir." Anthony felt something ominous in the air.

"I am Obadiah Andrews of the Society of Friends. Thought I'd deliver our message in person." He gave Anthony a letter. "We debated thy application long," he said, a blunt kindness about him. "Conversion is a serious matter. Even a local man would serve a probation period, and thee is foreign-born. In two years, if thee still feel inclined, write to me again." With a nod, he drove off.

Wait two years to marry Charity! Anthony flung the Friends' letter into the fireplace. A bigoted old Quaker might keep him dangling, but Charity would not. He must not call her people "bigoted"—and Charity would send a comforting message. Any minute, a boy from Blue Clay Farm would ride to the door.

He picked up board and crayon, but could not draw. Eben arrived, and he went outside to help unharness Lightfoot.

"Travelling feller dropped into store and kept me," Eben remarked as he unfastened the traces. "He said it's all over Boston, John Quincy Adams and other peace delegates are meeting with British delegates in Flanders."

"At Ghent?" Anthony inquired.

"That's right. Adams's been against Mr. Madison's war from the start. A cold man, some say, no feeling in him. But he's got brains enough to outsmart the British, by cracky." He gave Lightfoot's flank a light slap, and she ran to the new shed. "Now what do you want me to do?" he asked.

"Wish you'd work on the new water wheel."

Consulting Anthony's design, Eben took measurements for the buckets which, set into the rim of the great wheel, would catch water pouring down from the sluiceway and by sheer weight compel the wheel to turn.

"There'll be a deal of argument at Ghent," he said as he cut into a board.

"Do you think they'll agree on terms soon?" Anthony inquired.

"Gorry, no. We'll lick the British good and proper before we make terms."

Anthony said nothing. Nobody wanted peace more than he. But he knew, better than Eben, how the British would try to crush American industries, when peace gave opportunity.

Eben went home for noon dinner. Anthony stayed at the mill. Clouds were piling up in the leaden sky, and his shirt felt as damp as if he had walked through rain. An hour later, mist blotted out the trees and fields until the mill seemed an island in a gray sea. No use trying to set cement in the new wall of the dam in such weather! No use trying to keep a fire in an outdoor forge! Anthony told Eli Durgin and Ivory Oldfield they might go home.

Left alone, he went to the fireplace and retrieved the Friends' letter. It expressed what the elderly overseer had said, but in more formal words. Angered anew, Anthony tore it into bits. He decided to join the Todds for supper and later ride to Blue Clay Farm for a talk with Charity.

Spirits somewhat lighter, he saddled Gypsy, locked up.

Supper was a cheerful meal. Anthony found himself relishing the cold ham, baked potatoes, blackberries smothered with heavy cream.

"Guess I'll take Ruddy for a run," Betsey said afterwards.

"Keep inside the yard," her father charged. "Heavy sea turn's blowing in."

"And you, Anthony," Sary Ann called as he started up the box stairs, "don't think of sleeping on that wet riverbank tonight. Stay here."

Up in his small room, Anthony lighted a candle and looked himself over, making sure he was tidy enough to call on Charity. He could hear Sary Ann and Min putting things to rights in the kitchen. Somone drove into the yard.

Presently Betsey climbed the steep stairs. "Letter from Blue Clay Farm, Anthony. Man that brought it said there's no answer needed." She clattered down.

Anthony had seen Charity sign her name, the day they met in Matthew Gragg's office. Breathing hard, he opened what he knew must be her letter.

"Dear Anthony Bryce,

Thee has received a reply from the Society of Friends, I am told. Regretting the decision more than I can say, I must abide by it. That thee and thy mill prosper will ever be the wish of

CHARITY DAMON"

The words swam before his eyes. Charity had not written them, he told himself. She would never write as if they must be separated for all time. But she had! The bigoted old Quakers had persuaded her to throw happiness away.

Pacing the floor, he felt hemmed in. He went part way down the stairs. The family were in the front room, Min was occupied in the buttery. He hurried down, and through the kitchen.

Only Ruddy, nose between his paws and one eye squinted, saw him go outside.

He saddled Gypsy, walked her out of the yard, turned her in the direction of the mill. Everywhere, the fog wiped out fences and landmarks, lights in village houses showed a ghostly dimness; but the mare trotted, sure-footed. The fields, when he reached them, were a sea of mist, and the river a murmuring sound.

In the new shed, he tossed fresh straw down; hung Gypsy's saddle and bridle on hooks. Then he unlocked the mill. In his despair, he did not bother with a lantern. He had taken pains, before he went to the Todd house, to close the upper story windows; it seemed a deal of trouble to climb up there now. On a stormy night, the pair of windows on the ground floor of the old part of the mill would give air enough. He laid his hand on a sash.

The window wasn't quite shut—and the catch was open! Queer, he thought, as he shoved the window up and propped it with a stick. The opposite window, to his relief, was securely locked. Nothing was amiss except that, disturbed by the letter from the Friends, he had neglected to close one window properly. And what did it matter, what did anything matter, now that Charity would not marry him!

On his way to bar the door, he fell against a great bale of raw cotton that stood in the middle of the space. Rubbing his shin, he undressed and tumbled into his narrow bed.

Sleep seemed unattainable. He raged against all who would wreck young people's happiness. He turned and tossed, unable to keep his mind off the action of the Quaker overseers. Had Mark Badger had a hand in the decision? He wished he could talk with Shad.

The river's murmur turned louder, and he realized there was an incoming tide. A bat flew in, circled the space with a loud flapping of wings, flew out again. An owl hooted. The air felt chilly, and he drew up a blanket. . . .

Voices roused him.

"What do I break open?" someone asked.

"Small cabinet. It's nailed to the wall, above the cot in far corner. Designs'll be inside." There was a clinking sound, as if someone had set a lantern down.

Anthony bolted upright, reached for his boots. Mark Badger stood outside! Eben must have told Dominicus, who had told Mark, where he kept the designs.

"Likely anyone's in there?" the first voice drawled.

"No," Mark said. "Bryce has a room in the village. I went into the yard and saw a light in his window as I came by."

When he stole down the stairs, Anthony realized, he had forgotten to snuff out his candle. It would burn to the last drop of tallow. Eben and Sary Ann thought him safe in young Eben's room; but he was alone in a remote meadow, a log from the fireplace his only weapon. Men had killed his father to get a design!

"Anyone else sleep here?" the unknown voice inquired.

"Nobody but a runt of a feller'd run from a whisper, and he's gone off. I was over here, while ago. Ladder sets by the lumber pile. I got in through an upper story window, nosed around, pushed this window up so we can use the short ladder."

Anthony took his hand off his boots and stood erect. A vindictive man waited outside, meaning to steal his designs. An unscrupulous man, perhaps touched in the head! He reached up and unlocked the cabinet above his cot; unlocked the metal box and took out all the papers; relocked box and cabinet. On bare feet he went to the bale of raw cotton, and stuffed the rolled papers far down inside. He stole to his water keg, washed all crayon marks off his drawing boards. Then he crept to the window. Fog was still too thick for the men outside to see that it was propped open, he thought.

"Afore we break locks, there's a point or two to settle," one voice said.

"What's to settle?" Mark sounded surly.

"The man I'm selling designs to thinks I come by 'em honest. He pays me well. Of course, you don't get anything."

Mark burst into a loud laugh.

During that laugh, Anthony removed the stick, lowered the window sash until it was as he had found it. He pulled on his boots.

"All I want," Mark said, "is to drive a trouble-maker out of this village. He's slow about taking a hint, but guess I can start him travelling. If not one way, then another." Mark's laugh had an evil echo.

"So we break a lock. I skip back to my boat with the papers. And that's all?"

"That's all, Jake. Except that if you ever connect my name with the business, I'll tell the sheriff such a story—"

"My word'd never count against yourn," Jake broke in. "I know that. Anyways, soon's I'm paid for these designs, I'm heading West."

"Wind's freshening," Mark said. "Fog'll clear, if we don't hasten. You go up, first." Something bumped against the clapboards.

Crouched in the shadow, Anthony waited, a log in his hand. A lantern gave an eerie light as the man who must be "Jake" raised the window and put a stick under it. Anthony let him step inside, waited until Mark was astride the sill. His left hand gripping Mark, he wheeled and struck Jake with the log.

Jake went down surprisingly quickly. Not sure he had really knocked Jake out, Anthony was dealing a second blow, when Mark slipped out of his grip. Before Mark had got both legs outside, Anthony gripped again, dragged him in. Mark made a sudden twist and began to run.

Anthony picked up his log and went after Mark, filled with scorn for a man who ran.

Back and forth, Mark ran; behind the spinner that showed dark against the white pine wall, across to the window and back to the opposite window, around the bale in the middle of the floor, under the workbench, forward to the door. He managed to kick Jake's lantern and put out the light. He stumbled over Jake's still form, recovered himself, and slid along the wall.

Near the cot bed, Anthony caught him. Mark whipped out a knife, gashed Anthony's hand; he ran forward, unbarred and opened the door.

Anthony followed him outside. The fog had lifted slightly. He could see Mark, twisting like an eel as he ran, and gained steadily on him. When Mark headed towards the limepit, Anthony raced after him. But another form appeared beside Mark. Had Jake only pretended to be knocked out! Suddenly Anthony's throat felt dry.

Something whizzed by his ear, and his shoulder burned. Mark had found the broken rock, left ready for the morning's masonry. He and Jake were hurling stones, freshly broken and knife-edged.

Anthony was the hunted, now. Two men were on his track, throwing stones that rained around him. No trees or bushes screened him, and the sky was growing lighter. He must get to the river side of the mill, gain the high bank's shelter, then swim across the stream. Keep clear of the quicksand! he warned himself.

He turned left, then right. He crouched and crawled; he stood erect and raced in a zigzag path; fell flat and wriggled. But always one of the two spied him, and the stones rained down. Twenty paces, and he'd be beyond the quicksand . . . fifteen paces now. His face felt stripped of skin, his head and hands dripped blood, his breathing came in wheezes. He staggered on. Ten paces more, and he could leap into the river, dive out of his tormentors' sight. Bent double, he reeled on. His head felt suddenly as if it had been cracked open, and he stumbled.

"This village ain't healthy for foreigners," Mark taunted. "Understand?"

Unable to see, struggling to get his breath, Anthony reeled on. His legs sank under him, down into wet ground. He heard a sucking sound . . . he heard Gypsy's high-keyed snort.

The dizziness eased. He felt cool—and free from pain, at last.

Little Old Man

WHEN SHAD left Forks Village, he cut himself a hickory stick; flicking Queen Anne's lace and goldenrod as he walked, he followed the path of the sun. At night he slept in a grove of pine. At dawn he looked for a cow with teeming udders, and trudged on. Sometimes he begged, but oftener he stole his food, sharing it with chipmunks, squirrels, now and then a young deer. Spirits brighter under the open sky, he travelled west as far as Vermont; went south into Bay State. Homesick for the smell of the sea, he headed east.

In Maine, one day, he built a fire alongside a brook that ran through pine; he set out a row of fresh-laid eggs, half a dozen ears of new corn. Letting the wood burn to flaky ash, he heard a crunching of pine cones.

"Howdy," a man with a pock-marked face said.

Shad wasn't too pleased, but remembered his manners. "Howdy," he returned.

The stranger held out his hat, well-filled. "Let's share," he said.

Shad peered in. If they'd been huckleberries, even high-bush blue, he'd have shaken his head. But the berries were low-bush, deep blue, clean as a whistle.

"My name's Shadrach Nye," he said by way of assent. "What's yourn?"

"Sometimes Ned, sometimes otherwise, but to you I'm Nick." The stranger spoke in a sing-song drawl. Doubling his long legs under him, he winked.

"Ye're welcome, Nick." Shad tucked the eggs and the corn into rosy ashes.

Shad and Nick travelled together, though sometimes they went different ways for a day or night. One afternoon Nick pulled out a hank of twine.

"I'll cut a twig," he offered, "and make you a sling."

"What for?" Shad asked, skipping to keep up with the tall man's stride.

"For killing. With a sling, you can get a bird—or a dog that's annoying."

"I don't go in for killin'," Shad said, curt. "But ye can make me a sling."

"A little sling for a little man," Nick drawled in his sing-song way.

"There was David—" Shad stopped right there.

Nick got out a patch of leather and, after a while, handed Shad a sling.

Shad aimed at barndoors, at chimneys; he advanced to hornets' nests. And then, one day, he hit the lettering on a milestone.

"Pretty good for a little old man! Now let me try." Nick squinted at a rabbit crossing the road. A twang of the string—and the rabbit stopped running. "You get a kettle," Nick said with a grin, "while I skin him."

Shad stole a kettle, carrots, onions—and they feasted on rabbit stew.

They came to a settled community. "Seems like I can't breathe." The words were barely out of Shad's mouth, when a burly fellow gripped him.

"Shadrach Nye, I'm sheriff here. You come along with me!"

Shad peered up at the fellow's badge. It was genuine. "What for?" he asked.

"For stealing," the sheriff shouted. "Whatever you do in Bay State or Granite State, you don't trick sheriffs in the District of Maine."

Shad counted on his fingers: the kittle, carrots and onions, a pie or so. Nothing to make such a fuss about! He turned for a word with Nick, but the pock-marked man was running.

"I'll ketch up with ye," Shad called. Then he trotted along to jail.

The sheriff yanked his long-skirted coat off him, turned the pockets inside out, felt up and down his breeches, examined the bandanna bundle.

"Where did you hide them spoons?" he thundered.

"Spoons?" Shad queried.

"Them silver spoons you took last night from a poor widow's home."

"Sheriff!" Shad protested. "Whatever'd I do with silver spoons!"

The sheriff slammed the thick-beamed door, by way of answer. Shad heard the great key turn in the lock. Getting out of the old-time jail was no trick at all; but, falsely accused, he meant to stand trial.

A jailer, stout as a hogshead, came with a bowl of gruel.

"How soon Court meets?" Shad asked briskly.

"Soon's judge gits ready. And when he's through, ye won't be so sassy." The fellow rattled the keys on his chain.

Shad tasted the gruel—it wasn't cooked to suit him. He inspected the pad which served as a bed. Its smell annoyed him. Jailers never thought, he reflected as he got out his blade, of looking under the inside sole of a shoe; never knew a big lock was easier to tinker. A few minutes' work—and he stepped outside, carrying his bowl of gruel.

It was dark by this time and a dog, big as a colt, barked sharply.

"Good doggie!" Shad coaxed, setting his bowl down on the ground. The animal lapped up the mess. "Good doggie!" Shad praised. "We'll sleep in the open."

He found baked ham and crusty new bread in a pantry next door. A blanket was hanging on the sheriff's clothesline. He took straw from the barn. "Good doggie," he coaxed, patting the great head, "ye can have half my bed for keepin' me warm." Snuggled close to the dog, he was asleep in no time.

A jailer's kick waked him next morning. "Tell sheriff, he better git a new lock for this no-account jail," Shad said.

They padlocked the door that evening. Shad found a rotted log near the window, cut his way out, and slept in the yard with the dog.

Court met in the morning.

Things went against Shad from the start. He was described by the sheriff as a dangerous criminal . . . with wizard powers. He had aided the British . . . should be hanged. . . .

"Land sakes!" Shad protested.

The judge shook his white-wigged head to silence him.

There was a stir, as a woman came forward. " 'Twan't him took my silver," she cried. "I saw thief. Tall feller with a pock-marked face!"

"That's Nick!" Shad said, indignant.

The sheriff gave him a dollar, by way of amends, and the sheriff's wife fed him boiled lobster.

"I'll find that rascal of a Nick," Shad promised, "if it kills me."

"Seen a tall feller with a pock-marked face?" He asked the question a hundred times, and Nick's trail led him through half a dozen villages, a wood, and down to the river's edge. A man was hauling a boat in.

"Seen a tall feller, pock-marked face?" Shad asked once more.

"He wanted my boat, but I was taking taters to Portsmouth fort. He must of got one, next place along. Anyways, time I got back, he was shoving off."

"Which way?"

"Up river. 'Gainst tide, and pulling hard for New Hampshire side."

"How much to row me across?"

"Current's tricky, fog's coming." The man considered, Yankee fashion.

In the end, Shad gave up the sheriff's dollar. Part way across the river, he got out his sling and aimed at a whitecap, unable to tell, in the evening fog, if he hit it. " 'Tain't easy," he said as they neared the New Hampshire side, "to ketch up with a feller on a night like this."

"Look for a boat, name under tiller is 'Judd.' Letters are faded." The boatman drove an oar down to keep things steady, while Shad hopped ashore.

Climbing the bank, he found the fog thicker. No use trying to follow Nick. He slipped into a barn, curled up in the warm sweet-smelling hayloft. A rat scuttled across his arm. He roused, peered out a window, but the fog was still thick. He curled up—until a banging shutter annoyed him. Must be a wind, he figured, and wind would scatter fog. He sat up and pulled on his coat.

Outside, the air was sharp for August but not quite so thick. It was about four o'clock in the morning, Shad judged. Hurrying along the riverbank, he looked at the name of every boat. He passed Blue Clay Farm . . . passed Forks River Landing. A man couldn't get far in fog, and Nick must be somewhere around. Then he spied a boat in a cove. Four faded letters—J-U-D-D. Queer, how Nick was taking him close to Tony's mill, just where he had aimed to be. Suddenly, he stopped short. That Nick, who stole a widow's spoons and let him take the blame, said something about a little job to do when the weather was right. He got a letter at a post office, the day before they parted, said he'd soon be heading for the West.

Shad ran in the direction of the mill, through woods and rough places, over stonewalls and picket fences. Halfway across the last field, he heard Gypsy's frightened neigh and ran faster still. He saw a light bob. Tony's candle never capered so! A trespasser's lantern? Close to the mill now, he heard voices and leaned against the clapboards near the open door.

"The designs are here somewhere." That was Mark Badger's voice!

"Nothing in the cabinet, I tell you." Nick's drawl!

"We've got to find them, Jake."

Jake! Shad nearly spoke out—from pure disgust. Then he realized that Mark and Nick were stealing Tony's designs. Where *was* Tony? Asleep at Todd house, most likely. What to do? Shad tapped his forehead, he pulled an ear. Maybe if he waved his red ribbon, he'd get some notion! Before he had his bandanna open, an idea came.

Stones were easy to find, and he filled his pockets. He took the sling out of his coattail, tucked a proper stone into the hole in the leather patch. Before he pulled the string, he ran behind the mill and let out a madman's shriek. That would make them come outside, he thought as he raced back.

Mark was the first to come through the door—and Shad's stone missed. He might have to let Mark go, but he'd get Nick! His second shot hit Nick's knee and made him stumble. Now Shad sent stones so fast that whichever way Nick turned, he was pelted. At last he fell, exhausted. Shad got a rope and trussed him tightly.

"There was David and Goliath!" He felt entitled to quote Scripture.

And then for the second time he heard Gypsy's frightened neigh. She was down by the quicksand! "Tony!" Shad cried as he ran, an iron band around his heart.

Tony was buried to the armpits in quicksand, deaf to his call. Shad tugged this way and that. Might as well try to uproot a tree! And each lapping wave brought the tide higher! Tears streamed down Shad's face.

Then Gypsy pawed the ground, and he knew what to do. He contrived a harness, one end under Tony's armpits, the other end fastened to the mare's collar. He found a long plank and, making a bridge from solid earth, pushed it towards Tony.

"Now Gypsy, pull as you've never pulled in your life!"

Between them, inch by inch, they wrested the limp body away from the sucking sand and steered it onto the plank. When Gypsy's collar broke, Shad saddled her and knotted the traces of his harness to the stirrups. When he slipped and felt himself being sucked in, he grabbed the traces and bade Gypsy pull; when he turned faint, he lay flat and rested.

A pale dawn was breaking when at last he had Tony on solid ground. He bent over the limp body, heard a faint heartbeat.

"Gypsy!" he cried. "Ye can pull Tony up the steps, and right inside. A floor that'll hold a loom'll hold up a hoss. Just wait till I tie that knot tighter. There, now!" Inside the mill, he stripped Tony, and got him on the cot. He built a fire, heated water for washing the bruises, piled on blankets. And he pondered.

"I never liked women," he said aloud at last, "but Tony's got fever. There's nothing like Quaker nurses, and Charity's the best of 'em all." He went outside and patted the mare's neck. "Gypsy, we'll go to Todd house, send Eben back. Then I'll hitch ye to a wagon and we'll git Charity."

He was in the saddle when he heard Nick moan.

"Ye deceivin', murderin' no-account Nick," Shad called. "I'll let sheriff know where ye are. And don't think ye can run. Them knots were tied by a little old man!" His heels touched the mare's sides.

Charity woke to find herself feeling cold, as if all warmth had gone from the earth. Then she remembered brother Obadiah Andrews' visit.

Was it true, the senior overseer had asked, that she permitted the stranger who worked for Eben Todd to call at her house? Yes, she had said. Was it also true that she considered being the foreigner's wife? Yes, if he became a member of the Society of Friends. Hour after hour, brother Obadiah admonished: the stranger was judged unacceptable . . . she must wed within the Society. . . . In the end, she yielded, wrote to Anthony.

A girl *should* have satisfaction from following the path of duty; but she felt none. Footsteps sounded on the walk outside, and milkpails clinked.

Hilda came with hot water. "Ten minutes, and I'll bring trays up."

"I'll be ready." Charity planned her day as she dressed. The milk must be skimmed and the butter-making started, vegetables cut up and stewed and put in crocks for winter use. . . . She listed things to do, as if she could never find enough to fill the day—all the long days that lay ahead. Then she went to the sickroom.

Elisha lay back on the bolster Hilda had tucked behind him, his skin white as the linen, blue veins standing out on his poor helpless hands. His pale eyes showed faint response as she took the chair beside him, drew up a table and gently gave him the hot porridge.

Hilda came back. "Shadrach Nye's here," she said, "I'll feed Lish."

"Shad in some trouble again?" Charity went down.

Shad stood on the doorstep. "Ma'am, ye're needed for sickness," he said. "I'll drive ye."

"Who is sick, Shad?" she inquired wearily.

He eyed her gravely, fingers twisting his shabby cap.

"Tell me quickly," she bade. "I'll go if I'm needed."

"Ye're needed," Shad returned promptly. "Errand of mercy. Mark and 'nother feller most stoned Anthony Bryce to death. Then he missed drownin' by a hair. He's clean out of his senses with fever."

She had promised not to see Anthony. But Friends never refused a sick call! "Can't Sary Ann take care of him? Or Lucy Lane?" she asked.

"No, ma'am! Only Charity can save Tony—if he ain't dead."

She called up the stairs to Hilda, went for her bag of medicines, put on cape and bonnet. "Hurry!" she bade, following Shad to the wagon. "Drive fast as thee can!"

They rattled up the lane, along the highway and through the village.

At the mill, she knelt by Anthony's cot. His face was a sorry sight; his head, fiery hot; his chest heaved with the labored breathing. But he *was* breathing! Briskly, she gave orders for hot water, a warming pan, the mustard plasters that kept pneumonia away, broth she could heat, two cots and bedding. The invalid must not be moved . . . Lucy would stay with her through the night.

Eben nodded, strode off. Shad helped her clean Anthony's wounds more carefully than had been possible in half light; he waited on her while she smeared on healing essences, and he helped her with the bandaging.

Looking down at the battered face under the wet fair hair, Charity felt she had never loved Anthony as much. But when he was out of danger, she would slip away. He need never know she had nursed him.

Eben came back. "Lucy'll be here before nightfall." He set down a chair for her to sit on, tiptoed off. Shad filled the warming pan Eben had brought with red-hot ashes. Carefully, she tucked it inside the blankets; put mustard plasters on Anthony's back and chest.

Slowly the terrible breathing grew easier. But the patient suffered from strain on lungs and heart, and he tossed violently.

It must be afternoon. At any rate, Eben had gone off a second time, brought a great basket of food. Charity ate while she watched. The patient still tossed; delirious, always liable to throw the blankets off. But he was better, she thought thankfully, as she wiped sweat from his forehead.

"Wonder where Tony hid them designs," Shad remarked.

Charity saw him reach up to a cabinet above the cot. He walked about, prying into every corner. "Mark and Nick been pretty thorough," he said.

She became aware suddenly of the disorder around her. Cotton fluff, tools, torn paper, logs and what-not, made a wild hotchpotch. She had walked through the clutter without even seeing it!

"Eli's hell-bent on finishin' dam." Shad looked out through the open door. "Nick and Mark," he went on, "used up his store of broken stone and he's had to crack more all mornin'."

Until Shad mentioned it, Charity had not heard the hammering outside. Occupied with nursing Anthony, she had been blind and deaf to all else. Now she heard a moan, and glanced at Shad.

"It's Nick, and he ain't goin' to die, lessen sheriff hangs him."

Charity bowed her head. She had walked by an injured man. Been blind and deaf to everything but Anthony.

The sheriff came and took the man outside away. Shad was mighty pleased with the sheriff's praise. Eben told Charity how Shad had driven Mark off, captured Nick, and rescued Anthony. "If Tony comes through," Eben added solemnly, "he'll owe his life to Shad."

" 'Twas the mare saved Tony," Shad protested. He grew shy when Charity tried to thank him, not used to folks being grateful. "Guess Eben and I better clear up a mite," he said. And presently the mill looked fairly tidy.

Charity got a little of the hot broth down Anthony's throat. He opened his eyes. "Cotton fibre . . . papers . . . Mark . . ." The words sounded confused.

But Shad ran to the huge bale standing in the middle of the floor, reached inside, drew out a roll feathered with white fluff. "Tony," he cried, "papers are safe."

Anthony gave a faint smile and closed his eyes. When Charity laid her hand on his forehead, he fell into quiet sleep.

Eben discussed the matter of bringing charges against Mark Badger.

"Tain't a mite of use," Shad said. "Who'd take Tony's word 'gainst Mark's? Who'd take *my* word? Blamin' Mark for Tony's gittin' hurt might put Tony in worser light. Give Mark rope enough and he'll hang hisself, is my advice."

It would also be Simeon's advice, Charity surmised. Seeking punishment for others was not the Friends' way. And they would not know what part Mark had played in the night's evil business until Anthony was better. She felt sure, now, he *would* be better.

"Guess I'll hump along." Eben looked thoughtful as he rose. "I'll drop in at the fulling mill, see what John Welsh has to say about Mark." He went off.

Lucy came.

"I'll take the first watch," Charity said.

"Do not fail to wake me for my turn." Lucy lay down on one of the cots Eben had brought, and quickly fell asleep.

Charity saw a shadow in the doorway. Shad sat on the step, a musket Eben had given him across his knees, thin shoulders hunched as he peered into the night.

Seated by the cot, she thought about Anthony. He had been ready to comply with requirements for admission to the Society. Mark's opposition, Obadiah Andrews had said, was mainly responsible for his being rejected. In spirit, Anthony was more a Friend than Mark. Wasn't something wrong with a group that let members' actions be controlled by the will of a single misguided man? Uncle Simeon had often said that Forks Village Friends, isolated from the world, had allowed themselves to be shackled by an outworn past.

In the morning, Lucy chided, "Why did thee not let me take my turn?"

"I was not weary." Charity replied.

Lucy looked thoughtful. "The patient is out of danger, and thee can ride home with me when William comes."

"The patient is still delirious," Charity objected.

"Why don't ye go?" Shad called from the doorway. "I can nurse Tony now."

Charity glanced from one face to the other. Now Anthony was slightly better, Shad was jealous; Lucy thought it unseemly for her to be at the mill. And she had intended to slip away before Anthony could recognize her!

He groaned, restless suddenly, and threw off a blanket. When she laid her hand on his forehead, he quieted. She would not leave, she decided.

Presently William came. Lucy and Shad argued. But Charity let Lucy and William drive off without her.

Later in the morning, she heard Eben's cart rattle up to the door.

"Morning, my dear," Sary Ann said.

Had Lucy sent her? Were there three against her now? Charity watched Sary Ann bend over Anthony.

"I saw John Welsh," Eben was saying. "John asked what Bryce done to merit attack. Without mentioning Mark, he made it plain 'twouldn't do to cast suspicion on respectable villagers."

"What'd I tell ye!" Shad chuckled.

Charity felt Sary Ann's arm around her. "Eben, never mind about Mark now," she said. "I want you to drive Charity home to rest. But mind, mid-afternoon, you're to bring her back." She shook a warning finger at Eben. "Lucy sent me over," she went on. "But when it comes to nursing, nobody's like Charity." Her eyes had a warm look.

Shad scowled, Charity noted.

When Charity came back in the afternoon, Anthony was so restless that it took both Shad and Sary Ann to keep him on the cot.

"He's been out of his head," Sary Ann said, "and we couldn't quiet him."

Charity put her hand on the hot forehead, brushed the damp hair back as she spoke Anthony's name. In a few minutes, he lay still.

"I'll send more food over," Sary Ann promised before she went away with Eben. "You have Shad, and don't need Lucy or me tonight. My dear," she led Charity back from the door while Eben fastened Lightfoot's traces, "if you love someone and he loves you, don't let anyone separate you, whatever seems to hinder. Look at my Eben! Some'd say he ain't much for a woman to count on. But I wouldn't find life worth living —without my Eben."

Watching the patient, while Shad guarded the doorway through the night, Charity made her decision: she would marry Anthony, if he still wanted her. Let the Friends read her out of Meeting! Times had changed. The earlier Charity Damons, if they were alive, would oppose Anthony's being rejected because of the will of one misguided man. They would be on the side of machines; they would fight to better the lot of the poor. As she, too, would fight!

In the morning, Anthony waked without fever. He was ravenously hungry. Charity let Shad feed him, while she related what the loyal friend had done.

" 'Twas the mare saved ye, Tony," Shad protested again. "Them loom designs are safe, like I told ye. 'Member?"

Anthony did not remember. Once more Shad reached down inside the bale. "Tony," he said as he handed the roll over, "I've changed my mind about this mill. When folks start stealin', there's always something worth takin'. And Daniel Webster couldn't tell ye truer."

Anthony laughed and began to ask questions about progress made while he was sick. Eli had worked like a beaver, Shad told him, but the blacksmith hadn't showed up and he didn't know where to find another. . . .

"Thee must not use up strength in serious talk," Charity protested.

Anthony grinned, seeing she was anxious. "Just to amuse me," he begged, "let Shad tell me about this Daniel Webster everyone speaks of."

"Ye don't know 'bout our Black Dan!" Shad cried, perching on the box beside the bed. "Well, I'll tell ye, best I can.

"Dan come from over Franklin way, a few year back, and set up a law office in Portsmouth. Folks liked him from the start. Him and Jeremiah Mason got the cream of the legal work. They rode round on circuit cases. Often as not pleadin' on opposite sides, spite of travellin' together.

"Dan was the one brought crowds. He has a voice'd draw maggots out of cheese. Coal-black hair, eyes dark as mountain pools. When word went round he'd be at a trial, farmers'd drop their scythes and run to hear him. Women'd leave the bread in the oven. 'Tis said, hunters'd let the bears go by 'em to hear Black Dan plead. Well, he got famouser and famouser. Two year come Independence Day, he made a speech 'gainst the war and Mr. Madison's policies. That speech got him 'lected to the Congress. Peace Party. And now Black Dan makes laws for the whole country."

"I was thinking," Anthony put in, "even before Mark tried to steal the loom designs, of going to see Daniel Webster. Eben said he's in Portsmouth now."

"But I doubt he'd help ye," Shad said. "Dan's Federalist, and Federalist ticket don't favor domestic mills."

"It can't do any harm to see him," Anthony rejoined. Then he reached for Charity's hand. "Either Shad or the Lord brought thee to me."

She noted his use of the Friends' speech. "Shad was the Lord's instrument," she said, smiling, "and thee should lie back on the pillow. Don't go!" she called when Shad started towards the door. "Thee belongs to Anthony and me, now."

"I need my cat-nap." He went off with a grin, evidently resigned to sharing Tony with Charity.

Anthony found he had strength to put his arm around Charity and draw her close.

"I never knew," she told him, "how much I loved thee until I saw thee ill."

"And now it is not mad to ask?"

"No, I am wiser. But even after I'm read out of Meeting," she added earnestly, "at heart I shall be a true Friend."

"True friend," Anthony whispered, his head against her, "I cannot live without thee."

Bad News, Dan!

IT WAS early September when Anthony sailed down river to see Daniel Webster. Charity would have had him postpone the journey; but he refused to be invalided longer, especially as Webster must leave soon for the Emergency Congress President Madison had called. The gundelow was heavily laden that morning with provisions for men at the harbor forts, and sail crowded the river. Up and down the waterside men tossed caps in the air and cheered for the brigantine, "Portsmouth," built at the local Navy Yard and now declared to have put safely to sea.

Climbing the steep street of the river port, Anthony felt tense excitement around him. The town was filled with strangers, many of them seamen from the vessels held in port by the blockade. He paused to watch a huddle of lads lined up beside the barn-like old State House.

"Purty good drill for farm boys," an aged man beside him said.

Anthony nodded. "Can you tell me," he inquired, "where Daniel Webster lives?"

"Dan ain't home now. Went through here to his office an hour ago. Market Street, over that way—second story."

"Thank you, sir." Anthony realized that the time was not favorable for promoting arts of peace. While he was ill in August, the British had landed an army on the Maryland shore, marched on Washington; burned the Capitol, the President's Palace, and other public buildings. But he would point to the lads drilling without arms or uniform, dependent for equipment on their mothers' looms and blacksmith's forges;

and he would tell Daniel Webster how much more effective these willing defenders would be if the country had mills to outfit them.

He climbed the stairs, steps echoing. In an office, sparsely furnished except for books, a man sat at a desk, dark head bent.

"Mr. Webster?"

"What can I do for you?" The face under the black hair was sallow, the eyes lacked lustre. Not as striking a face as Anthony had expected of New Hampshire's orator.

"My name is Bryce," he began. "I'm building a water-power loom for a cotton mill. Mill men would feel greatly encouraged, sir, if they had your backing."

The Congressman showed no warmth. A few persons thought something should be done to favor mills, he said in a weary tone. As for himself, the Constitution did not, in his opinion, confer on the government the power of changing the occupations of the people; and agriculture and commerce formed the backbone of the nation. He was not the enemy of manufactures, but wages had soared above the point where labor could be procured advantageously; and he felt no desire to push capital into new channels faster than the general program of wealth and population propelled it.

In spite of disappointment, Anthony felt drawn to Daniel Webster.

"It's the Union I think of," the Congressman went on, and his dark eyes flashed as he explained that the country had lost its Navy in a war it should never have embarked upon, and its currency was disordered. He rose and paced the floor, hands clasped behind him. New England opposed Mr. Madison's policies, he said. Newspapers, even some of the clergy, advised secession. He halted, his sallow face lighting. "New England must not secede. New England must stand by the Union . . ."

He was only an average-sized man in a small bare office.

But Anthony could picture him before the nation's Congress. The magic voice rose and fell in moving cadences as Webster spoke of the wonderful liberated land, the sacrifices that had made it free, the right each man had to be free. Freedom, however, depended on strength, the coast lay unprotected. . . .

An army officer burst in. "Bad news, Dan." He removed his pompommed shako, and the face above the high-collared blue coatee showed tense. "The enemy, we hear, plan immediate attack."

"Governor Gilman has ordered the militia out?"

"It's not enough. Citizens are arming, under command of General Montgomery. And the selectmen have named a Defense Committee, with you as chairman."

"I'm due in Washington." A worried look showed on Webster's face as he explained that political enemies would gladly smirch his name if he failed to join the Emergency Congress at the first possible moment. Ten days was the shortest time in which he could make the journey.

"In Washington, men will debate cold policies," the officer pleaded. "Here in Portsmouth men are ready to lay down their lives, and they will have more heart for knowing that Daniel Webster is with them. If Portsmouth is saved, the entire New England seaboard will be less endangered . . ."

A clatter sounded on the stairs. A sailor saluted briskly. "The Commandant of the Navy Yard sends his respects to the chairman of the Defense Committee, sir. He desires to inform, two British seventy-four's stand inside the Isles of Shoals. A frigate advances to larboard. We hear the enemy plan to burn the town and wreck the new warship 'Washington,' almost ready to leave her ways."

Webster wheeled. "How many local defenders?" he asked the army officer.

"Three thousand, with more reporting every hour. They meet, picks or shovels under their arms, in Market Square."

"Get me a shovel!" Daniel Webster cried. "I'll lead the citizens to the forts. You in the chair," he turned to Anthony, "are you with us?"

"Yes, sir."

"Defenders from outside the town go to the ropewalk barracks," the army officer instructed.

Down on the street, lines of men carrying muskets or old-fashioned side arms showed where the ropewalk lay. Anthony fell into place. The lines inched forwards towards a long shed turned hastily into a camp. Men seated on coiled cable tested gun sights, filled powder horns, cleaned muskets. Here and there, squads drilled.

"Handier with gun or shovel?" a young officer asked, when Anthony's turn came.

"Shovel," Anthony said, remembering he was to marry a Quaker.

"Go to Fort Constitution on Great Island. Ferry leaves in half an hour."

Anthony stopped at a stationer's, wrote briefly to Charity and to Eben; then hurried down to the waterfront. No cheering or cap-tossing now. Men went quietly about their business, faces grim.

Anthony gave his letters to the gundelow skipper. "I'm bound for Fort Constitution," he explained.

Respect showed in the riverman's eyes. "I'd go with ye, lad," he said, "if I wan't needed to keep the fighting men's bellies filled. Yes, I'll deliver your letters. Ferry lies t'other side of the schooner."

Anthony ran along the waterside.

Men clad in broadcloth and in homespun were among the crowd on the ferry. Anthony found himself between a lad in a muck-stained shirt and a bronze-skinned fellow who smelled of fish. As the sail spread, they were swept into the current. Great Island lay like an outstretched hand in the wide river harbor. A toll bridge on the other side, the fisherman said, connected it with the mainland. Its thumb and little finger bulged with earthworks; and the stone fort at the tip of the long middle finger was Fort Constitution.

"Where are the enemy vessels?" Anthony inquired.

"They stand off Isles of Shoals, sometimes this side, sometimes t'other," the fisherman said. "We'll see 'em from Great Island."

The ferry bumped against a wharfside. An officer gave instructions. There were tools for men who had none; food for those who had left their homes without taking time to eat. The main undertaking was a Martello tower, being built under the direction of Colonel Walbach to reinforce batteries in place, with a revolving gun that could rake the beaches to the south, where the enemy might try to land.

Anthony picked up a shovel. He was soon made aware that he had not regained full strength since his illness. His back ached, his legs felt unsteady; but he kept at work. Men sweated all around him as, brick by brick, the circular tower rose. By evening good progress had been made; but the hostile ships still stood off the Shoals. Would their longboat keels, under cover of darkness, slide over New Hampshire sand? Would morning show ranks of redcoats advancing?

Anthony's hands grew raw. Gnats and flies tormented him. He worried lest Charity cast him off for not leaving the protection of New Hampshire entirely to the Lord. With brief rest periods, he worked far into the night.

In the morning, the beaches were still bare. The warships stood off the Shoals, their great sails billowing. Word came that spies disguised as native farmers were trying to learn the strength of local defense. Anthony was allowed a snatch of sleep and then assigned to cutting peat in a swamp a mile or so away. After the peat was cut and carted, he was pressed into hod-carrying for the tower masonry. He helped lay the peat over the circular fort's *terreplein*.

A bundle from Sary Ann brought fresh clothing, warm

blankets. Eben wrote that Portsmouth vessels had taken refuge in the upper river. Eli Durgin had finished the new dam . . . Ivory Oldfield had gone to make guns . . . Shad slept at the mill, guarding the premises.

Charity's letter came at last. Uncle Simeon had visited the farm. When she told him their plans, he showed no displeasure. He meant to keep a watchful eye on Mark. She thought often of the young man doing a patriot's duty. . . . No reproach! In his relief, Anthony burst into song.

He was set to rolling cartridges. The men called him "Tony" now and he felt he knew them well. Men from Berwick, Eliot, and York, in Maine. But mostly New Hampshire men, full of New Hampshire talk: the yield of crops, the high price of corn, the good luck that brought schools of mackerel so close to shore this year, the pay that different towns allowed defenders.

Every now and then, news of the outside world arrived. The Congress considered moving the nation's capital inland for greater safety. A driver from the South brought word that the enemy had attacked Baltimore, and an American, held prisoner on one of their vessels through the night fight, had written the words for a song: *Oh say, can you see by the dawn's early light. . . .*

On Great Island, the work that remained was getting the cannon in place. Men had time to laugh or wipe their sweat away. But the seventy-four's still stood off the Shoals.

And then a report went around that the new gun would not turn. A blacksmith, expert with gunnery, had been borrowed from a brigantine held in port, but he could not manage the thirty-two-pound gun. Had all their work gone for naught!

A worried-looking officer came down from the ridge. "Anyone handy with the mechanism of a cannon?" he asked.

Nobody answered. Anthony had never worked with weapons. If the artillery men, aided by the smith, couldn't manage the gun, it seemed unlikely that he could. Then it was reported that the hostile ships, one mile nearer, were clearing decks, as if preparing for action. Machinery was machinery, whether it made cloth or swung a cannon, Anthony reminded himself.

"I'll try, sir." He heard half-hearted applause as he stepped forward.

The space within the tower was small, and the artillery men went outside, leaving Anthony in full charge. He looked things over; changed the angle at which the gun was set on its pintleston, oiled points of friction. The cannon would not move! He made new calculations, but they proved useless. Finally he took the carriage gear outside to examine it in clearer light.

Lookouts in the meantime reported that the enemy ships showed further signs of action. All around him, tension mounted. White-lipped volunteers spoke in hoarse whispers.

Anthony whipped out his handkerchief to mop his brow, keep sweat from dropping into the machinery. A bit of grit scraped his forehead. If the wind had blown sand into the handkerchief in his pocket, it might have blown a grain into the gun carriage parts! Breathing hard, he took the gear apart, cleaned it, put it together again and carried it inside.

The cannon muzzle swung! "Tony's saved Portsmouth!" men cried. "Spies'll spread word we got a revolving gun."

Men from Berwick, Eliot, York. From Durham, Dover, Exeter, Rye, or Portsmouth. They were his brothers now. Some recalled his fight with Steve. A few knew he had barely escaped death in quicksand. One or two had heard that he worked in a cotton mill. "Hooray for Tony!" they shouted.

For a time, the great warships moved back and forth across the harbor entrance. Then, after firing a single gun, they dipped below the horizon.

When the volunteer defenders were at last permitted to leave Great Island, there was high praise for Daniel Webster, chairman of the Defense Committee. And there was high praise for Anthony Bryce who had set the gun revolving.

Before boarding a gundelow, Anthony went to see the brigantine captain who had loaned his blacksmith. Yes, Paul Driggs could go to Forks Village for a spell, the shipmaster said. With the blockade spread like a net all along the coast, he wasn't hoisting anchor. And maybe the smith would learn a trick or two from the young man who had managed the balky cannon.

In high spirits, Anthony sailed up river. He planned to set Paul Driggs to work. And then, as soon as he could get cleaned up, he would call on Charity.

End of a Year

SARY ANN, tucking a pie into the oven, looked up as he came in. "My boy, I'm thankful you're home!" She eyed him, proud as if he were her son.

"Shad got jealous of a ship's smith I brought along," Anthony told her. "Said as long as I had the squint-eyed feller I didn't need him, and he'd take a holiday. I stopped at the store for a word with Eben, and here I am."

"And you want to see Charity." She nodded understandingly. "Kettle's boiling and I'll send hot water up. Better eat a bite before you go."

At Blue Clay Farm, Hilda answered his knocking. "Come in! Charity's upstairs, I'll call her."

In spite of the woman's warming grin, Anthony felt uneasy as he waited in the best room. What if the sour-faced overseers had worn Charity down in his absence, persuaded her it was wrong to wed according to her heart's choice! What if Hilda came back with word that he must leave at once!

Then Charity was flying to him. "Anthony!" she cried. He bent and kissed her.

She led him, after a minute, to the long sofa. Uncle Elisha was poorly, she told him. Mark had gone on a mysterious journey, and Rachel Foster was acting strangely. "Anthony," she burst out, "I could not bear to deceive the Friends and explained that we mean to wed."

"They were harsh?" he asked.

"Oh no. Brother Obadiah thinks anxiety over my uncle, or the wicked war, has addled me, and I need a long rest. Lucy was sterner than he."

"And you gave in?"

"Indeed not." She sat proudly erect. "I told them that many of our rules are outworn. That Anthony Bryce made proper application, and they should welcome new members. That a woman has a right to wed the man she loves. But oh Anthony —" she leaned against him, "I'm to be admonished twice each week until I perceive my error. I begged brother Obadiah to have me read out of Meeting now, but he claims I will yet see the light. Reproaches are harder to bear than anger. Let us marry at once!"

Marry at once! He was not able to support a wife. He looked into Charity's eyes. "We'll marry as soon as the mill turns out cloth, and that may be in a few weeks."

"It frightens me," she whispered, "to think of thee off in the lonely field, and Mark around."

"Mark may have learned caution. His mate got a long sentence, barely escaped hanging. Besides, I have Eben's musket now," he reassured her.

"Hark!"

Light thunder sounded overhead. When another roll came, Charity rose. "Primrose, one of the cows," she explained, "is nearing her time. She's afraid of thunder and if she gets too frightened she may lose her first calf."

"I'll go along with you," Anthony said, amused. "I'll need to know about nervous cows."

Charity led the way to one of the smaller barns, some distance from the house. The thunder sounded nearer. By the time they reached the barn, the swollen cow stood rigid, eyes wide with terror.

"Thee is in no danger, Primrose." Caressing the animal, Charity turned her so she would not see the flashes in the sky, coaxed her to lie down; and drawing up a milking stool, she sat beside her.

As the storm came nearer, Anthony pulled the wide doors half shut. No rain fell; but the branches of the trees swayed in the wind, leaves fluttered down. Then a blinding flash tore the sky apart, and thunder cracked.

"I fear some building was struck," Charity said. "Is there sign of fire anywhere?"

Anthony stepped to the doorway and scanned the horizon. "I see nothing but a man pacing the hilltop."

"He is the watch." During a storm, Charity explained, everyone stood ready to help a neighbor whose house or barn was set on fire by the electric fluid. In the village, the volunteer fighters of the fire company would have horses hitched to the new engine.

Presently the wind died, and the electric disturbance passed on. Rain fell steadily, the dry earth sucking moisture in. When Anthony slid the doors back, the air smelled clean.

"How beautiful everything is!" Charity said, her eyes shining as if she saw more than the wet hillside. "No Damon was ever born who did not love Blue Clay Farm."

Anthony's gaze followed hers and, for the first time, he saw the beauty of the big gray house sheltered by the grove of pine; of the gnarled old trees on the slope, the phlox, goldenrod and asters. He felt closer to Charity, suddenly, than if he held her hand; he was seeing their future home together, he realized, as she saw it.

No Damon was ever born who did not love Blue Clay Farm, she had said. He had supposed he could never bear to live in his wife's house; now he resolved to overcome his petty pride.

"Does thee realize," he asked after a minute, "what it means to marry me?"

"It means I marry the man I love."

"I may be slow in learning Friends' ways."

"And *I* may need to learn some of thy ways."

"What if I burst into song, or into profane words?"

"Thee knows I enjoy thy singing," she said, eyes shining. "As for the other, I shall not hear it."

Working with Paul Driggs at the mill, Anthony felt more urgency than ever for getting the loom completed. He was glad when Shad came back from a week's wandering, eager to help. A few days later, Paul laid down his hammer. "That's the best I can do." He squinted at the mass of wood and metal. "I'll help you move the thing inside. Then I'll go back to my ship."

The great clumsy loom was a failure from the start. Anthony bent over it, changing this and that. In the end, he drew a new design with a shuttle better adapted to carrying coarse yarn.

"Guess ye'll want another smith soon," Shad remarked one morning.

"And I haven't an idea where to find one," Anthony groaned.

Shad cocked his head to one side. "Ever since Mark tried to steal them designs, Tony, I've knowed they's sense to 'em," he piped. "Ivory Oldfield's made guns enough to outfit the county. Lessen he helps here, I'll fire his house, burn up that bed-ridden old woman of his. And I'm off now to tell him."

Ivory appeared next morning. The ring of his hammer renewed Eben's interest. He brought Thomas, who was working at the store until he left for the school at Exeter.

Eben and the red-haired lad whipped the baled cotton to get it clean; they put it on the carding machine to comb the fibre smooth, and then on a device that turned the loose roll into rovings. They passed the rovings between cylinders which lengthened them. And finally they set the flier spindle twisting. By the time Thomas went off for school, they had a mountain of yarn ready for weaving.

The second loom was a failure, like the first. The cam would not turn, the shuttle was unsatisfactory. Eben soon lost interest. Anthony toiled on, except for First Days, when he rode to Blue Clay Farm.

Frost blighted the flaunting goldenrod and Queen Anne's lace. Trees stood stark against November skies. The harvest in, villagers celebrated in thanksgiving. By early December, the river froze and lads skated on it. Snow covered fields with a protecting blanket. Housewives set out Christmas puddings and fruit cake.

"Guess we can smith as well as carpenter," Shad announced one morning, working the great bellows to get the forge fire started.

Presently he and Anthony were hammering small parts out. Shad lived at the mill now. With a fire roaring up the stone chimney, he found the place cozy. To please Anthony, he kept Eben's gun loaded and handy; but he took more pleasure in his sling.

The last day of the year came. Sary Ann had charged Anthony to be on hand for supper. He stopped work at five o'clock and, pulling on his sheepskin jacket, watched Shad bend over the fire. Both Charity and Sary Ann had given Shad holiday invitations, but he preferred his own fare. Now he ladled a spoonful out of the pot, blew on it, tasted it, smacked his lips.

"Shad, you know Sary Ann wants you to come to supper," Anthony said.

Shad gave a shrug. "Whatever'd I do at a family table? I'd ruther stay here with my knuckle of beef stew." He stirred the pot, a picture of content.

"Well, good night." Anthony opened the door.

Outside, the wail of the wind gave him an eerie feeling. The fields were a chartless blue-white waste, and he could hardly tell whether the swirling flakes came from the sky above or the drifts around him. He fixed his eyes on a village light. Toes under his snowshoe straps, he struck out.

When he opened the Todds' kitchen door, Ruddy barked a greeting. Betsey, roasting chestnuts over the fire, called out that young Eben had sent a letter.

Sary Ann came from the pantry, hands white with flour. "We let Min and Joe take the night off," she said. "Soon 's Eben beds down the cattle, I'll dish up."

His feeling that something threatened was nonsense, Anthony told himself as he climbed the box stairs. Sary Ann had kept the door at the foot open, so that his small room was comfortable. Hot water waited on the washstand.

For supper there was oyster stew, fried chicken, hot buttered biscuit, mince turnovers with cheese. Afterwards they drew chairs around the fire. Sary Ann picked up her knitting, Betsey sat with her hand on Ruddy, while Eben read aloud young Eben's account of how Andy Jackson's army were keeping the British out of New Orleans. "Read that part again," Sary Ann said, "about how he thinks of us often and hopes his letter gets here for Christmas and—"

Someone drove into the yard. The door opened and Hilda came in, red-eyed, wrapped in shawls. "Lish is dead," she said grimly. "Anthony, I come for ye afore Mark takes charge."

He had started for the door when Sary Ann handed him Eben's boots and jacket. "Tuck that bearskin in good," Hilda charged as he jumped into the sleigh. "And you, Geranium, get a wiggle on!" She slapped the reins.

Through the lighted window Anthony saw Mark, standing by the fireplace in fur cap and jacket, a look of triumph on his long-nosed face.

"Charity don't know I went for ye," Hilda told him while he unwound the bearskin.

Stamping snow off his feet on the doorstep, he entered the house and flung the door of the best room wide.

"Anthony!" Charity exclaimed. She stood at the farther end of the fireplace, deep circles under her eyes. "We're talking," she said, "about the—the burial. I want Uncle Elisha laid in the hilltop graveyard. Mark says he must go to the village vault until spring comes."

"Snow's drifted too deep for grave-digging, three to six feet," Mark returned, surly. "Ground's frozen, foot or two more."

"It's hard enough," Charity protested, "to—to leave Uncle Elisha in sweet earth."

"This time of year," Mark retorted, "corpses do as well in a vault."

Only Charity's look of warning kept Anthony from knocking the man down.

"My father died in midwinter," she went on. "Grandfather too. Both times, the snow was deep but the men dug a grave."

"It won't matter to Lish, either way," Mark rejoined.

"I'll dig the grave," Anthony burst out.

A sausage-like roll lay coiled on the hearth at Mark's feet. Intended to keep cold air from coming in under the door, it was filled with bits of lead. Mark eyed the weighted roll.

Muscles taut, Anthony waited. The room seemed very still. Then the door was thrown open, and Hilda tramped in. Crossing in front of Mark, she stood by Charity's side.

Mark moved away from the puddle the snow on his boots had made. "Elisha goes into Friends' vault till spring." His tone challenged anyone's right to dispute his authority.

"Men on the place'll dig a grave for Lish, if they have to use rock-blowing powder." Hilda snorted.

Mark gave Hilda an ugly look. "Undertaker has his orders," he said.

"Mark Badger," Charity spoke steadily now, "thee is manager here. But I am mistress. I'd like a grave dug. If thee refuses to have this done, I'll ask another."

"No man on the place dares disobey me."

"I'll ask Anthony Bryce, to whom I am promised."

"Promised!" A wild gleam showed in Mark's eye. He picked up the weighted roll and threw it.

As it hurtled towards him, Anthony reached and caught it. He saw Mark dive forward, beside himself with anger. Waiting until the man was close, Anthony gripped him, pinioned his hands to his side, dragged him towards the window. At his signal, Hilda raised the sash. Anthony managed to lift Mark and then, as if he were getting rid of an insect, dropped him into the snow.

He turned to Charity. "The man is unbalanced, not fit to be allowed on the premises."

"I hear the undertaker's sleigh," Hilda put in. "Anthony, you talk to him. And here's my advice! You and Charity best be tied legal at once."

Dearly Beloved

CHARITY had seen Elisha laid to rest under blankets of sweet brown earth and clean white snow in the hilltop graveyard. Returning to the house, she had offered the other mourners fitting hospitality of rich fruit cake and steaming tea. After the guests' going, the house seemed still.

Anthony threw fresh logs on the fire, took the chair beside hers. "In Boston," he said, thoughtfully, "you could be married within the Society."

She nodded. The broader-minded Friends of Bay State's capital would regret her union with an outsider but condone it. "I love this village where I was born," she said softly. "I love the people. More than this, I want to show the Friends here that I feel I'm right. Timothy Carr will marry us."

"He will," Anthony returned. "I called on him yesterday and learned that Mark has tried to dissuade him from performing the marriage ceremony. The pastor thinks Mark has lost standing in the village. You're sure you don't want to be married in Boston?"

She shook her head. "I want to be married here."

"There's another thing you should understand," Anthony went on. "I hoped to be making cloth before we married. I've nothing to give a wife but good health and willingness to work."

"The best form of wealth," she said with a smile.

"We may have to scrimp for years."

"The Friends esteem thrift."

"Suppose I'm unsuccessful with the mill, a failure?"

She laughed and reached out her hand. "Thy success is the

only thing I would take chances on."

Moving his chair closer, he put his arm around her.

On First Day she drove alone to Friends' Meeting House. She had not attended in several weeks and as she took her seat beside Lucy, she was aware of the stir her appearance caused. On the men's side as well as on the women's, everyone thought admonishment had prevailed. During the long silence with which Meeting began, a sister coughed; across the aisle, a brother blew his nose. Then a bench squeaked as a brother got to his feet and gave thanks for a straying sister's return to the fold.

The Spirit moved Charity to speak. All eyes on her, she rose. Her words rang out through Meeting House:

"I, Charity Damon, declare that this Society errs in permitting actions of members to be controlled by the will of a minority. Since my betrothed was denied membership because of the opposition of only one overseer, I shall marry without the approval of the Society. Knowing that by this act I lose my own place here, I now leave Meeting." Head proudly high, she walked to the door.

Within the week, she stood beside Anthony in the Reverend Timothy Carr's cold parlor. Over her drab gown, she wore a white cashmere shawl. A Quaker bonent hid her curls; she held a Bible in her hand. Howling winds were the only music; but on the window panes Jack Frost had worked his scrollery in white, and icicles, iridescent in the morning sun, threw rainbow colors at her feet.

Snow-covered roads had kept Simeon from being present. But Hilda stood there, and Lucy who wept beside her William. Sary Ann and Eben had come. Shad shuffled in. Thomas, home from the Exeter school, stood in the doorway with his mother. The Reverend Timothy Carr rubbed the palms of his hands together and gave a wintry smile.

Head bowed, as she listened to the prayer of an alien faith,

Charity wondered if any Damon had ever been married in such scant company. From this hour she was an outcast in Friends' eyes. They would speak of her harshly, and when they saw her, perhaps turn their heads away. She must pass by the Meeting House, knowing she had forfeited the right to enter.

"Dearly beloved, we are assembled here . . ."

Hearing the words of the marriage ceremony, she felt lifted above petty fears. She would make her life a shining example, prove the rightness of marrying where the heart bids.

"Two persons come hither to be made one . . ."

These were beautiful words. Hearing Anthony's firm response, she tried to make her own sound as clear. A ring was on her finger. Lucy kissed her. Sary Ann was saying, "We wish you all happiness, Mr. and Mrs. Bryce." Thomas passed with a tray, and glasses of mulled cider were raised. "To the health of bride and groom!" Eben called.

"We thank ye," she managed to say.

Anthony pressed her arm, and she smiled up at him. She was Anthony's wife, no matter what lay ahead!

On Sabbath Day morning, Anthony waked early, as usual, ready to leap from a narrow cot. Then he remembered: this was not the small room over Sary Ann's kitchen but a chamber at Blue Clay Farm. Charity was still asleep, her curls spread over the pillow. Careful not to rouse her, he went to the window.

The snow-covered pine trees stood white against the gray sky; ice fringed the riverbank. He let the sash fall softly, stirred the smouldering ashes in the fireplace to warm the room before Charity waked.

They breakfasted by a roaring fire downstairs. And as soon as the sun was high, they slipped their feet into snowshoes and toured the farm; down to the wharf, up to the hilltop graveyard, back through the woods.

Sleighbells jingled as they returned to the house. "Lucy and William are bound for Meeting," Charity said as they went inside. "I shall hold my own Meeting each First Day morning. Any of the household who care to may worship with me."

He went into the best room with the others. They sat, in the Friends' way, men on one side, women on the other. Later in the morning, he forgot himself and broke into the pedlar's song. Hilda said it was a godsend, after the gloom of Lish's dying, and Charity smiled.

As they sat by the fire in the afternoon, Charity said, "I wish I could put some of my money into the mill." He felt thankful that the terms of her father's will did not permit her to make investments before she was thirty. He would hate to use his wife's money!

The one subject they refrained from mentioning, this first Sabbath Day, was Mark Badger. Mark had not been heard from since the evening he was dropped out the window, but Anthony was not so foolish as to imagine he was through with the surly manager.

Next morning, as he pushed his snowshoes over white fields on his way to the mill, Anthony felt a glow he never had known. Even the sky seemed near and friendly. In the village, shutters were being thrown back and smoke curled from chimneys. At the mill, Shad had hot coffee ready. In spite of a solid breakfast, Anthony accepted Shad's mug gratefully.

"Been hitched two days and still seems to like it," Shad observed.

"I only wish you were as well off," Anthony returned with a laugh.

Shad shook his head gloomily and plunged the emptied mugs into water made by heating snow. "Guess I'll go up river and look at some eel pots," he said when he had cleared up.

"All right, Shad." His friend still resented the marriage a little, Anthony thought as he went outside to the water wheel.

He spent an hour or two hacking ice off, and then opened the floodgate so that water pouring down through the sluiceway could set the wheel moving before new ice formed.

Returning to the mill, he made sure that the warp threads lay smooth over the yarn beam. He dropped oil here and there, as usual, connected loom and water power.

There was a rasp, a click. The shuttle stirred! It moved across the warp threads, forwards and backwards. The heddles lifted alternate threads, forming a passageway for the shuttle. Yarn crawled over the cylinder at the rear.

Hardly daring to breathe from fear of ending the spell, he glued his eyes to the mechanical finger. His head felt hot and his hands grew cold. Sweat poured off his nose. And still the shuttle moved! He looked down. Cotton sheeting was winding around the cylinder that made the cloth beam. And the loom still purred. One inch . . . two inches . . .

He heard a scratch. The shuttle slowed its movement; it quivered and, half way across the warp, stopped dead. He bent over the cloth beam. There were nearly three inches of strong cotton cloth! A gash showed in the warp where the shuttle had torn the threads. But the loom *had* operated. What happened once could happen again.

The place was cold as a tomb, he realized suddenly. He had forgotten to throw logs on the smouldering ashes and they had burned out. Jubilant, he built a roaring fire. Then he set the shuttle on a spot where the threads were smooth. It did not stir. Over and over, he tried to get the power, generated by the water wheel, through to the shuttle. The loom seemed a monster, defying him. But it had functioned. The general construction must be sound. Only, somewhere, something blocked motion.

He toiled until the fading light of the short winter day halted work. Banking the fire and preparing to shut down for the night, he remembered the major defect in the English water-power loom: the shuttle, moving so much faster than when thrown by hand, got tangled in the warp threads. His father's last invention was a dresser intended to keep the warp smooth. Could he design a dresser?

First he must discover what blocked motion.

At Blue Clay Farm, he told Charity the story.

"The loom will come alive again, dear Anthony," she said, eyes brimming. It was queer, he thought, the way women cried from joy *or* sorrow. He hadn't wept when the loom operated; but he could have shed a bucket when it stopped.

"Has thee told anyone the news?" Charity inquired.

"No. Shad will see the cloth, when he gets back from his eel pots. But Shad can be trusted with a secret. Eben will have to know, and I'll warn him not to tell his brother or anyone. Of course, I must inform Simeon."

"Not a soul else!" Charity charged.

"You're right," Anthony agreed, "though I wouldn't mind the villagers finding out that I'm not quite the ne'er-do-well Mark has led them to think."

The spectre they had refrained from mentioning was out in the open now. "Where is Mark?" Anthony asked. "I haven't seen him around."

"He had business in Maine. Winter is our dull season."

What was the man up to? Anthony wondered. He said nothing, not wanting to fret Charity. Presently the cat came in from the kitchen and rubbed against his legs.

"Periwinkle approves of the master," Charity said with a smile.

Except for her horse, named after a saint, all her animals bore the names of flowers, Anthony thought, amused. He bent to stroke the purring Periwinkle. Seated with Charity before the fire, he forgot Mark.

In the orange-red flames he saw rows of spinners and looms, in a long brick building lighted with many windows, turning out cotton cloth that filled a need of people all over the land.

Bells Peal!

A THAW turned the January world to slush. The mercury dipped, and villagers slipped on ice, the older ones breaking their bones. Fever broke out. Doctor Owen Butler travelled from house to house with his leeches. Some of the stricken, however, sent for Charity who disapproved of bleeding. Shad went roaming and returned with a frozen finger. "What's a mite of frost bite?" he protested when Anthony showed concern. "Over to Great Bay, man crossin' ice in warm spell was drowned. I'll just stick my finger in snow."

Word arrived that Andrew Jackson's army had defeated the British near New Orleans, routing more than twice their own number. Sary Ann, torn between anxiety and pride, at last received the letter that said her son was safe; and Eben, by way of thanking the Lord, sent the parson a load of firewood.

Whatever happened, Anthony went to the mill at dawn. The loom still baffled him, but he recalled that his father's machines had balked for months and then responded to a touch. In early February, he had Ivory Oldfield install the Benjamin Franklin lightning rods and he made other plans for spring. Through the winter he had got along with only two ground floor windows, but by summer he would need another pair. And he wanted stairs, so that supplies now kept in the cellar could be equally accessible in the drier upper story.

In the middle of February, the news came that the war had ended; on Christmas Eve, British and American delegates had agreed to terms of peace. Everywhere bells pealed in rejoicing, flags tossed; there were illuminations, banquets, fancy balls.

Thankful that fighting had ended, Anthony worried over

what would happen to struggling American mills when trade with Europe was resumed. And what would Simeon do?

Within a week, Charity thrust a letter from Simeon into his hand. "Do read it aloud," she begged happily.

Simeon sent greetings to them both. "Boston has celebrated victory so whole-heartedly," he went on, "that many people are blind to new problems. It is folly to deny the crisis for domestic mills. Several factories closed their doors within an hour of receiving word of the peace, but such action seems hasty. I advise keeping on with the Forks Village mill for a time and am sending a man well-informed in matters of machinery, one John Guppy, to look into the situation. He will visit various mill seats and, if all goes well, should arrive in Forks Village about the tenth of March . . ."

Two weeks in which to save the mill!

John Guppy arrived on a raw windy morning. A runt of a man with deep-set eyes that missed nothing, he climbed down from a rig hired at the Landing.

"Guess you heard, direct from Mr. Damon, he wants me to look things over, Mr. Bryce."

"Yes. Shall we go to the river first?"

Water fell freely over the dam, great chunks of ice occasionally sending up geysers.

"Now the wheel." Anthony showed Simeon's inspector the sluiceway. As he opened the flood gate, water raced down, the wheel turned.

"Water supply, first rate." Guppy nodded approval.

Inside the mill, Shad had a fire blazing. Coming in from the raw March air, Guppy plainly enjoyed the coziness and let Shad take his outer coat.

"I'll show you our entire process," Anthony said. He pointed out the frame on which they whipped raw cotton clean. He picked up a wad and let the various machines in turn comb it smooth, narrow it into slivers, lengthen the slivers, wind them on bobbins, and twist them into strong yarn.

"First rate," Guppy said, turning to the loom.

There was always a chance, Anthony thought, remembering machines in his father's shop which had behaved unpredictably. "The loom has operated only once," he said. "Here's the product."

Guppy examined the strip of sheeting with interest. When Anthony connected the transmission rod, Guppy watched, short body tense, eyes shooting everywhere.

The shuttle did not stir. Again and again Anthony tried. It was maddening to be kept within a hair of success.

Guppy spoke at last. "You've gone as far as any of the men experimenting with the power loom," he said kindly. "Mr. Lowell's been working on machine-weaving for two years, and hasn't put a yard of cloth on the market."

"Lowell!" Anthony repeated blankly, trying to hide his disappointment.

"Yes. Mr. Francis Cabot Lowell. He visited England before the war, became so interested in cotton manufacture that he's organized a company and built a mill outside Boston. He is a wealthy man, able to afford expensive toys. You've gone as far, I judge. I'll tell Mr. Damon." Guppy held out his hand.

"Be sure ye tell Simeon," Shad charged, voice shrill, "how Mark Badger tried to steal Tony's designs. Means there's sense to 'em."

Guppy nodded, amused by the little man's loyalty.

Anthony watched Guppy drive away. Simeon wasn't likely to back him, now the British were definitely trying to crush American industries. And there was nobody else. This wealthy Boston man, who was also working on the power loom, wasn't likely to help him. "Lowell," Guppy had called him. Lowell! Something in Anthony's brain clicked. "Mr. Lowell" was the man who had talked with his father, asked countless questions! Yes, "Lowell" was the name he had tried to recall, the day he rode in the stagecoach from Boston to Portsmouth. He wouldn't forget again.

Two weeks passed, and no word came from Simeon. There were days when Anthony felt hopeful, days when he was plunged in despair. Money in the Portsmouth bank was low. Eben was interested in machine-made shoes.

The ground thawed, and horses wallowed in mud. Crocuses showed their heads in Charity's garden. Down by the river, pussywillows swelled. Workers in the brickyard were turning clay, after the winter's weathering. Mark stalked back and forth, self-important; and when he met Anthony his eyes showed contempt.

At last the expected letter arrived. Heart pounding, Anthony opened it.

"Be assured," Simeon wrote, "I have looked thoroughly into the matter of cotton manufacture. At some future time, the Forks Village mill may prove useful. For the present, I commend thy ingenuity and advise ceasing operations . . ."

Charity showed she was disappointed but refused to be down-heartened. "Uncle Simeon is right to be prudent," she said, "and thee is right too. The loom will weave cloth in good time."

Anthony groaned, knowing that "in good time" meant when the Lord saw fit. These Quakers, so close-fingered with their money, so free with their trust in the Lord! Yet Charity's faith heartened him.

"Think I'll go to Boston to see a man named Lowell who owns a cotton mill," he told her. "And the shipowner, James Lester, owes me some wages."

"Do go!" Charity said. "Stay long enough to look into all matters that interest thee. And bring back news of Uncle Simeon."

Anthony arrived in Boston on an evening in early May. Next morning he collected the money due him on Long

Wharf, learning that the senior officer of Lester Brothers had gone to New York. He wrote a letter to Francis Lowell and, later in the day, called at Simeon Damon's house.

"A kinsman in hired lodgings!" the Quaker protested, sending his coachman for Anthony's luggage at once.

Anthony had enjoyed the independence of his boarding-place but yielded with reasonable grace. And he found himself relishing Simeon's talk.

Everything, Simeon said, pointed to a great trade revival. "Thee should have been here in March when commercial vessels were first permitted to put to sea. Whole fleets, loaded with two years' produce, spread sail. And wharves were crowded with people shouting good luck to the ships they expect to bring prosperity . . ." Vessels from Europe were due any time. With everyone eager to buy, preparations had been made for auction sales. . . .

Not once, Anthony noted, did the white-haired trader mention domestic mills!

Crossing the Common next morning, Anthony saw a lad race by. "Ship came in!" the boy cried. "First ship bringing foreign merchandise!"

Anthony quickened his own steps but by the time he reached the wharves, sales had begun. The auctioneer stood on a raised platform. "Cashmeres, Scotch broadcloths!" he bawled to the crowd surging around him. "What'll ye bid?"

"Fifty dollars . . . One hundred . . . Two hundred . . ."

"Sold for four hundred. Next lot is cutlery."

"Three hundred . . . eight hundred . . ."

Bids were called out before the wares could be fully cried, such was the fever to buy. Fresh bales and boxes were brought. Keys and clocks, guns, pistols, hardware, calicoes, muslins, sheeting and shirting, were cried. Women joined the crowd, but buyers were mainly wholesale dealers or agents.

Anthony felt a hollow in the pit of his stomach, as he heard the bids. How could American mills survive the craving for foreign goods? He turned away and as he climbed the hill, a man stepped up. "Retail sales start tomorrow on Cornhill," he said, excitement in his eyes. "First chance to buy in years! Pick up all you can. What you can't use, you can sell."

Day after day ships came in, close on each other, like bears after honey. Anthony paced back and forth from the wharves to Cornhill. The sales made him miserable, yet he could not keep from witnessing them. He spent his evenings with Simeon who took keen interest in the day's prices and was buying, through an agent, for his own Cornhill shop.

Anthony missed Charity more and more. Although he wrote daily, only one letter had come from her. He wished she had journeyed to Boston with him. He had proposed this, but she insisted that the farm needed her.

A note came from James Lester. Would Mr. Bryce dine with him, three o'clock of the following Tuesday, at Exchange Coffee House?

Word came also from Francis Lowell, who would be happy to see John Bryce's son at his Waltham mill on any morning of the following week.

Anthony seized quill and paper. His letters written, he stumbled through dark streets to post them. But he did not talk with James Lester, the following week, nor with Francis Lowell.

Life or Death

THROAT distemper broke out in Forks Village, the day Anthony left for Boston. It appeared in a cottage near the Landing, spread to houses on the high street, and then to farms. Doctor Owen Butler prescribed leeches and purges, claiming the disease was caused by fever in the blood. Within four days' time, half the village were taken, children and the aged were dying.

One of the afflicted was Lucy's month-old infant. Charity wrapped a woolen cloth, saturated with a solution of salt and vinegar, around the baby's neck. Through the night she kept watch, renewing the cloth, administering balsam of fir. Slowly the swollen throat became normal, and the gasping eased. By morning, Lucy's child was out of danger.

Even before word spread that Lucy's child was safe, Friends and world's people were calling for Charity. She went wherever she was needed. Bad drainage caused the distemper, she said, bidding women see that their men-folks cleaned the outhouses. Day by day, the epidemic abated.

"Thee does not get sleep enough," Hilda warned her.

Charity paid no heed. At the end of the week she had a swollen throat and fever, but forbade word being sent to Anthony.

Shad heard of her illness and hurried to Blue Clay Farm. "She can't swallow any food, her throat is so swollen," Lucy wailed. "Hilda and I use the saturated cloths and give herb tonic. But we don't have Charity's healing touch. Doctor Butler came and wanted to bleed her. He'll insist, if she doesn't get better. He claims the epidemic is almost over, due to his treatments with purges and leeches."

Shad stood on one foot and then on the other. He wiggled an ear, tapped his forehead, scratched his chin. "See ye tomorrer, mebbe," he said as he trudged off. When he reached the highway, he paused. The stagecoach had gone, but if he walked, taking rides when he could, he'd likely get to Boston by nightfall. He looked north where the road wound towards the tree-shaded village, the cool mill, and the falls.

"This is Tony's wife and a matter of life or death," he said aloud as he took the road leading south.

The day turned warm. He sweated and panted, but by noon had reached the boundary between Granite and Bay States. Only one ride so far—wagons travelled the wrong way! The fragrance of a horse chestnut tree in bloom halted him. He eyed the shady space underneath, the petals fluttering down. "No," he said to himself, "I better hurry, so Tony gits to Charity afore Doc Butler kills her."

Counting milestones, he plodded on. Now and then a dog barked from a doorway, a fox or skunk crossed the road. Hunger plagued him. But he went on. "Less'n twenty mile to go," he told himself at last.

In the very next village, a rough hand seized him. "Shadrach Nye, I'm sheriff here, and you can stop a while."

"What for?" Shad asked in his routine way.

"Stealing a ten-pound cheese. County Court'll try you."

Shad felt sad as he trotted along. Sometimes, playing with locks amused him, but the game was inconvenient now. "Mr. Sheriff, I'm savin' a leddy's life," he pleaded. "Lemme off today, and I'll come back tomorrer."

"I ain't letting you slip through my fingers," the sheriff thundered.

They searched his clothing, emptied out the contents of his bandanna bundle, but didn't think to look under the insoles of such shabby shoes. Down in the jail's dungeon, they shackled his legs to bolts stapled into the floor beams; they wrapped his hands in iron chains fastened to the wall.

"There now, guess you're with us till Court meets next week." The sheriff eyed him with relief. "You can have your trash." Throwing down the bandanna bundle, he strode off, his two assistants behind him.

Darkness hindered Shad for a while, but at last he made out a small high window. There'd likely be a grating to cut through, he figured, but things didn't look too bad. The chains were so snug around his hands, he had to wriggle three times as long as usual before he was rid of them. He bent to feel in his shoe—and then he heard a clatter. By the time the heavy door was opened, he stood with his back against the wall, hands wrapped in chains.

"This'll do for a table." A jailer placed a high stool in front of him; set a hunk of bread, a bowl of soup, a dipper of water on it. "Guess you can lap—like a cat," he said with an unpleasant grin.

"I eat my victuals at reg'lar hours." Shad pretended to scorn the food. "What's the time?"

"Five o'clock, and this is all you'll get afore morning." The door slammed.

Shad sniffed the soup. It was poor thin stuff, but a body had to have something in his belly to travel on. He picked up the bowl and drained it. As he munched the crust, he figured he'd got to reach Simeon's house in time for Tony to catch the morning stage. Say he got out of jail at half past eight—and he couldn't leave afore twilight. Four mile an hour, and he'd be there by one o'clock. He eyed the stool and snickered. Jailers had no imagination! Nothing'd be better to stand on, when he worked at the window.

Using the file edge of his steel blade, he began to nick at his leg irons and had lost track of time when he heard footsteps. He stood erect.

The jailer pushed a man in. "Sheriff says this feller don't have the spirit of a worm, and handcuffs'll do for him. I'll take the stool away till tomorrow's breakfast."

Shad could have wept when the jailer carried the stool off. And he had no desire for company. Now he must figure out new plans. He eyed the newcomer for quite a while as he sat on a low box, head slumped.

"Pile of cornhusks in the corner's only bed in this tavern," Shad began. "My name's Shadrach. What's yourn?"

"Tim," the spiritless fellow answered.

"I'm here, matter of a mite of cheese. What's your line?"

"Hosses."

"Hoss thief. My, that's bad. They can hang a man for makin' mistake 'bout hosses. But listen, Tim. I got to reach Boston afore dawn. Matter of life or death. Ye're most as skinny as me, and we can wriggle through winder." He swung his arms to show they were free, drew out his blade. "Come over, Tim, and I'll unpin them bracelets," he said.

"You ain't Shadrach Nye?" Tim asked in awe.

"That's me." Shad took pains to be modest. "Now here's my plan. Soon's I git my legs free, I'll stand on your shoulders while I file winder gratin'. I wriggle through, lend ye my blade so ye can nick footholds in them beams."

Tim nodded approval.

The leg irons were tougher than Shad expected. When at last he stood on Tim's shoulders, removed the curtain which covered the window, and peered through, the stars were fading.

"Land sakes!" he shook his head, dismayed. By the time he had cut the grating through and climbed out, a gray dawn was breaking. He looked at his blade and heaved a sigh. He had never let it out of his possession, but a promise to lend it was part of the price of his freedom. "I can't wait till ye climbs out," he called to Tim. "I live at Eben Todd's mill, t'other side of Forks Village. Swear ye'll git this piece of Swedish steel back to me?"

Tim swore.

"Then watch out!" Shad tossed the blade in. Scurrying over

the road, he had a lost feeling without the blade in his shoe.

The watch was crying eight o'clock when he arrived at Simeon's door. Too late for Tony to get the stagecoach! Rueful, he stood on tiptoes to reach the knocker.

Simeon and Anthony were talking in the drawing room, when Sappho answered the knocker's pounding. Hearing Shad's shrill voice, Anthony rushed to the hall.

Shad stood winded, weary-eyed, his bleeding fingers twisting his cap. "Tony," he gasped, "Charity's got throat distemper and 'less ye stop him, Doc Butler's certain to kill her."

Anthony was about to dive out the door, when Simeon laid a hand on his shoulder. "The stage has gone, but a schooner hoists anchor for Portland this morning. I'll persuade her skipper to stop at Portsmouth."

He sent his coachman off to the wharf. He also engaged his physician, Dr. Aaron Winthrop, to go to New Hampshire with him.

A river gundelow dropped the four men off at the Damon wharf, early next morning. Tortured all the journey, remembering that Charity's parents had died from the distemper, Anthony gazed at the big house. A plume of smoke curled from its chimney, but there was nothing to tell him whether Charity breathed or not.

Simeon went up the hillside, the Boston physician beside him. Anthony followed with Shad.

"Doc Butler's rig's over by the barn," Shad pointed out.

The local physician's presence did not prove that Charity was alive. Anthony dreaded taking a step forward.

"The Lord be praised!" Hilda said, when they reached the door. "Now Doc can put them leeches he's got on Charity's ankle back in their bottles."

She was alive, they had come in time! Anthony would have rushed up the stairs, but Simeon held him back.

"Better let me talk with Owen," he said. "I'm native-born."

Owen Butler came down presently, hurt pride showing in his face. He bowed coldly as he passed. And then Dr. Winthrop went up to the sickroom.

Charity was in delirium from high fever, Simeon gravely told Anthony. They must wait until the crisis was over. All day long, the battle in the sickroom went on. Downstairs, Anthony paced back and forth; when the house seemed too confining, he went outside and paced the hillside. He had no appetite for food, no thought except for the sick girl. At nightfall, they said he might see her. She smiled faintly when he took her hand.

The next afternoon Dr. Winthrop pronounced the danger over. "Think I'll spend the night with friends in Portsmouth," he said as he packed his things, "and travel by stage to Boston in the morning."

Anthony walked down to the wharf with him.

"Rest and good care are all your wife needs now," the physician said. "The woman, 'Hilda,' is competent, and I've given her full instructions."

The gundelow ploughed through choppy water and bumped the wharfside. A twinkle showed in Dr. Winthrop's eye as he shook hands with Anthony.

"Your child," he said, "should be born in early December."

A child! Charity and he were to have a child! Not waiting for the gundelow to push off, Anthony raced back to the house.

A few days later, still in a glow over Charity's recovery and the news about the child, Anthony harnessed Gypsy. Simeon had said he would like to see the cotton mill, and this was a convenient time.

Though it was a rainy morning, they stopped at the brickyard. Mark showed them the weathered clay, cut and ready for the ovens.

"Sales holding up?" Simeon asked.

"Can't meet the demand," Mark replied, self-important. "So many wooden structures have got afire, been looted afterwards, everyone wants to build with brick. I need an extra hand. There's a man in Maine might do."

"Hire him, if he's available," Simeon said.

Mark was sufficiently respectful to Simeon, Anthony noted, and plainly considered the ne'er-do-well beneath his rancor.

They drove on. Near the Landing they saw Eben, and stopped to take him along. He seemed downcast. The shoe factory enterprise was probably in difficulties, Anthony thought, as they drove on to the mill.

"Mornin', folks!" Shad greeted them.

This was Anthony's first visit to the mill, since the journey to Boston, and it seemed damp and chilly as they went inside. "I'll start a fire," he offered, thinking of Simeon.

Simeon shook his head. "I only want to look at the machines," he said.

"Tony, I'll open flood gate, set water wheel goin'." Shad ran outside, came back.

Anthony put the spinner through its paces, while Simeon watched. He felt neither agitation nor hope when he went to the loom; but he poked about, oil can in his hand, from habit.

A small metal band seemed tight, and he loosened it. Parts had an unaccountable way of changing tension. Connecting the power, he braced himself for failure.

There was a whir. Jerky at first, it grew steadier. Heddles rose properly, as the shuttle moved—forwards and back, forwards and back.

"Land sakes!" Shad let out a whistle.

Eben got up off the bale he sat on, eyes bulging.

Simeon pulled out his watch and counted: "One minute . . . two . . . three . . ."

With a ripping of threads, the shuttle stopped. Anthony freed it from the torn warp, set it on smooth yarn. He heard a whir that became a hum, a steady purr, as if the loom were a contented cat.

There was the tight metal band, he realized. Also, the other time that the loom had functioned, there was no fire. The morning John Guppy came, the place had been as cozy as a kitchen on baking day. Somehow he had overlooked allowing for expansion from heat. He had needed this cold rainy May morning to discover his errors.

The shuttle stopped. Anthony freed it again, set it over untangled warp—and it moved. Cotton cloth began to wind around the cloth beam.

"We have a power loom!" Simeon boomed.

"Land sakes!" Shad exclaimed once more.

Eben paced the floor, eyes glowing. "Shoe factory ain't panning out. Meant to give up there, anyway. Tony, I'm going to work here with you," he said.

The shuttle stopped again. Anthony wished he could reduce the speed of the loom. "I need a dresser," he told Simeon. "Some way of sizing the warp to keep it smooth. And I need a device for controlling speed."

"Can thee devise such machines?" Simeon inquired, eyes sharp.

"I'll try," Anthony returned with thumping heart.

"If thee has success," Simeon went on, "I might invest further."

"By gorry, clean forgot I'm due to meet my partner," Eben exclaimed. "I'll tell him I'm quitting shoe factory." He strode off.

At the pharmacy Eben told his brother, as well as his partner, the news. The currier, buying a package of snuff, overheard and told the cobbler next door. The cobbler told the postmaster, who told the inn-keeper. Presently everyone in the vicinity of the Landing knew that Eben Todd's newfangled loom could weave cloth.

Folks chewed the situation over: "You said, Simeon's turned fool. . . . I never. I said Simeon's smartest lad ever grew up in this village. . . . Them that been calling the mill 'Simeon's Folly' better change their tune . . . Simeon couldn't of done this alone. Nor Eben. The hired feller done it. . . . Him we been calling a ne'er-do-well? Maybe Charity didn't get tooken in, after all . . ."

Hour by hour, word spread. The selectmen heard, a sheriff from Maine, a reporter for the Portsmouth paper. It was said that Simeon meant to build a mill half a mile long. How the women would get out of hand, with no cloth-making to fill their time! All stories agreed in one respect: folks that had bought shares would get their money back, doubled.

Anthony and Simeon, trying to find the exact speed at which the shuttle tore the warp threads, forgot time. When at last they drove home, they passed smiling faces. Everyone wanted a sight of Simeon, who had not been afraid to back a mill. Everyone wanted to greet the Englishman who was making it possible for folks to get rich. At the brickyard, workers waved. In the house, Hilda beamed.

Only Charity, permitted to sit downstairs for the first time, looked grave. "Is it wise," she asked, "for all the village to know?"

Anthony barely heard the question, his hopes too high for caution.

I Ain't Forgit

SHAD stood in the mill doorway, peering at the sky. Might be a storm before morning, he figured, and if much more rain fell, the path to the spring would be miry. He picked up a couple of pails, scurried down to the hollow. When he came back, he stacked wood beside the chimney.

From the doorway, he looked off towards the village where dim lights flickered. This time of year, with the days longer and fewer candles needed, folks stayed up later. Now the lights were winking out. Folks had put on nightcaps. Shad felt pity for people who lived huddled under roofs.

Middle of May was a pleasant time for roaming, he reminded himself, but he wouldn't go off until Tim brought his blade back. Without that bit of Swedish steel, he wasn't taking chances with jailers' traps. Besides, he had Tony to think of. Great shakes would be doing, now the loom was come alive. He must tell Tony to watch out for Mark, who'd likely be up to tricks again. But things were safe for a day or so. Everyone knew, Mark had set out for Maine this very afternoon to hire an extra hand. Though that didn't signify so much.

Lightning streaked the sky. Distant, Shad decided. And the mill was protected, now Tony'd had the new rods installed. He was sure to waken, if a storm came close. He shut the door, pushed the bolt across, stripped off his jacket.

Passing by the loom, he stopped and laid his hand on it. How Tony loved that mess of wood and metal! Even when it was most cantankerous, Tony loved the loom like it was a child he'd brought into the world. Shad touched a bit of fluff.

Must be quite a lot of waste cotton around, after the day's doings, but he'd sweep up, early morning.

Walking on towards the cot in the far corner of the new extension, he thought of all that Tony would do, now the loom was panning out. Tony could have the pair of windows he wanted in the downstairs part of the extension, a flight of stairs, other things. Sitting on the cot's edge, Shad made sure the red ribbon was safe. He kicked off his shoe, which hadn't felt right since he loaned Tim the blade that fitted under the insole. Tim'd certain keep his word! Shad stretched out, a blanket over him.

Outside, the wind was freshening. Thunder cracked now and then, but nothing to worry over. Shad thought of Tony, turned to a different man; of Eben, grown lively, and Simeon not traveling back to Boston soon's he'd planned. It was pleasant to rest after the day's doings. Water rushing over the dam sounded like a lullaby.

A crash waked Shad. He jumped out of bed and ran to the window that looked towards the village. No bolt from the sky had fired barn or cottage, no rain fell. Everything was quiet, but something smelled queer. Must be oil that Tony spilled, Shad thought, sniffing. He went for his shoes.

By the time he got back to the window, a flash streaked the sky. In the piece of a second when night was brighter than day, he spied a man running. Only Mark Badger ran with that wide-straddled gait. Why was Mark here, when folks saw him start for Maine around four o'clock? Why was he running? Why was the smell of oil so strong? And a thread of flame creeping along the floor?

He'd better make his legs move, get out of the fire-trap, Shad realized. He dreaded fire. Maybe if he took the short cut, he'd catch up with Mark. Shad grabbed his sling and pulled the door wide.

Then he remembered the loom Tony loved. He remembered how Tony fought with Steve. "I ain't forgit how Tony stood up for me," he said aloud. "First thing, I'll save the loom." He dropped the sling.

His legs felt lively now. He ran to the bulkhead outside to get into the cellar. The wooden covers were in flames! He'd have to find another way. Then it seemed, near the door, that Tony cried: "Shad, don't go inside!"

He halted dead. Tony wan't anywhere around. He was only imagining again! No reason to fret, he told himself. With all the rattling overhead, rain would fall any minute. Bound to. He went inside and shut the pair of windows to prevent a draft that would fan a flame. He heard a sizzling and snapping in the cellar underneath. If he ran for help, anything might happen while he was gone.

A ribbon, orange-colored, crept towards the loom. Grabbing a rag, he smothered it. How much heat would it take to twist the loom? Silly to have such ideas. Cotton fluff around would burn, but the floor beams were eight inches thick. And any minute rain would fall. Bound to.

He stamped out another ribbon of flame. Never a fire started but someone saw it, he told himself, swallowing fear. Soon as ever flames swept from the burning bulkhead up into the night sky, someone would see. Someone tending a sick child or cow, or someone waked by thunder. And the new engine would come racing over the fields, bringing the smart young fire fighters.

He went to the window. No rain as yet, and no racing engine. A spark fell on the loom's warp threads; he sprang to smother it. If the sparks landed higher, he couldn't reach them so easy. He eyed the bales of cotton fibre that stood around; hard-packed, slow to burn. Not easy to move, them five-hundred-pound bales! Shad tapped his forehead, pulled his ear.

An idea came. Taking a log from the stack by the chimney, he managed to coax it under the corner of a bale. A log under the opposite side, and he could roll a clumsy bale wherever he wanted. Sometimes a log slipped out of place and he had to begin again, but at last he had the bales so they made a wall; the loom behind, in the new extension where floor-boards were set so close, flames could never get through. He poured water over his wall.

A good idea to fill the pails from the river! He wriggled through the narrow space between a bale and the wall. Fire cut off his way to door or windows! Terror in his heart now, he pulled the mattress off the cot and used it to smother the tongues of flame licking hungrily at his wall. If the tight-packed bales once caught, they'd burn like hickory. But he wouldn't let them catch, Shad vowed. Choking, almost blinded, he fought the fire.

The glass in the windows cracked and fell apart. He could not prevent the draft that already was fanning the flames. But the bulkhead was sending up a glow! Someone in the village would see that the mill was on fire.

As he fought the flames, Shad put his mind on pleasant things. Green grass under a blossoming fruit tree, cool petals fluttering down. The ripple of a lively brook. A stretch of crusted snow, and sleighbells jingling. . . .

His breeches caught; slapping out the blaze, his hand got burned. It was hard to breathe, with smoke so thick. And the roar of the fire was enough to drive a body crazy. Shad grabbed a blanket and threw it over his head. Any minute, now, the fire horses would come galloping.

The bales of cotton began to burn. The floor of the old part of the mill fell through. The floor of the extension would go next, carrying the loom with it!

He'd done his best, the Lord knew, but he couldn't save the loom. All he could do now was tell Tony it was Mark, not the electric fluid, that set the mill on fire. Well, he'd just cut a hole in the wall, same as he'd done time and again in a jail, and wriggle through.

He had stooped before he remembered. The blade wasn't in

his shoe! Tony's tools would do. They went, when the floor fell through! He was alone, imprisoned in a fire-trap. . . .

Down in the place it wasn't polite to name, everything was warm as folks said. Eggs would roast to a turn, no blaze under them. Coffee in the pot would boil of itself. He'd soon get the hang of things, Shad thought.

There was plenty of food. Cupboard doors stood open; chickens on the shelves, pies, cheeses, milk and cider. Tim came running through the blue-yellow air.

"Brought back your knife, like I swore," he said with a bow.

Shad took the thin blade. Folks were crowding around, glad he was with them. "But you can't break out of jail—here!" they cried.

A fellow whose breath was smoke pointed to the badge on his red uniform. "Shadrach Nye," he said, "I'm the sheriff. Whatever you do on earth, you don't get out of jail—down here."

Shad found himself in a cell that had every sort of lock contraption. If he laid a finger on the wall, it rattled a warning. His hand-cuffs were bracelets of fire; his leg-irons, forks of electric fluid.

He went slowly for a while, wanting folks to think Shadrach Nye had met something too much for him. Then, just when the crowd was losing hope but before they started for other fun, he surprised them. A wave of his red ribbon, a twist of his steel blade. And he was free.

"Hooray for Shadrach Nye!" the crowd roared. "Hooray!"

The sheriff jingled his great keys and breathed out clouds of smoke.

"Hooray!" the crowd cried again. "Shadrach Nye can break out of jail—even down here!" The shouting rose to the copper-colored sky.

* * *

Anthony tossed in his sleep, bothered by a noise like the buzzing of a bee. The sound grew louder. "Anthony . . . Anthony . . . Anthony . . ." He roused and ran to the window.

"The mill is on fire," William called. "My mare's being harnessed."

Anthony jumped into clothes. Boots in his hand, he ran down the stairs.

"Shad sent warning?" he asked as they raced up the lane.

"Don't know." William was tight-lipped. "Lucy was giving the baby three o'clock feeding when my brother rode up. Engine had started, Noah said."

If the engine reached the mill soon enough, Anthony thought as they galloped over the highway, the danger wasn't too great. The loom stood in the extension, and new wood was slower to burn. How Shad would fret!

"Electric fluid's been playing all night," William said as they rocked along. "Gentle as firefly's flicker. Didn't seem like it struck anywhere."

"Where's Mark?" Anthony inquired, a new tightness in his throat.

"Went to Maine to hire a man. I saw him start, round four o'clock."

They had topped a rise. Fire lighted the sky.

"Hear church bell?" William asked. "It's a call for more help."

They tore through the village, and over the road beyond. The reek of smoke grew stronger. And then they saw the mill, wrapped in flames. The mare shied, unwilling to go nearer.

"I'll get out here." Why did the men around the mill stand idle? Anthony wondered as he ran. When he reached them, their faces seemed pale discs, in the glare.

"Sorry we can't do anything," one of them told him. "Blaze got too much headway. Never saw wood burn faster. Looks like oil was poured on."

"Where's Shad?" Anthony demanded hoarsely.

"We ain't seen him. He must have gone off."

Shad had not gone off! He was too interested in the success of the loom.

"Let's step inside." Moving forward, Anthony heard angry protests.

The fire captain touched his arm. "These men'd do anything in reason," he said, "but I wouldn't ask one of them to step inside. We've got wives and children to think of. Sorry you lost your mill, young feller, and just when things was panning out. But we can't help it."

He too had a wife, Anthony reminded himself, and expected a child. But Shad was inside the mill!

"I'll go in alone," he said. "Ask the men to set a ladder under the window!"

The men stood back. "It's wanton self-destruction," someone cried. "Nobody could survive, inside."

"Half of floor's caved in," the captain warned. "Roof'll go any time."

Anthony had seized a ladder. When the men saw they could not dissuade him, they wrapped him in wet woolen, played the hose around him as he climbed.

"Shad!" he called from the window ledge. "Shad!"

Only the roar of the fire answered. Dense smoke prevented his seeing anything. Then a fresh spurt of flame lighted the entire interior. The old part of the mill was ruined, floor to rafters. The extension was as yet intact, a row of cotton bales making a barrier between the fire in front and the machines in the extension. Shad had fashioned that wall to save the loom! Somewhere behind it, Shad lay!

As he went inside, Anthony thought again of his wife and child. For a minute it seemed he could not go forward. The men were right: nobody could survive in here. But Shad!

It was certain death to step on wood. A wet blanket around him, he crept along the stone of the foundation; passed the wall of baled cotton, passed the loom. Shad lay on the cot in the far corner. Wrapping the mattress around the small limp figure, Anthony started back.

Timber crashed around him. The baled cotton had begun to burn. The mattress around Shad caught, and he had difficulty in smothering the flame. The hot stone of the cellar burned through his shoes. Once he lost his balance, almost falling into the furnace below.

"Hurry!" worried voices called. "Roof's going to fall!"

Blinded, choking, knowing his clothes were burning, Anthony crept forward with his burden. Only a few yards more to go! The wall beside him crackled. He could not breathe. Only a foot or so to the small space that was his exit to safety! Friendly hands reached for his burden, helped him through the window, at last.

Down by the river's edge, away from the heat of the fire, he bent over Shad. There was a faint heart-beat. Holding the small hand, Anthony felt a slight pressure.

" 'Twan't 'lectric fluid started the fire," Shad whispered. " 'Twas that Mark! I saw him runnin'." The whisper, the fingers' pressure, ceased.

"Shad!" Anthony cried. "Shad!"

No answer came from his friend.

They buried Shad in the Damon graveyard.

"Here on the hilltop he'd not feel shut in," Charity said, bending to lay lilies on the new mound. Anthony drew her back until she stood, one hand in his, the other resting on the chain looped between granite posts to keep cattle from encroaching on the sanctity of the burial place. "Shad lost his life trying to save the loom," she added softly. "We want him near us."

Anthony nodded, head bowed. As long as he lived, he would yearn for the sight of Shad's young-old face, the sound of his high-pitched "Land sakes!"

Short Interlude

SIMEON announced, next morning, that he must return to Boston.

"What about fixing responsibility for the fire?" Anthony inquired.

"I'll call on the selectmen this afternoon," Simeon replied, grave.

Anthony did not accompany Simeon. His burns were severe and, in spite of Charity's healing ointments, he suffered considerable distress. With events occurring so rapidly, there had been no opportunity to plan for the future. Waiting for Simeon to return, he knew that a crisis in his affairs had arrived.

The older man did not appear until supper time. He had stopped, he explained, to inspect the brickyard again, particularly the ovens.

"The selectmen think electric fluid caused the fire," he remarked as he dipped his spoon into the hot chowder. "And William believes this to be the general opinion."

"Lightning rods had been installed," Anthony pointed out.

"I know, but the selectmen consider that the mill site, so close to the river, invites lightning. And the rods, they tell me, might have got out of line."

Hilda, carrying off the big tureen, halted to put in her word. "Anyone can see that Mark set the fire," she sputtered, "and without poor dying Shad having to tell 'em so."

"Officials," Simeon continued, "are obliged to judge according to the facts. The facts in this case are that a score of persons saw Mark drive off to Maine, in the afternoon, but nobody had a glimpse of him afterwards. We know he intended going as far as Saco to engage a new man."

"When Mark heard about the loom," Hilda declared with a dark look, "he set out earlier'n what he'd planned, taking pains to have folks see him go. Nightfall, he rowed across river, fired the mill, then rowed back to Maine. And he's got something more up his sleeve. Didn't he take boxes and barrels along? Didn't Rachel Foster set out, same time? Visiting her aunt in Portland, she said. But the postmistress hears where Rachel's name is 'Badger' now."

"Mark has married Rachel!" Charity exclaimed.

"Only 'cause he couldn't get Charity Damon!" Hilda marched off, leaving the door open a crack in order not to miss anything.

"We can't prove that a wild flash of the electric fluid did not strike the mill," Simeon pointed out. "Men of the law will not accept Shad's word. Indeed I expressly advise against recourse to law. The law can neither restore the mill nor bring Shad back to life."

Anthony felt appalled by Simeon's attitude. "You mean Mark is to go unpunished?" he asked.

"Unless we have evidence of his guilt," Simeon observed, thoughtful. "Mark, if guilty, will suffer in good time."

In good time! The mill and a life were gone. And Simeon would calmly leave punishment to the Lord! With difficulty Anthony restrained himself. At last the meal was over. They went into the best room where Hilda had lighted a fire for Charity.

Presently Hilda burst in with a letter for Simeon. "Just come," she announced, eyes snapping. "Postmistress knew Mark's writing and sent it right over."

Simeon broke the seal, scanned the lines, then flung the page down. "Mark is dishonorable," he declared, "to desert when the ovens are being started."

"Didn't I say he was up to something!" Hilda crowed.

"The men in the yard had much rather work under William," Charity said.

Simeon fumed about Mark's lack of honor. "By this act of leaving us, Mark brings suspicion on himself," he said. "But I doubt if a New Hampshire sheriff can bring him back from the District of Maine," he added. Thoughtful, he picked up Mark's letter and reread it. Then he looked at Anthony.

"And what does thee intend to do, now the mill is gone?" he asked.

Anthony, who had hoped Simeon might suggest rebuilding the mill, felt dismayed by the question. So he had nothing to show for the year's work but charred wood, twisted metal, the new grave! Charity was waiting for his answer, her face pale in the firelight. Hilda dallied by the door.

"There are several possibilities," he said slowly.

"I make a definite proposal," Simeon announced. "I think thee could be a satisfactory manager here at Blue Clay Farm."

Anthony could not believe his ears. It was incredible that Simeon, who understood almost better than anyone the importance of the new machines, could suggest his taking charge of a brickyard.

But the Quaker went on: "William Lane understands the practical end of the business. We need someone to have general oversight . . ."

While Simeon talked, Anthony glanced at Charity. Her pale face had lighted. In her heart she wanted her husband to have charge of the brickyard, the herd and barns and rolling acres, the schooner at wharfside! No Damon was ever born who did not love Blue Clay Farm, she had told him.

"Thee could become a leader in the community," Simeon was saying. "If so inclined, serve in the State Legislature . . ."

They dangled a worthy life before him, and many men would covet his opportunity. But he must refuse. Even now when he hated to disappoint Charity! He was not meant for the land, like Damon men. His muscles and bones, the very blood in his veins, would fail him. Yielding now, he would be false in the end—to Charity as well as to himself.

"I appreciate your confidence," he answered Simeon, "but William will make a better manager for the yard than I. He'll learn the general oversight."

Simeon stared, a perplexed expression in his keen blue eyes. "But thee," he persisted, "what does thee intend to do?"

Until this moment, deluded by the hope that Simeon would rebuild the mill, Anthony had had only vague plans. He made a decision now.

"I mean to see if Mr. Lowell will employ me in his mill."

"Thee knows friend Francis?" Simeon inquired.

Briefly, Anthony explained that he had met the Boston man in England, but forgotten his name. "John Guppy spoke of him, the day he came to inspect the loom. I wrote to Mr. Lowell, while I was in Boston, and he was good enough to reply." Anthony reached for the letter in his pocket.

Charity read it, then handed it to Simeon.

It took the older man a little time to adjust to the new circumstances. In the end, he seemed satisfied. "Of course, Charity and thee can live in Boston with me as long as convenient," he said. "That is, if Francis offers thee employment."

Anthony felt reasonably sure that Mr. Lowell would employ a man trained in an English mill; but Simeon's invitation disturbed him. Waltham, the seat of the mills, was ten or eleven miles out of Boston; he could not manage so long a daily journey. Neither could he bear being separated from Charity. Yet, in her uncle's home she would enjoy comforts he could never provide. The daughters of Boston Friends would welcome Simeon's niece.

He felt her hand in his. "Anthony, it takes a wife to plan. I shall live in Waltham with thee. Uncle Simeon will drive out often to see us."

"Any home I can provide," he said quickly, "will be humble, compared with yours or your uncle's."

"No home is humble where people live happily."

Her words took a load off his mind, but her happy laugh touched his heart.

"Let me suggest," Simeon was saying, "that thee engage the humble home for no longer period than one year. By the spring of 1816, conditions may be ripe for a cotton mill here in Forks Village."

"Away from the farm only a year!" Charity exclaimed. "The time will seem a short interlude in our lives."

All The Twenty-Four States

In Waltham

D*ING–DONG, ding-dong, ding-dong. . . .*

Roused from sleep, Charity lifted her head. She was in Waltham on the Charles River, she reminded herself; the bell must be the cotton mill's, and at its first clang Anthony would have gone. On the street outside, people were hurrying by. A wagon passed so close, its wheels might be rolling through the house. Someone was running.

Ding-dong, ding-dong. . . .

The bell had been cast in Paul Revere's copper-rolling factory, Anthony had said. How clear it sounded—though the mill was half a mile away! People still hurried by. . . . Not so many now.

Hilda came into the bedroom. "Here's hot water." She set the pitcher down.

"I can scarcely wait to see my new home," Charity said as she sat up.

" 'Twon't take ye long," Hilda remarked darkly.

Charity laughed, remembering how Anthony had led her up the stairs the night before, fearing she was over-tired by the journey. In no time, she had fallen asleep. The room *was* small, with the bed reaching almost from wall to wall. A pair of ladder-back chairs stood by the dormer windows, small chest between; the washstand in one corner, candlestand in the other. And this was every stick of furniture the room could hold!

"Hilda, I don't see how thee did so much in the week before we came," she said.

"I scrubbed, inside and out." Hilda nodded vigorously. "I'll bring tray up," she added as she stepped toward the door.

"Indeed, not. I'll be down in about ten minutes." Charity sprang out of bed.

The room might be small, she thought as she dressed, but Hilda had freshened every inch. The walls were covered with left-over rolls of paper she had found in the attic at Blue Clay Farm and sent with the furniture. Curtains fluttered at the windows. The floor, painted blue, was covered with a white hooked rug. She put on a freshly starched white cap and ran down the narrow box stairs.

Hilda had set her breakfast on a table in the tiny front room. The house must face the south, for sun poured in both windows.

"Milk ain't so creamy as ourn," Hilda said, "but best there is. I told the milkman to call regular. Seems queer not to have our own cows."

"We won't mind," Charity rejoined.

A loud din drowned her words.

"Stagecoach for New York," Hilda shouted. "Goes by regular."

The small house shook as the horses thundered by. The street, Anthony had said, was part of the Great Road. It nearly took one's breath away to be able to look out, see people bound for Worcester, Hartford, New York. And what clouds of dust the stage had raised!

"Sandy stretch runs through here," Hilda told her. "Some folks call it 'Waltham Plain.' "

A new clamor sounded. An army of cows must be coming, if one judged by the grunts and bellowing. Presently a man's shout rang out: "Keep in the road, pernickety critter!" A whip lashed the air.

"Drovers taking cattle to Brighton slaughter sheds," Hilda explained as the animals ploughed through the dust. "The sheds were built in Revolution to feed Washington's army and still do a lively business."

Perhaps it was just as well, Charity thought, that they were likely to live in Waltham only a year.

After breakfast, she and Hilda tried every possible arrangement of furniture, although there was little choice. "This doll's house ain't no place," Hilda complained as she eyed the three small rooms, "for the mistress of Blue Clay Farm."

"It will do very well," Charity said, "and I'm going to look around outside."

The houses were set close together. Only a few feet of ground lay between her new home and the fences marking boundaries on either side. There were no flowers, no green lawn. She would sow grass seed, get asters, zinnias, other quick-growing things. Ferns, brought from the woods and placed against the cellar wall, would make the cottage look cozier, she thought, as she picked her way through weeds to the small building that served as a barn.

She had not let Anthony know how hard it was to leave Gabriel behind. "The barn has only one stall," he had told her, "and Gypsy will be more useful." Anthony was right. Gabriel had never been hitched to cart or carriage. Yet, giving Gypsy the lump of sugar she had brought, she longed for Gabriel.

Anthony had said he would not come home for noon dinner. Charity spent the early afternoon putting her clothes in drawers and closet. By four o'clock, she sat in the small front room, her knitting in her hands. The road ran so close to the house that people almost brushed against the glass of the windows as they walked by. And they were all strangers. In Forks Village, she rarely saw anyone she had not known for years.

She was not so silly as to be homesick, she told herself. But what was there for her to do in Waltham? At Blue Clay Farm, she had been responsible for men and maid servants, all the animals, a dozen enterprises. In this box of a house, Hilda could put things in order in half a morning. The tiny garden she planned would take only a little time. She could not knit baby garments, day in and day out. What was there for her to do?

A carriage halted outside. A man who looked like hired help sprang out and held the horse's head while a lady in sprigged calico and a little boy stepped down. They were knocking at her door. She had callers, her very first day in Waltham!

"I'm Mrs. Horne," the visitor announced when Hilda brought her into the room.

"Do be seated, Mrs. Horne." Charity rose and offered a chair.

"Think I will set for a minute. This is my younger son. Solomon, bow to the lady."

Wrinkling his nose, Solomon made a bow.

"There's a stool by the fireplace. Mind, children should be seen and not heard!" his mother charged.

Solomon fixed his gaze on the ceiling.

"My husband has a farm out Beaver Brook way, Mrs.—?"

"Bryce," Charity said, watching the caller spread the folds of her gay calico over her chair.

"Before I was married, I lived in next house but one," Mrs. Horne went on, "and when storekeeper told me folks was moving in here, I said to myself, 'Becky Horne, when you drive in to the village, drop in on the newcomers.' Waltham folks are friendly, Mrs. Bryce."

"Thee is kind to come," Charity said.

"Quaker?" Mrs. Horne inquired with a start.

"My family have long been members of the Society of Friends."

"You don't say!" The guest's eyes were taking everything in: the small high-backed sofa, the bright hearthrug, the pair of wall chairs, the table with the family Bible. "You've got nice things," she summed up. "Time was, Quakers were trouble-makers, but nobody minds if a few come to Waltham now."

Charity picked up the knitting she had dropped in courtesy to the caller.

Solomon was getting restless. "There's a nice cat worked into the hearthrug," his mother told him. Young Solomon scowled and eyed the cat.

Hilda brought a tray, and Charity poured the tea.

"Servant?" Mrs. Horne inquired when Hilda had left the room.

"Hilda has been with me since I was born." Charity handed her guest the cup of tea, and offered Solomon a cookie.

A dray drawn by a pair of oxen went by, leaving a cloud of dust.

"Drivers dread sandy Waltham Plain more'n midsummer rash," Mrs. Horne said. "It's worst in dry weather like this June afternoon. Blows in doors and windows. But sand never harmed anyone. Healthy place, Waltham is, and some folks live to be ninety years old, even a hundred. When you're used to things, you'll be thankful you came here."

Thankful! She would always feel she was an outsider, Charity thought.

"There's pretty scenery around," Mrs. Horne continued. "Hills and woods and ponds. Elegant country seats, too. Folks can't agree which is handsomer, Gore or Lyman place. Gore place belongs to Senator Gore . . ."

Charity repented her earlier resentment. Any newcomer to Forks Village would be subjected to questioning. If Mrs. Horne had never known any Friends, how could she be expected to understand them!

"I'll have you meet some of the ladies I know," she was saying.

"Thee is kind and I thank thee," Charity returned, "but we'll not be here very long."

"I know." Mrs. Horne nodded. "Storekeeper told me your husband works at the new cotton mill. Nobody expects the mill to last very long."

"What does thee mean?" Charity inquired, puzzled.

"That newfangled loom they count on is just a rich man's

toy. Waltham folks don't put a mite of stock in it."

"It's a wonderful invention," Charity retorted. "The mill proprietors mean to manufacture cotton cloth so cheaply that everyone can buy it. They mean to make our country independent of foreign factories."

"I'll tell you something that clever rich men don't know." Mrs. Horne patted a fold of her sprigged calico. "Women don't want cloth manufactured in this country, Mrs. Bryce. They want imported goods, even if it's dearer. Would I enjoy this gown as much if the calico was made in Waltham? Certainly not. I like to say, 'This is imported goods. I got a piece off a bolt the storekeeper had.' Besides, the Honorable Christopher Gore tells us American prosperity depends on buying from abroad."

"He must have a dull brain," Charity flared, forgetting Friends' tolerance.

Mrs. Horne bridled. "He was Governor of Bay State before he was sent to the Senate in Washington. He knows more than Francis Cabot Lowell, Patrick T. Jackson, and all the rest of the Boston Manufacturing Company, as they call themselves, put together. Time was, women bought bags of Carolina cotton at the grocer's, wore themselves out, spinning and weaving. Nowadays, except in war time, ships bring cloth ready for the making up. Imported goods are bound to stay the fashion." Her eyes snapped.

Charity let her knitting fall. It had never occurred to her that Anthony and the others at the mill might perfect the loom, manufacture cloth cheaply—but be unable to sell it. Was Anthony doomed to fail in Waltham?

"Storekeeper told me," Mrs. Horne ran on, "he'll have more imported goods next week. You're not one of the long-nosed Quakers. Let me buy you a piece of something lively, 'stead of that drab you're wearing, and you'll look pretty as any of 'em."

Charity held her tongue. She felt grateful to the talkative

little woman from whom she had learned something very important to know.

"Ma," Solomon interrupted, "I'm hungry."

"Have a cookie!" Charity held out the plate, and Solomon took one.

"I declare, forgot I meant to stay only a minute." Mrs. Horne rose. "My folks'll want cold meat and preserved peaches this June evening."

Charity went to the door with her guests. "I thank thee, Mrs. Horne, for coming to see me, and I am glad to meet Solomon."

"I enjoyed my visit." The caller beamed. "I'll drop in again and bring you a piece of imported goods. You have a friend in Becky Horne! Now I think of it, there's a sewing-bee at my house next Wednesday. Come and meet my friends! See the nice dresses they wear, all imported goods!"

"I shall be there," Charity promised. From the window, she watched Mrs. Horne lift her sprigged calico as she climbed into the carriage. Solomon waved, and they drove away.

Indeed she had work here in Waltham, Charity thought. She must persuade women like Mrs. Horne to buy American-made goods. And just an hour ago, she had wondered what to do with her time! Neither foreign manufacturers, local politicians, nor empty-headed women were going to defeat Anthony—if she could prevent it!

She would accept all the invitations that came and, wherever she went, drop a word in favor of American-made goods. She would not worry Anthony by telling him that silly women wanted only imported frippery.

But, she wondered, did he know?

We Want Imported Cloth

WHILE CHARITY was still asleep that morning, Anthony had eaten his breakfast and hurried down the street. A stream of people turned into the half-mile lane leading to the Boston Manufacturing Company's Number One mill, and he walked with them. The mill was built of brick; its basement and four stories had rows of shining windows. The yard was ample, with a convenient well-house. He was seeing the type of mill, Anthony realized, of which he had often dreamed.

He paused to look at the river. The falls, lower than in Forks Village, disappointed him. The dam was built of wood, a foot-bridge running along its top. The Charles was much narrower in Waltham than in Boston, but boats lay by the waterside.

Turning away, he entered the mill. A man guided him to the basement wheelroom, where he found Paul Moody. The master mechanic stood beside a loom which ran unevenly and presently halted.

Anthony stepped forward. "My name is Bryce, sir."

"The new English mechanic?"

Anthony nodded.

"We've been expecting you. Here's our loom, if you care to look at it."

Anthony gave close scrutiny. The machine was less clumsy than his own. They needed a better way of sizing the warp, Mr. Moody explained, to keep the threads from snarling.

"I was working on that problem when a fire wrecked my New Hampshire mill," Anthony said.

The proprietors would be glad if he'd continue to work at

the problem, Moody said. He went on to tell how Mr. Lowell had contrived a small model of the water loom, solely from memory of what he had seen in England. Working in the back room of a Boston store, a hired man turning the crank by hand, he had completed the machine only the previous autumn. As yet, it was far from perfect. For one thing, there was this matter of snarling threads. He had obtained a drawing of an English dressing machine but would like a better model.

Seated by a workbench in the wheelroom, Anthony realized that his problems had been the problems of all men trying to weave cloth by water power.

Later in the morning, Mr. Lowell came to greet him. It was a pleasure, the Boston man said, to employ the son of the inventor from whom he had learned so much. His goal was to perform the entire operation of cloth-making under one roof. He and the other proprietors had plans for a machine shop, a bleachery and dye-house, suitable boarding places for women workers, a library and a school for employees' children. They considered financial profit but were equally interested in the welfare of the community.

Though not more than forty years or so of age, Francis Lowell seemed too frail a man to be the guiding spirit of a great enterprise. His face showed kindness as well as intelligence. Anthony's gaze dropped to his hands. Yes, they were sensitive, as he remembered them.

He was very fortunate, Anthony was reflecting, later. He admired his employers; he liked his work, and received the very high wages of a dollar and a half a day.

Then another worker sat down beside him. "Did you know," he began, "this mill hasn't sold a yard of cloth yet? Ships are bringing more foreign goods than ever. Just yesterday I heard a man tell how British prices will fall below cost of American manufacture. This mill may have to close and leave us looking for other work soon."

On the day of the sewing bee, a neighbor drove Charity to the Horne farm. This was her first view of the outskirts of Waltham. She saw rambling houses, neat gardens, a pond or two, Mackerel and Prospect Hills. From the top of Prospect Hill, the neighbor said, ships could be seen in Boston Harbor, ten miles away.

Mrs. Horne was waiting at the door when they reached the farm. "You call me 'Becky,' " she said, "and I'll call you—?"

"Charity."

"Sober-sounding name, but easy to say. Charity, come in and meet my friends."

The sewing bee was for a neighbor's daughter soon to be a bride. Half a dozen women worked on a patchwork quilt; others hemmed towels and napkins, or overcast the long middle seams of sheets. Charity was reminded of the days when the sisters sat in the spinning room at Blue Clay Farm. These women chatted about country dances, hayrick parties, the shops in Boston. They seemed overjoyed by the prospect of wearing new clothes.

"We've had nothing but homemade things," one of them told her, "for years. Now the war is over, we want fancy cloth. We want Scotch muslins and calicoes. We want English broadcloths."

"Half a century ago," Charity remarked, "our grandmothers refused to wear or buy anything made in Britain."

"Our grandmothers!" Becky laughed merrily. "My dear, *we* keep up with the times."

"It is timely to be patriotic," Charity replied. "Did thee hear that President Madison wears only American-made cloth?"

The others were not impressed by the question, but they seemed amused by her Quaker speech. They showed her the fancy patterns of their own new gowns: a muslin with green sprigs on a white background, a bright Scotch gingham, a blue and pink calico. "All imported goods," they said proudly.

"The dresses are very pretty," Charity rejoined, "but they'd be still prettier if the cloth were made in the United States."

Back and forth the good-natured banter went, as needles flashed.

"We'll get Charity on our side before long," Becky declared.

"Indeed I mean to get thee on my side," Charity rejoined.

"I'm on your side," a gentle voice said. "I won't buy imported cloth. And my husband works at Mr. Lowell's cotton mill."

Charity felt satisfaction as she was driven home. She had gained a dozen new friends and one ally!

By the end of June, her yard was a green bower, with flowers poking heads up everywhere. She and Anthony often sat outside through the evening. But, mindful of Paul Revere's bell, they climbed the stairs to the dormer-windowed bedroom early.

Charity began to organize a group of women, mostly mill employees or employees' wives, who agreed to campaign in the interest of domestic-manufactured cloth. Their slogan was: "President Madison wears only American-made cloth, and we follow his example." She gained no headway in weaning Becky Horne from her craze for foreign goods, but the two remained friends. She accepted all the invitations that came to her; and wherever she went, she spoke a word for American-made goods.

Anthony worked feverishly through the summer, receiving high praise from Paul Moody and indeed from Mr. Lowell. They made progress with new inventions. And yet a feeling of gloom sometimes hung over the mill. Ships from Europe brought goods into Boston every week. As the flow of cash dwindled and purchasers were forced to ask for credit, prices fell. Nobody wanted domestic cotton when the finer imported goods could be had for the same—or less—money. American mills, one after another, closed their doors. By autumn, the great Rhode Island mills had idle spindles.

On a visit to Boston in October, Anthony went into Mrs. Isaac Bowers' shop on Cornhill. All customers commended the quality of the Waltham samples, the widow told him, and did not complain of the price, twenty-five cents the yard; yet they pushed the samples aside and asked for imported goods. Her shop, Anthony knew, was the only one in Boston that even tried to sell domestic goods.

Charity now went about less. The cradle in which she had lain was brought from Blue Clay Farm. Anthony refinished the outside, painted the inside pale blue. Charity had blankets, pillows, tiny garments, ready.

The child came into the world early one morning in December. For once, Anthony ignored the summons of Paul Revere's bell. At last he was shown a rosy mite, his son. It was noon before he remembered Simeon and dispatched a rider into Boston with the news that Simeon Damon Bryce was born.

One evening, some six weeks later, Anthony and Charity were in the kitchen, admiring the baby in the hooded wooden cradle. "See, Anthony," Charity said, "he has thy hands. I believe he will be a mill mechanic."

They talked of Anthony's trip to Boston the day before. Simeon had told him that the price of imported cotton sheeting, such as the Waltham mill was making, might drop to fifteen cents the yard—and no American mill could possibly compete. "Mark my words," Simeon had declared, "no other factory has as much capital, as able men in charge, as the Waltham mill. If it fails, all American mills are doomed. And the current year, 1816, is bound to be the crucial time."

"Can nothing be done?" Charity asked.

"Mr. Lowell will spend most of the winter in Washington," Anthony told her, "trying to get a tariff bill passed that will give our infant industries some protection."

"I hoped," Charity said, "the struggle would be over when the power loom was perfected."

"Perhaps," Anthony returned slowly, "it is only beginning."

It was no news to him that not only men with selfish interests, but also silly women bent on wearing imported finery, might wreck the cause of the mills!

"One of the proprietors," he continued, eyes on the fire, "has suggested my joining Mr. Lowell in Washington for a while. He thinks someone with first-hand knowledge of the situation in England might help swing opinion to the side of the tariff bill. My expenses would be paid, also my wife's—if she cares to go with me."

Leave the baby to go to Washington! And just when she was resuming her campaign in Waltham for the cause of American-made cloth! But Anthony would need her with him. It was nonsense to worry about the baby. Hadn't Hilda taken care of her, as well as of her own brood of nine!

"Anthony, I'll go with thee," she said firmly.

Crucial Year

BY WAITING for tolerable weather with passable roads, Anthony and Charity accomplished the journey to the Capital in only ten days' time. Darkness hid the landscape on the February evening that the stage dropped them at their boarding-place. A waiting servant led them up a path and through a doorway. The glare of the room they entered half-blinded them. Presently they made out a portly landlady behind a desk.

A room had been reserved for Mr. and Mrs. Bryce of Massachusetts. "Fifteen dollars a week for a gentleman's bed and board, his candles, and firewood," the landlady said condescendingly. "His wife is extra."

The price seemed monstrous dear to Anthony.

The gentleman would do well to remember, the landlady went on, that the Capital was crowded; high government officials, as well as foreign emissaries, considered themselves fortunate to be accommodated in her establishment.

There was little alternative. "Very well, madam. Will you kindly send word of my arrival to Mr. Francis C. Lowell." Anthony wrote an address.

"Pompey!" the landlady cried, clapping her hands. "Pompey!"

A young Negro came to carry the message. Another servant gathered up their luggage. Following him, they saw that two or three ladies, very fashionably attired, had joined the company of men now grouped around card tables, chess and backgammon boards.

Next morning Charity wore a drab gown as usual, a kerchief covering her neck and shoulders, a cap over her bright curls. No woman could have been more plainly garbed; but the men at the dining-table paid her marked attention. She was even lovelier since the baby's birth, Anthony thought, as he watched the gentlemen on either side converse with her.

A message waited from Mr. Lowell, who was happy to learn of the Bryces' safe arrival and would call upon them in the afternoon.

"We have the morning to ourselves," Charity exclaimed. "I can scarcely wait to see where Quaker-born Dolly Madison lives."

The air felt raw when they went outside. Anthony turned his collar up, Charity drew her cape closer. "The gentleman who sat beside me at table is a Congressman," she told her husband as they picked a way through the mud of Pennsylvania Avenue. "I said a word about the need for domestic-made cloth, and he seemed favorably impressed. But look at that ruined building!"

There were many blackened walls, though a year and a half had passed since the British burned Washington, and much of the rubbish had been carried away. "I can picture the enemy marching," Charity said, "carrying long poles capped with the balls of flaming cotton they tossed through windows."

They reached a shell of a building standing in a field near the Potomac River. Drays laden with hickory posts, carts filled with sand and lime, lumbered by. There was great activity everywhere.

"The President's Palace, sir," a workman said in answer to Anthony's inquiry. "We'll have to give it a few coats of white paint to hide the scars made by fire."

Charity gazed with great interest at the wrecked mansion. "It was from here that Dolly Madison fled, the British close upon her," she told Anthony. "And she saved Gilbert Stuart's portrait of Washington, the State silver and valuable documents, hiding them in her chaise."

They inquired where the President lived, while the official residence was being restored, and presently stood in front of an imposing brick house with a rounded end. "It would please me to have a sight of the First Lady," Charity said. They looked for some time at the windows, hung with fringed red curtains; but no high-turbaned, low-bodiced Dolly Madison appeared.

Shivering in the cold, they walked on. Anthony wanted to see the new Congress Hall, at the other end of Pennsylvania Avenue. Arm in arm, they braced themselves against the wind that swept down the long avenue, through gaps between buildings, and across vacant areas intended to be "circles" or "squares." Everywhere, they saw reconstruction work. Smart turnouts drawn by high-stepping horses passed, the drivers erect on box seats, the ladies inside wrapped in furs.

At last they reached a building set at the foot of a hill and evidently only lately completed. A tide of people surged back and forth, long lines of vehicles waited. Officers with gold braid and burnished side arms appeared in the throng. Occasionally, ladies with escorts swished by. Couriers carrying fat dispatch cases mounted horses and galloped away.

"Probably they'll place the permanent Capitol on top of the hill," Charity surmised. "Anthony, I'd like to see a New Hampshire face. Does thee think Daniel Webster is here?"

The Representative from New Hampshire, a friendly bystander informed them, was due any time. Many of the lawmakers lived in Georgetown, considering the comforts of the older settlement well worth the daily three-mile stage ride.

They waited until the stage pulled in, watched the passengers step down.

"There's Daniel Webster!" Charity exclaimed as a black-haired man appeared.

He paused. "Madam, I hear a New Hampshire voice?"

"My home is near Portsmouth, on Forks River."

"Indeed. You come to Washington on a matter concerning New Hampshire?"

The Congressman's interest diminished when he learned that temporarily they lived in Massachusetts. He bowed cordially, before he strode off.

"Daniel Webster disappoints me. He did not say he had met thee before. Nor thank thee for aiding with the Portsmouth defense," Charity said, indignantly.

"And little wonder," Anthony rejoined. "Everybody aided with the defense. The morning I called at his office, enemy warships stood off the harbor. I'd like to know if he has changed his views about mills since then. . . . Maybe we'd better ride back. That seems to be our stage over there." He steered Charity around a puddle.

Mr. Lowell came in the afternoon, looking wearier than ever. He told Anthony that Daniel Webster, New England's spokesman, was not in favor of a tariff protecting the new industries. Virginia-born President Madison was on their side. Another Virginian, Thomas Jefferson, who had once called mill-owners unpleasant names, was with them. They must win, however, the support of a third Southerner, John Calhoun of South Carolina. Calhoun not only had remarkable personal influence; he was chairman of the Committee of the Currency and deeply interested in raising enough revenue to keep the nation out of debt.

An informal hearing was to be held before a committee interested in the tariff bill. If Mr. Bryce, with his first-hand knowledge of England, could make it clear that Britain meant to crush the young industries and thereby wreck American finance, the prospects for a tariff law would be improved.

"I'll do my best, sir," Anthony responded.

Mr. Lowell expressed the wish that his guests should enjoy their stay in Washington. Invitations, he told them as he departed, would reach them.

The invitations came. Escorting his wife on her social rounds, Anthony picked up useful information. It delighted him to find that Washington ladies admired Charity's quiet manners; that the gentlemen flocked around, declaring her Quaker bonnet the prettiest headgear in the Capital.

As for Charity, she was shocked to see at one of Dolly Madison's "drawing-rooms" that the famous lady's cheeks were painted, her person adorned with vain ornaments. But there was great friendliness and courage in the face that smiled upon a fellow-Quaker so kindly. And Dolly Madison wore her finery in the service of the nation, Charity reasoned.

She thought often of her baby. "What if the little fellow has croup!" she would fret. "Hilda knows what to do," Anthony reassured her.

He conferred regularly with Mr. Lowell about his speech. Every morning, in the privacy of their room, he read to Charity what he had written.

"Make it so simple," she counselled, "that the dullest-witted cannot miss thy meaning. And along with the dull facts, tuck in words that will rouse the best in men and move them to action."

Corridors of the Congress Hall were thronged, the day of the hearing. Mr. Lowell led Anthony and Charity through the crowd. "The President," he told them, when a modest little man in wig and old-fashioned knee breeches passed. Then a dignified white-haired man approached.

"Good morning, Francis," he said.

"Good morning, Christopher." Lowell presented his youthful guests to Senator Gore, who greeted them cordially.

"I warn you, Francis," he said after a minute, "if your tariff bills gets as far as the Senate, I'll vote against it."

"I warn you," Lowell returned, "we'll win, in spite of you."

After Waltham's distinguished summer resident had passed, he admitted that having the Senator from Massachusetts against them made their task extremely difficult.

The committee room they entered was well filled. Mill-owners from the various States were being given opportunity to express views, Lowell said. John Calhoun came in, a tall gaunt figure. A moderator took charge.

One after another, speakers rose; demanding protection against foreign guns, coal, clocks . . . nails, glass . . . cotton and woolen cloth. . . . Anthony was amazed by the number of interests represented, and mills from Maine to Maryland were equally hard hit.

"In Rhode Island, where I own a cotton mill," a broad-shouldered fellow shouted, "more than a hundred mills have had to close and throw thousands of deserving people out of work. During the war, we served our country by producing much needed cloth. Are we to be rewarded by losing our shirts?"

A dozen men spoke, the others in the room approving or dissenting. The air grew stuffy. Anthony heard Mr. Lowell, beside him, cough. Charity slipped her hand in his. The speeches went on, and the noisy protests or applause. Each moment his ordeal came nearer. At last Mr. Lowell signalled.

"I lived in English mill towns until I came to the United States, less than two years ago," Anthony began as he rose. "I know that British mill-owners, also agents, shippers and merchants, mean to maintain British manufacturing monopolies. With my own ears I heard a member of Parliament declare that the States afford a far more profitable market than if they had remained a clutter of colonies; that they must be kept dependent on Britain's factories and, to that end, their infant industries wiped out . . ."

With war ended on the continent of Europe, he went on, thousands of British fighting men were thrown back into the ranks of laborers. Mill-owners could lower wages, reduce costs, until all American industry was crushed.

"The right to have our own mills," he declared, "is part of liberty . . . " He pointed out that cotton grown in the South, turned into cloth in the North, then sold to the rapidly developing West, could be a means of uniting the scattered sections of the country. What one industry could do, others could do. But no industry could survive without a tax on imported goods and wares!

There was hearty applause when he sat down. Later, Lowell said that the speech was even more effective than he had hoped. With politics subject to unexpected turns, however, it was idle to speculate how the proposed tariff bill would fare.

Invitations continued to arrive. Lowell urged the young Bryces to linger in Washington, insisting that they had earned the holiday. Yet more and more often, Charity spoke of her baby.

"Do you mean," Anthony inquired after a gay reception one evening, "you would as soon be at home as here in the Capital?"

"Now thy work is done, I mean I'd rather be at home," Charity answered.

Next morning, Anthony booked places on the stage for the North.

"Young'un ain't had a sick hour," Hilda reported on their arrival.

Young Simeon had grown in their absence. He stretched and blinked and smiled engagingly. When Charity picked him up and cuddled him, Anthony thought the two made the prettiest picture he had seen.

For a few days he and Charity were content with settling down. Then they began to fret about the fate of the tariff bill and pored over newspapers. The bill was still in committee, the Fourteenth Congress being occupied with other matters. What if the bill failed to become law! And just when one of the proprietors had found that he could sell Waltham sheeting through wholesale dealers who bought eagerly at auctions. The price, thirty cents a yard, allowed for commissions and gave the company fair profit. But if foreign sheeting dropped to fifteen cents, as was threatened, what could the Waltham mill—or any mill—do! Unless there was a tariff!

Becky Horne called promptly to learn what ladies in the Capital wore. "I'll get me a piece of storekeeper's paduasoy and make me a gown like Dolly Madison's," she announced. "And to think a Quaker should be telling me!"

Ice on the ponds broke up; sleighs were stored away; horses struggled with muddy roads. When Anthony learned that the tariff bill had reached the House, he tossed in his sleep and lost his appetite. Wherever there was a mill, discussion was hot. With Senator Gore against the tariff and Francis Lowell backing it—Waltham had never known anything like it.

The story of what happened in Washington reached Anthony at last. The bill appeared certain to meet defeat, when one of its supporters rushed to the office where John Calhoun was busily writing and begged him to rally the party forces. Calhoun laid down his pen and hurried into the House. Refuting Daniel Webster's argument that the country was not ready for manufactures, he defended the tariff bill. Voting was close. But the bill was through the House!

When it went to the Senate, Waltham people talked more heatedly than ever. Anthony and Charity fretted. Then word came that the bill was passed and President Madison about to sign it.

Relieved from the long strain, Anthony worked with even greater zeal. At home he played with his son, and sang merrily. Hilda, hands on hips, hummed along with him; while Charity looked on, smiling.

The tariff was too low, Lowell said when he returned, and Daniel Webster had imposed a time limit. American mills were due for a struggle, but at least they were not crushed at the start. The Waltham company now laid plans for a larger building, housing for workers, a three-story machine shop.

Anthony's pay was raised to the astonishingly high sum of two dollars a day.

His ease of mind was marred when he heard Hilda say, one evening: "Our time in this box of a cottage's most up." They had lived in Waltham almost a year, he suddenly realized. Simeon had said no word about a mill on Forks River!

"I must set out some roses and a few hardy perennials," Charity remarked.

Anthony felt grateful for her wordless surrender.

We're Headed West

DURING THE following spring—this was the year 1817—Charity found it hard to stay away from her windows. Day after day, poverty-ridden folks passed; afoot, on rawboned nags, in rickety carts with pots dangling. Most of them looked as if little but hope was left to them. If she inquired where they were bound, they would say: "We're headed West, ma'am."

One rainy morning she saw a famished-looking family trudge by, the mother carrying a child about Simeon's age. "Hilda," she called, "hungry people are outside our door. Thee will invite them in."

"Floor's just washed up," Hilda objected. "Poor folks bring sickness."

Charity glanced towards young Simeon. "Thee will invite the wayfarers in while I carry the baby upstairs," she bade as she stooped for the boy.

Presently the little company were swallowing bread as fast as she and Hilda could slice and butter. Charity brought out the cold roast, the pans of milk, a tin of cookies. When she saw that the baby wore only a ragged shirt, she gave him one of young Simeon's warm outfits.

"Please sit by the fire to dress the child," she invited the tired mother. While the other children dried their wet clothes, she persuaded the father to tell his story.

He was a weaver, he said, and lived north'ard near a woolen mill. The yarn was spun by machines at the mill, and brought to their cottage door. They set it up on looms in the kitchen. He earned thirty-five cents a day; his wife earned thirty cents, and each of the three older children, something. As soon as the cloth was woven, the mill agent brought their pay and more yarn. It was a good life.

But the mill closed down. He didn't know why. Some folks said it was the fault of the English, but that didn't make sense as the war was over. He couldn't find other work. Couldn't pay for the cottage rent or the meat and milk and flour. Rather than be thrown into debtor's jail, he started out.

"We're headed West, ma'am. The British burned the village of Buffalo, I hear, but there's land near by to be had for nothing. . . . Walk all the way? Certainly, ma'am. We'll get on by ourselves far as Albany. Beyond, we'll join up with a larger party—'count of Indians. I aim to be settled afore winter."

Charity turned to the mother, whose face was less forlorn now that her children were fed and dry, and took the woman's worn hand in hers. "Thee is very brave," she said feelingly. She watched the gallant party trudge off. The woman held the baby; the father carried the next youngest, in spite of the roll of blankets on his back. Each of the other five children toted a sizable bundle.

"Why have more mills closed down?" she asked Anthony.

"Because, without a power loom, they can't compete with foreign goods."

"Not with the tariff?"

"Not with so low a tariff. Here in Waltham, where we have the power loom, we survive by making heavy sheeting which can be sold easily. Even we could not compete in ginghams or fancy goods."

Charity looked around her home: the floors covered with bright rugs, the dishes and silver shining, pantry shelves piled to the ceiling. Her husband was well paid for work he loved. Her baby was bursting with health. Hilda hunted for ways to please her. Her home was an island of comfort.

The passing before her door had always fascinated her; now it made part of her life. She fed famished migrants, heard their stories as she bandaged sore feet, sometimes gave counsel. Dawn to darkness, she was kept occupied. It was useless to campaign for women to buy only American-made cloth; except in Waltham, people had little money for anything.

Prices rose. Even with Anthony's good pay, she had to figure carefully. Beef that had been eight cents the pound was now fifteen cents. Sugar soared to twenty-five cents, coffee to thirty-seven. Sometimes she was moved to give the meat or pudding intended for her own dinner table to hungry wayfarers.

As spring advanced, the processions grew longer. People from Massachusetts, from the District of Maine, even from her own New Hampshire, were journeying West to escape debt. An entire community of twenty-two families passed, intending to found a township on the banks of the Mississippi River. All thoroughfares leading to the West, Charity learned, were similarly thronged.

"The people who pass now are not mill workers," she told Anthony as they sat in the garden. "They are carpenters, painters, cobblers, even storekeepers and fisherfolk."

"When one group of workers lose their occupation, other groups suffer," Anthony explained. "If weavers stop buying shoes, shoemakers can't pay storekeepers, and storekeepers can't employ carpenters or painters." The hard times were not entirely due to British efforts to crush American industries, he admitted. The country had outgrown its former way of living and not adjusted to a new way.

Grit blew in through doors and windows, and sifted down the chimney flue. Charity saw it on the long white bolster when she waked in the morning; fine as pumice powder, hard as anthracite. It drifted down on the food they ate. No screen was fine enough to keep it off the child. Young Simeon, now in his second summer, began to have coughing spells.

"You should go to Blue Clay Farm for as long as windows have to be open," Anthony urged.

"I'm needed here," Charity said. "My discomfort is nothing

compared with what the people who walk through the sand must endure. Either Hilda or I can harness Gypsy, take Simeon to play by one of the ponds or in the woods." Nevertheless, she thought of the farm longingly.

Drivers of carts had learned they were welcome to wet their parched throats at the well of the cottage with a garden. One morning a wagon pulled up outside. Charity heard the squeak of the well rope, heard Hilda speak with a stranger.

Presently Hilda rushed in and pointed out a front window. "See that wagon!" she cried. "It's loaded with Waltham sheeting, driver told me. Most times, goods goes to New York by water, but this is a rush order for Indiana."

All day long, Charity thought of the wagon rolling West. She pictured life in the new settlements: at first, half a dozen huts in rough fields; then a cluster of cabins, neat farms around them; and finally the village with church and store. Beds would take the place of rushes laid on floorboards, but nobody expected the luxury of sheets. What woman in far-off Indiana, between farm work and caring for her big household, had time for weaving bed linen! Occasionally, however, she would long for comforts. Her daughter a bride, and no sheets to carry to the new home. Or when company came; bear meat dangling, plenty of greens and potatoes, johnnycake in the oven—but no smooth sheets to lie on. And then, one day, a wagon turned up, loaded with Waltham sheeting.

"Does thee have any idea," she asked Anthony when he came home, "of the joy thee gives a woman who sees sheeting after years of doing without?"

He laughed, glad she was proud of him. "And what about the aid and comfort you give travellers?" he rejoined.

"When we left Forks Village we never guessed we were meant to help the settlers of the West," she said thoughtfully.

The migrants continued to plod by; shuffling, limping, or walking sturdily. The road became a trampled ribbon, gold in the morning, gray at night.

President Monroe, making a good-will tour, arrived in Boston in July and was brought to Waltham by the committee in charge. After his visit, newspapers referred to Waltham as "the most notable mill center in Bay State."

Many visitors now came to the mills on the Charles. Sometimes Anthony was assigned to talking with them. Occasionally they asked him why Mr. Lowell hadn't wangled a higher tariff while he was about it. They complained that the twenty-five per cent duty would not save the mills. If you could not get a big ship by an enemy blockade, Anthony pointed out, you slipped a small vessel through. And this *was* war, as much as if men-of-war stood off the seaboard.

He assured discouraged men that as soon as the Waltham machines were perfected and patented, they would be available to all. When he left Forks Village, Anthony had considered his year there wasted; but every hour had value now. For one thing, he understood other mill men's difficulties: lack of capital, poor equipment, jealousy, loss of workers from injuries—and yes, from fire.

Orders for cotton sheeting came in so fast that the company had to register them. They laid plans for a bleachery, a print shop, a dye-house. Mr. Lowell constantly strove to influence lawmaking bodies to pass legislation favorable to mills.

In August, the word came that Francis Cabot Lowell had overdrawn on his scant strength for the last time. To Anthony it seemed that another friend had been sacrificed with Shad. Without Mr. Lowell's leadership, would the mills go on? he wondered. At last he learned that the remaining proprietors considered the enterprise well enough launched to continue.

All through the fine autumn weather, groups of migrants passed Charity's door. The road seemed to her less sandy. It was as if each traveller brought a little soil on his feet and, trampling it in with the granulated particles, left something of himself behind.

Oil of Spruce

CHARITY waved as she drove away from the Beacon Hill house, knowing that Uncle Simeon would watch from the window until her chaise had turned the corner. She felt glad she had taken time for a meal with him. It was sad to see him looking older. Yet everyone had to age. Wasn't this the year 1821! Seven years had passed since she met Anthony, more than five since her eldest son was born. And she herself was twenty-three.

"Gypsy, thee is not so young, either. Watch out thee does not stumble." She took the reins shorter as they went down the hill, noting that Boston had changed too. Fine mansions on Park Street, the Common no longer a cow pasture, much filled-in land, and footwalks everywhere!

At Tremont Street she halted the mare to check her shopping list. She had everything needed for the house, down to the tin of China tea. For the migrants, who still trudged by her door, she had snuff, which weighed little and heartened men bound for wilderness; she had balm of Gilead, and the pectoral balsam of liquorice that kept coughs away. But she had forgotten one thing!

"Gypsy, we can't start for home without oil of spruce. I want to stop at the pharmacy on Washington Street." She flicked the reins.

The Washington Street shop had none of the remedy. "You'll find it at the little store off Pudding Lane," they told her.

Pudding Lane! Anthony would never approve of her going alone to the region of crooked alleys. Nor Uncle Simeon, who had wanted Plato to drive her to Waltham. But ever so many children needed the tonic that kept scurvy away, and a bottle given to a mother brought tears of gratitude. A Quaker must never be afraid!

"Gypsy, we go down Summer Street, make a left turn, a right, another to the left, and we are there."

It was after three o'clock, she reminded herself, and she would be late in getting home. Young Simeon was likely to pull the house down; three-year-old Tony was always up to something. But Hilda was competent to deal with them as well as with baby Shad. She smiled, remembering how Anthony had hemmed and hawed before suggesting their youngest's name. As if she had not always thought that Shad's loyalty more than made up for his wandering ways. As if she could object to any name Anthony wanted so much.

She felt drowsy, and the cobblestones threw up a suffocating August heat. The mare moved slowly, her flanks dripping in spite of the rest in Uncle Simeon's stable. The air smelled sour. She had never been in this lane, she realized with a start. Thinking about her children, she had turned off the beaten track. Well, Boston lanes went round and round; if she kept on, she was bound to come out somewhere.

The way grew stranger. Forlorn faces looked out a window, here and there. A dog in a doorway panted, the naked child beside him staring. The houses were so close, they seemed to press in on her. Down ahead, a hungry-looking man came up from a basement. Pleasant places, the oyster-cellars had once been, where people ate in cool comfort; but during the long years of hard times, they had turned into dens for thieves.

"Gypsy, go fast as thee can," she bade.

Perversely, the mare kept to a snail's pace, her slow clop-clop echoing back from the house walls. Now a sick-looking woman was coming up from a basement. Strangely, something about her was familiar. Charity found her thoughts running back to the days when she had charge of the spinning in an upstairs chamber at Blue Clay Farm . . . when Rachel looked out the window, eyes on Mark. But this unkempt creature with sunken cheeks could not be handsome Rachel!

As Gypsy came abreast of the cellar entrance, the woman's jaw dropped. She stared for a moment and then started to run. She was Rachel!

Let her go! Charity thought, remembering the unhappiness that had begun the day Rachel taunted her. But her happiness had also begun then. For seven years her life had been warmed by Anthony's love, while poor Rachel—

"Rachel," she called. "This is Charity. I want to see thee."

The woman ran faster, and Gypsy refused to hurry her pace. All around, people peered from windows with a look of wanting to seize the chaise and everything in it. Rachel still ran, her gait unsteady from weakness. When had Charity Bryce been afraid to aid a woman in need!

"Gypsy, thee will have to look out for thyself. Do not let anyone take thee without a struggle!" she charged as she stepped down from the chaise.

"Rachel!" she called, running after the ghost of a woman who ducked and dodged, stumbled but picked herself up and ran on, disappearing into a wall.

Charity found a narrow door, when she reached the spot where Rachel had vanished. "Keep out of there!" a rough voice warned from overhead. She paused, wondering what lay behind the forbidden entrance. She wore no jewels that thieves could covet; she had left her purse in a hidden pocket of the chaise. What if she had been sent into this lane for some purpose!

When she pushed against the door, it yielded. She stepped inside. The place was dark and airless. "Rachel, I want to take thee home with me," she called.

No answer! Reaching out her hand, she touched damp stone. Something that might be a rat slithered by, but Charity refused to be frightened. If she searched the cellar inch by inch, she would come upon the Forks Village woman in need of aid. Hands stretched out, she groped her way. She thought she heard strained breathing. "Rachel!" she said softly.

No answer! She stumbled against a bench and felt along it. Her hands touched cloth. "Go away!" a sullen voice said. But Charity sat down beside Rachel. She talked about her home in Waltham, the spare room overlooking the garden, her longing to have a visit from one of the Forks Village Friends she had known as a girl.

At first Rachel tried to draw away from the hand that sought hers, but she resisted less and less. At last she burst out: "Mark never loved me. He struck me, and I fell. My child was born dead."

"I am sorry." Charity stroked Rachel's uncared-for hair. "I have three sons and if it is any comfort, thee may cuddle one of mine."

Rachel began to weep, her sobs interrupted by hard coughs. "I was always jealous of thee," she moaned.

"It does not matter. Let us leave this unhealthy cellar and go home."

"Oh no, I might give my cough to one of the children." Rachel drew away. "Forget thee saw me," she begged.

Charity shuddered as she heard the racking cough. Indeed Rachel might bring disease into her home. But she must manage, some way, to nurse Rachel back to health. "I'll cure the cough," she said, drawing Rachel towards the door.

Like a wild thing tamed, Rachel let herself be led. Once outside, she knew better than Charity the winding way back to Gypsy and the chaise. They found the mare surrounded, her yellow teeth bared; she snorted angrily and tried to rear when a man with a tattooed face yanked at her bridle, while half a dozen others hunted through the chaise.

"Stand back, ye beggars that ain't fitten to touch a lady's carriage!" Rachel screamed. She reached for the whip in its holder. "Back, I say!"

"These people are only hungry." Charity laid a restraining hand on Rachel. "Let us give them the food they crave, and they will not steal. Here is the coffee . . . the tea and rice . . . dried apricots . . ." Soon all her supplies were gone. The crowd stared, hands holding packages, eyes showing bewilderment.

"Rachel, thee will sit beside me." Charity helped her into the chaise, took her own seat. "Tell me where the medicine shop on Pudding Lane is," she bade. "We must also buy more groceries." She felt in the hidden pocket under the seat. Her purse was safe! "Gypsy, thee gave an excellent account of thyself. But kindly move, now."

The crowd parted as the mare went slowly forward.

Charity avoided direct questions, on the ride to Waltham, but listened attentively when Rachel chose to talk. She pretended not to see Rachel's ragged gown, the broken shoes with bare toes protruding.

When they drew up beside the vine-covered cottage, Hilda came out. "I put the young'uns to bed," she said. Then her jaw dropped.

"We have a guest," Charity announced. "Rachel Foster."

"Merciful Moses!" Hilda gasped.

Bit by bit, as health returned, Rachel told her story. She had never been happy with Mark. "Soon as he went to Maine, he gave up all pretense of belonging to the Friends," she said. "Sometimes he crowed over how he fooled Forks Village Quakers. Other times, he seemed crazed, flying into black tempers." The Maine brickyard had closed because of the lack of orders. She and Mark went to Boston, but work was scarce. Mark left her. She found employment in a Boston coffee house. Times worsened and, one Saturday night, she lost her place. "I hadn't saved for a rainy day. When I got hungry, I joined a gang of thieves." She burst into tears.

"Never mind now," Charity counselled. "Thee will have

another chance for happiness."

Under skilful nursing, Rachel's cough vanished; the hollows in her cheeks filled out. She was becoming a handsome woman with fine dark eyes. One morning after they had fed a band of hungry migrants, she said: "I'm strong now. Think I'd like to go West with a family. One where there's a little girl, same age my own'd be." Her eyes lighted as she went on. "Five years old. And plenty of other young'uns, so the mother won't be jealous if the little thing loves me."

Now they scrutinized all the people passing by. But Rachel was never satisfied. The child was too large or too small. She didn't like the looks of the father, or the mother might be hard to live with.

As weeks passed she spoke more often of Mark. "A devil lives in Mark," she declared. "He boasted how he set Eben Todd's mill on fire."

"Mark admitted his crime!" Charity exclaimed, horrified.

Rachel nodded. "He bragged how he fooled Forks Village folks, making them think electric fluid struck the mill. But he poured oil on the cotton stored in cellar, set the fire, ran back to his boat and rowed across the river to Maine. When he learned Anthony found work in the Waltham mill, he hated him worse. 'I'll get even with him yet,' he swore. Charity, want me to make a signed statement afore I go West, saying how Mark set the mill on fire?"

Charity shook her head. "No signed statement will bring Shad back," she said. "As for Anthony, he is better off here in Waltham. Sometimes I think Shad is better off, in his hilltop grave."

As they put up jellies, made pies, or worked in the garden, Rachel would mention Mark. "He swore he'd get even with Anthony," she warned.

"Anthony is safe, the mill is guarded day and night," Charity returned. And she changed the subject, speaking of the child they were awaiting.

One October morning, a family came into the yard and asked for water. Carrying out a great pitcher of milk and a plate of cookies, Rachel's eyes were drawn to a fair-haired little girl. The child gave Rachel a trusting smile.

"How old is the little girl?" Rachel asked the mother.

"Five," the woman answered, "and I've eight more to care for."

"I want thee to share our noonday meal," Charity told the astonished mother. "Thy husband and the children, too."

When the party started off, Rachel walked with them, the fair-haired little girl's hand in hers. She carried her own bundle, like the others, and looked very happy. But her final words were far from cheering.

"Remember, Mark'll try to harm Anthony, in the way that'll hurt him most," she warned.

Rachel's body was healed, but not her mind, Charity thought as she waved farewell. The care of the little girl and change of scene would help her.

It was weeks before Rachel's first letter came. Charity turned it over in her hand. It was sealed with tree pitch that still felt sticky, and it must have been carried part of the way by pack-horse.

"The child," Rachel wrote, "grows fast. We stop for winter months at a settlement half way between Albany and Buffalo, called Cossitt's Corners. Spring, we travel on. Folks treat me well. Worst of things is men wanting wives. I say I'm married and not a woman to take two husbands. Never will I forget thy kindness. Remember about Mark!"

So Rachel's mind was not quite healed, Charity reflected. Or was there more danger than she had let herself believe? She had never troubled Anthony with Rachel's tale of Mark. But that evening, she told him.

Anthony's face darkened. "Mark's not crazy enough to come to a settled community like Waltham. Don't worry!" he counselled.

Yet Charity found she could not keep Mark entirely out of her thoughts.

Young Simeon and Tony had gone with Hilda to a children's party, one afternoon, and baby Shad slept in the cradle. Charity gathered her sewing things and sat down by the window. Snow covered the ground outside; a heavy fall for early December. Roofs and trees showed white under a sky that was clear blue save for small clouds scudding about, like dusters. Children coming home from school dove into the great banks of snow or pelted each other.

Charity knew almost everyone who passed, and nodded greeting. Life in Waltham had been kind, she thought, and the small cottage big enough for happiness. Samuel Ripley, pastor of the Unitarian Church, had invited her to worship with his flock. But she had remained a Friend.

She glanced down at her gown. It was blue, instead of drab, because the children loved color; but cut in Friends' fashion with full skirt and normal waistline. Quaker garb, adapted to present needs! At her throat she wore the brooch of garnets and pearls that had been Anthony's mother's. He had given it to her on their marriage day; for years she had kept the "vain ornament" in a drawer. Then she decided she should wear the brooch that gave her husband and children pleasure.

A snowball squashed against the window pane. She waved to Becky Horne's youngest, a tall lad now, and went to the door.

Young Solomon held out a letter. "Stopped at the post office and got your mail," he said.

"I thank thee. Do come in!"

"Ma promised to make apple dowdy." The boy grinned as he ran off.

Charity glanced at the letter's postmark. Who in Forks Village, except Lucy, would write to her? Unfolding the page as she returned to her chair, she saw the signature of Obadiah

Andrews, senior overseer of the Friends.

"Some time ago," she read, "Rachel Foster Badger wrote to us, making grievous complaint against her husband. We sent to the town in Maine where Mark Badger had lived. We found all Rachel said to be true, but have been unable to learn Mark's present whereabouts.

"We are convinced we erred in rejecting the application of thy husband, Anthony Bryce, for membership in the Society. We acted upon statements made by Mark and since proved false. It now appears that Anthony Bryce was more worthy of membership than the overseer who banned him.

"Wanting to make amends, we have replaced thy name on the list of members, and desire thy husband to make new application . . ."

The finely written page fell from Charity's hand. Rachel had loyally tried to make things right for her and Anthony, and in spite of advice to the contrary. As a result, Anthony was pronounced worthy of membership; she was exonerated for marrying outside the Society.

Supper over, the children in their cots and Hilda upstairs, she sat with Anthony before the fire. "News from Forks Village!" She smiled as she handed him the letter. And yet it startled her to hear him laugh when he read it. What had once been so all-important was now a subject for mirth!

"If you want me to turn Quaker, get out the Rules of Discipline," he said lightly, and went on with his whittling.

She had but to speak, and she could attend Meeting, even in Forks Village, her husband across the aisle that separated men and women. She need no longer feel outside. She looked at Anthony, whittling toys for his sons. She thought of him struggling with the Friends' "thee's" and "thy's," and did not like the idea. The pronouns of an earlier century, natural for her, would be artificial for Anthony. Besides, she loved to hear him sing. She loved his gay whistling when he romped with the children. Even his un-Quakerish expressions were dear.

Next morning, she wrote Obadiah Andrews that she was grateful for his diligence in searching out the truth. Once, she had urged Anthony Bryce to apply for membership in the Society, but she did not believe this desirable now. Especially as she disapproved of the rule forbidding marriage outside. "Since my husband is not to be a member," she concluded, "I realize I am not eligible for reinstatement."

Queer, how the feeling of being outside left her, now her status was the result of choice, not an unjust judgment laid on her!

A reply from the Friends arrived. She was in as good standing, Obadiah Andrews wrote, as if Anthony Bryce had been a Friend at the time of her marriage. The matter had been duly recorded, a copy sent to the Boston Society. . . .

She had made a beginning in opening the prejudiced eyes of Forks Village Friends!

That evening she said to Anthony: "I do not want my husband to become a Quaker. I like him as he is."

Victory over the Friends was unimportant, compared with the look he gave her.

Ice for the Torrid West Indies

SNOW squeaking under his high boots as he walked home, Anthony pondered on his new opportunity. Several of the mill proprietors had acquired a tract of land, with higher falls than those in Waltham, and bought rights to machines as well as releases for some of the workers from the parent company.

"Because of the skill you've shown in the wheelroom here," one of them had said, "we'd like you with us, Mr. Bryce, in our Merrimack River mill. Think the matter over for a week or two."

It was not unusual for Anthony to leave the mill early. When, as now, he had difficult calculations to make, he often did this in the quiet spare room. Hilda met him at the door, finger on lips. "Baby's asleep by the kitchen fireside," she warned. "Charity and the two lads drove with a neighbor to see where ice is cut."

Anthony nodded, went quietly up the stairs. Waiting for the logs to catch in the spare room fireplace, he recalled that he had told his son about a Boston company that cut blocks of ice from neighboring ponds, packed them in sawdust, stored them until summer, then shipped them to the southern islands so that children could cool the good pineapple juice they drank. He chuckled, remembering how his two lads had turned round-eyed over the idea that ice, which vanished from their fingers no matter how hard they clung to it, could go all the way to the torrid West Indies.

His mind reverted to the important matter. The new site was to be called "Lowell" in honor of the man considered a pioneer in American industry. The enterprise marked the beginning of a better era. "You'll go far if you come with us," the proprietor had said. But he would go far, if he stayed in Waltham!

What would Charity think? This was January, 1822. In six years and a half, she had grown accustomed to Waltham —the only home the children knew. Was it wise to uproot his family, even if he earned more money? When the children were tucked in bed, he and Charity would talk things over. Tossing another log into the fireplace, he sat down with crayons and drawing board.

Charity and the two lads came home. He heard the high childish voices tell how they'd seen where ice for West Indies children was cut. Hilda announced she was bound for the store, and the boys begged to go.

"It won't hurt them," Charity said. "The sun's still out."

The boys trotted off with Hilda, and the house turned quiet. He could go down and talk with Charity now. No, it would be better to wait until they had an entire evening to themselves.

He had worked half an hour when a cry came from the kitchen. Baby Shad was not in the habit of screaming! Anthony jerked the door wide.

"If you move," a voice rasped, "my knife might fall."

Mark's voice! Mark had come! Anthony sped down the stairs, through the parlor and into the tiny dining room. The door to the kitchen was closed. He must open it without alarming Mark!

"I watched that husband of yours go back and forth," Mark said. "I had chances to send a slug of lead into him. But then he might not have had time to know I got even with him. This way, he'll remember. Don't move, or I might get nervous, and there's things I'd like to say before leaving my sign on your beautiful face. You see . . ."

Only the door lay between him and Mark, but he must not startle Mark into throwing the knife, Anthony realized.

"Remember," Mark rasped, "it's that husband of yours I'm getting even with. Thinks he came out ahead of me—from the day I found him in the Portsmouth inn. When he sees the scars left by my knife—"

The baby screamed again and, trusting to this to cover noise, Anthony jerked the door open and flung himself on Mark. Mark had the knife at his throat. Anthony wrested it away. Mark kicked the cradle, and the baby screamed once more. Anthony got both arms around Mark. Somehow, Mark wriggled away and ran outside. Anthony ran after him.

Mark followed back ways. He jumped over fences, ducked behind trees, zigzagged into a barn. Close on him, Anthony drove him through a narrow door and into a henhouse. Mark broke the glass and bolted through a window. But Mark was only a poor scarecrow of a man and would soon tire, Anthony thought.

They reached the village outskirts. In open fields, Mark had the advantage; lighter than Anthony, he skimmed over the snow, where Anthony sank in. He was making headway! But Mark could have no lasting power, Anthony told himself as, warmed by anger, he plodded through snow. He was gaining now. When Mark fell, exhausted, he would pick him up, carry him back to the village and deliver him to the authorities. Officers of the law could deal with Mark!

Mark ran less steadily, heading for a grove. A pond lay beyond; and beyond the pond, a densely wooded hill that would offer shelter. Mark ran through the grove . . . started across the pond.

Anthony, close on him, had stepped on the frozen surface before he remembered: this was one of the ponds from which ice had been cut. Ahead of Mark lay a wide expanse, glazed with paper-thin ice. Anthony felt a moment's satisfaction over the prospect of Mark's running to death.

But he could not let any man die, unwarned. "Thin ice ahead!" he called. "You'll break through!"

Mark ran on.

Did he think the warning a trick to rob him of the advantage he had gained! Did he think all men as crooked as he was himself! Anthony made a trumpet of his hands. "They've been cutting ice here!" His words echoed from the hillside.

Mark ran on.

Anthony saw no farmhouse near. No rope, plank, or log. No tree with branches low enough for him to break off a bough. There was nothing to serve as means of rescue! For the third time, he called: "Thin ice ahead!"

Mark ran on.

There was a splash, an ear-piercing scream. And then, where a man had stood, there was only icy water.

Next morning, Charity sent a letter to Rachel, telling her she was free to wed again. "The Lord," she wrote, "has punished Mark."

In the evening, sitting with Anthony by the fireside and sewing on Waltham-manufactured sheeting, she spoke of a family who had passed by, in spite of the deep snow. "They lost their home," she said, "and want to settle on the banks of the new canal in New York State. They were afraid all land might be taken, if they waited till spring. Anthony, here in Waltham everyone has plenty. It seems unfair that in so many places people can scarcely keep body and soul together."

Anthony looked up from the toy boat he was whittling. "The power loom keeps Waltham prosperous," he said. "We can compete, in heavy cotton sheeting at least, with foreign factories because we have the loom."

Charity laid her sewing down. "Lucy writes that the local people are terribly poor. How I wish Forks Village had an industry to provide steady employment!"

Anthony's eyes rested on his wife's troubled face. Upset over Mark, he had not told her about his new offer. The Merrimack enterprise was a sign that times had changed; all businessmen were looking on mills with more favor. What if he could persuade Simeon to build a mill in Forks River! He decided not to mention his offer until he had been to Boston.

Simeon welcomed him warmly and inquired at once for his namesake.

"He's lively," Anthony reported, "and can't keep away from that kite you sent him. But I came on business matters. Charity tells me that Forks Village needs an industry. Farming won't support the community these times . . ." He explained the plan for mills on Merrimack River, pointed out prospects for sites near falls like those in Forks River.

"I've had two offers for my land there." Simeon's eyes showed a gleam. "In both cases, from men wanting to build mills. And yesterday, a third offer came from James Lester. How much capital is required?"

"We could start a mill with twenty-five to fifty thousand dollars."

"Twenty-five to fifty thousand! Indeed not." Simeon slapped his knee. "James once tried to make a wager with me. 'When it is known,' James declared, 'that Simeon Damon has bought a mill site, men will say he has grown too old for Boston trading.' To get my land, James must organize a company issuing shares up to a hundred thousand dollars. I'll accept part payment in stock. By the way, my neighbor, Daniel Webster, who now practices law in Boston, has come around to the side of the mills. He must draw the charter. What else can I require of James?" He paused, brows knitted.

"I know," he went on. "James must appoint my niece's husband Agent of the new Forks River mills. And erect the first building this summer!"

Home at Last

ON THE June morning of the year 1822, when the cornerstone of the new mill was to be laid, Anthony and Charity walked in the procession of guest speakers. As Anthony had been detained in Waltham to complete an invention, they had only just arrived in Forks Village. People in holiday clothes thronged the site of Eben Todd's old mill, and many of them nodded or called out greetings. It was a ceremonious occasion. The Free Masons were there, the farmers' Grange, the scholars of the school with their teachers. A military escort of two infantry companies and a band stood beside the new excavation.

Evergreen decorated the speakers' platform. As Simeon mounted the steps, the crowd burst into cheers: "Hooray for local lad made good in Boston. . . . Hooray for man wan't afraid to buy the mill site . . .!" The white-haired Quaker nodded in acknowledgment. The crowd cheered for James Lester, largest investor in the new mills. They cheered for other guests.

But it was Anthony's day. When he and Charity climbed the steps, the shouting rose to the skies: "Hooray for lad helped defend Portsmouth . . . Hooray for lad married local girl . . . Hooray for the Agent of our new mills!"

It was all hoorays, now. Anthony recalled an earlier time. Looking around while the band played, he saw Joe Furber, Matt Gragg, the others who had opposed him, years before. Reverend Timothy Carr again gave the prayer. Moderator John Welsh introduced Simeon.

"We celebrate a momentous event . . ." The crowd that reached to the riverbank, and the fields beyond, grew quiet when the white-haired Quaker began to speak. "We celebrate the founding of an enterprise which will afford workers fair treatment," Simeon continued. "Young women may earn good wages and yet be sheltered . . ." He expressed the hope that American industry would never be exploited by men greedy for mere wealth. "As the Waltham cotton mills are the model for Massachusetts factories," he concluded, "let our mill here in Forks Village be the standard-bearer for all in northern New England."

James Lester, president of the new corporation, was introduced. While he spoke, Anthony looked again at the crowd. He saw Eben and Sary Ann. Thomas Carr, grown into a tall young man, stood beside a comely girl. Dominicus Todd was there, Lucy and William, Obadiah Andrews who had bought shares generously. Quakers and world's people, all had come.

Then, off on the fringe of the crowd, Anthony seemed to see a shadowy figure in a faded long-skirted coat. "Land sakes, Tony," a high voice piped, "ye be havin' quite a time. Didn't I say, far back as when Mark Badger and Nick tried to steal the loom designs, there was sense in this mill!"

Anthony's throat filled. He reached for Charity's hand.

Presently his turn came. "We need the cooperation," he began, "of agriculture, of shipping and other commerce, *and* of mills for the full development of all the twenty-four States . . ." He spoke mainly, however, of what Eben Todd and other mill pioneers had undergone. "In the struggle to establish manufactures, men have fought for American independence whose names will never be heard. You know one man who gave his life, trying to save a mill. I refer to Shadrach Nye . . ." When he ended, the crowd were wiping their eyes.

Then the guests of honor came down from the stand and walked to the new excavation. James Lester and Simeon set the cornerstone. The band played *The Star-Spangled Banner,* while soil was shovelled on, and the crowd sang heartily.

Selectman John Welsh invited all to partake of the banquet to be served on the inn lawn, at shareholders' expense. The dignitaries rode in carriages; the crowd followed afoot, on horseback, in every sort of vehicle.

The banquet table was T-shaped. Landlord Asa Howland diligently saw that distinguished guests were seated at the top; the others scrambled for places. Anthony marvelled at the prodigality. There were soups and chowders; codfish, stuffed haddock, perch and pike, boiled lobster, fried clams. Duckling, pigeon, fowl. Pork, beef, lamb, a multitude of vegetables and relishes. Desserts made an endless procession of pies, custards, souflées, tarts.

At length the toasts began.

"To our Republican institutions!"

"To Agriculture, the basis of human sustenance!"

"To Commerce and Navigation, handmaids of Agriculture!"

"To our new Industries in all the twenty-four States!"

A dozen toasts, the last one to the Agent of the new mills, with the company shouting and the band playing!

That evening, Anthony stepped out of the big house to look at the hillside and the river. Judged even by the handsome estates around Waltham, Blue Clay Farm was an imposing place of residence. He turned and saw Simeon, wearied by the day's events, sitting by the window. Charity waved as she cantered by on Gabriel, a sedate horse now.

The sun was still above the horizon. Anthony went to the rose garden, cut an armful of long-stemmed blossoms, and walked to the hilltop graveyard. The burial place had been well tended. Moss around the base of the slab erected for Shad softened the granite's severity. Laying his roses on the grave, he lingered a while.

As he returned to the house, Charity cantered up, her feet on the ground before he could reach her.

"I can still dismount without aid, if I am the mother of three children," she said, laughing as she knotted the reins. "Gabriel, thee could always find the barn." She patted his flank, and the big gray trotted off.

They looked at the river, reflecting the bright colors of the sky. "Thee knows I am glad to be here," Charity said, "but everything seems different. And I miss Waltham. Does thee remember the night we arrived there and the cottage seemed just a box? And yesterday I hated to leave. But our Waltham friends have promised to visit us, and we can visit them. Does thee remember . . .?"

It occurred to Anthony that one of them would often be saying, "Does thee remember . . .?" The years in Waltham had not only given them a broader outlook but made a bond they might have missed, had they never left the farm.

The sun's rim dipped. They heard a songbird's note, the crickets' chirp, the wash of the river against the wharf.

"I miss the schooner that used to carry brick," Charity said. "It was sore needed for the post-war commerce, and would have rotted had we not sold it."

"We'll order a new vessel, and use it for pleasure."

"The brickyard has grown untidy. It reminds me of Mark."

Anthony slipped his arm through hers. "We'll turn it into smooth lawn."

"We need more cattle.'"

"Yes, and ponies for the boys."

"I am proud of my home. But more proud," Charity added softly, "of my husband."

He drew her close. The States had been good to him! He had Charity. In the house behind, their three sons slept—and already young Simeon wanted to know how old he must be to work in a machine shop. He had a mill. And, all over the land, other mills were rising, built of brick, with rows of shining windows, to serve the needs of the people.